COMMEDI

COMMEDIA MORTALE

Wayne Holloway

Influx Press
London

Published by Influx Press
Mainyard Studios
58B Alexandra Road
Enfield, EN3 7EH
www.influxpress.com / @InfluxPress
All rights reserved.

Printed and bound in the UK by TJ Books.
Published by Influx Press, London, UK, 2025.

Paperback ISBN: 9781914391545
Ebook ISBN: 9781914391552

Cover design: Jamie Keenan
Text design: Vince Haig

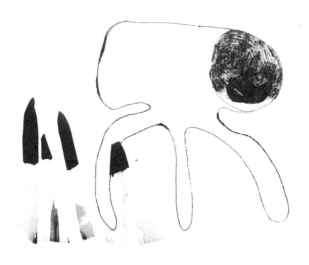

PROLOGUE

STREGONE

After an afternoon swimming in the river I was desperate for a cold beer. My tinnitus was equalised by the sound of rushing water, the experience of near silence in my head always energises me – only the crashing of waves surpasses it – but it was a steep climb back up to the road, hot and humid. The bar served Tuborg Gold on tap. A brand that speaks to me of nothing. A strong beer with a bitter, chemical aftertaste but cold and amber. So I ordered a *media* and sat outside on the narrow balcony with a zinc bar top overlooking the valley and the thread of road, town and terrace that bisect these mountains as they twist, turn and slope, becoming hills before running out onto the coastal plain. The balcony perches above it all, certain death below if it were to fail, and there is not one drinker who ever sits here that hasn't imagined how many people it would take for it to collapse under their weight or what misalignment of stars could bring about sudden disaster; steel rebar – compromised somehow – or rotting concrete badly mixed when first poured conspiring with temperature and humidity to precipitate catastrophic failure.

Sitting here was always a trip in itself.

I sit alone – it was my fate to do so – spaced out, buzzing from the sun, numbed by a day of doing nothing under it, punctuated by refreshing dips, the sense memory of that, of cool water on hot skin, distracting me from opening my book on a balcony held up as if by magic, a panorama of the whole valley at my feet, a scene so varied in shape and colour that it would make a fiendish thousand-piece jigsaw puzzle.

Sun softens the mind, enabling free association of words and thought. We respond to it as if swamped by drugs; a rush of serotonin our reward for providing the body with its daily fix of Vitamin D. Addicted to its pleasures, we are literally sun-spanked on peptides.

Two men come inside – I see them when I get up to order another beer – backlit by sunshine, momentary silhouettes that quickly resolve into people. The younger one is dark, with dense curly hair tamed under a jaunty bandana with a faded red and yellow pattern, a sleek black feather tucked behind one ear. He wears billowing blue pantaloons and leans on a dark wooden stick, which reminds me of an embossed Rastafarian swagger stick, redolent with meaning, but this one was more *Lord of the Rings*, its bulbous head a natural knot in the wood rather than something worked. A precocious stick. One last detail: he was wearing lime-green North African slippers.

Imagine preparing the props and wardrobe for a big scene in a blockbuster movie like *Pirates of the Caribbean*; so say there are three levels of detail or elaboration. Main players, featured extras, and then general background – think close-ups, mid- and wide shots – the latter having no need for jewellery or any small detail that would only be picked up in close-ups, so just the odd hat or scarf thrown in for colour variation. Featured extras were tricky: you could waste time on them, or indeed be caught out in the edit suite for overlooking them. They required some styling, props, but nothing too elaborate.

This guy was more of a featured extra. At a glance he looked the part from head to toe but wore no bangles and I didn't notice any earrings, necklaces or tattoos for that matter, something usually reserved for the main players as they were time-consuming to apply and a bitch to get right. The feather was probably his own touch. *Something he brought to the party.*

The other man was slightly older – or just more weathered – blond, thin on top with a light moustache and bare dirty feet, his ripped jeans more like ragged curtains framing each leg. He had a faraway look in his eye, whereas the darker one was intense, his eyes – olive-stone shaped and jet black – darted over every surface scanning the room. The blond's eyes were pale blue. Shifty, they didn't rest on anything for long, giving you the impression that he wasn't really looking at anything at all, his eyes were lit from elsewhere, reflecting a different scene altogether.

Asphalt sears the soles of your feet, literally hardening them for modern life on the streets, tempering them against slivers of glass and metal, diamonds of grit and stone, shards of brick, bones and the ooze of rubbish. These tempered feet are paid for in a silent currency of pain, paid in full and worn, if that is the word, worn with indifference, perhaps resignation, but never pride.

I returned to my spot on the balcony and picked up my book, *The House on the Via Gomito*, which was taking me weeks to get through, to the extent that I was bogged down in it, so any distraction led me to put it aside. The two men – *two men* sounds odd, they didn't strike me as such; although boys or youths was factually incorrect, there was something essentially naive about them – came out onto the balcony a few minutes later with two glasses of water and a single cappuccino on a small tray. We said hello and one of them mentioned the view. I offered a slight smile in return. I tried to focus on my book but I found myself drawn to their conversation. They spoke in a polyglot of Italian, Spanish and English.

Great spot isn't it? The blond gestures, sipping his water and whispers,

Almost a mirror.

The other one sipped the coffee before rotating the cup and offering it to his friend. He had an old metal tobacco tin and spent minutes sifting through the dark dry tobacco, finally rolling himself a cigarette. Through this action he sought to own time, shifting us all sideways in his direction. The blond prosaically smoked a straight, almost finishing it before his friend licked the paper on his.

I am really drawn to your energy, I feel your aura.

Said looking out to the mountainside opposite, as if addressing it and not his companion. (Or maybe he was talking to the mountains, it would make more sense?)

By his words and actions he ceded power to the younger man, despite his rollup being a disappointment. With his energy and fierce eyes I had expected the tightest, straightest pencil of a cigarette, something perfect. In fact, it was badly made – bulging in the middle – amateur, a hastily prepared last-minute notion rolled on the hoof as it were by a set dresser or prop assistant seeking to make a good impression with her (unnecessary) attention to detail and her understanding of background action and its unpredictable on-screen visibility.

The cigarette trailed loose threads of tobacco, he didn't even pinch them off. When he finally lit it they flared away trailing tiny sparks. It smoked badly and he had to suck hard to keep it going. With a simple look, a raising of eyebrows, the blond could have rebalanced the scene in his favour, but he didn't.

Here, have one of mine…

Would have clinched it. Instead he continued…

I felt it as soon as we met.

I should say that this is a rough translation of what he actually said, two sentences cobbled together from three languages. *Almost a mirror* might have been *take a look at yourself in the mirror*; whether literally in reference to the mountain opposite or figuratively, meaning take a look at yourself. I didn't invent this bizarre phrase – I'm not putting words in his mouth – that would have been odd, to want to do that, to make up something like that just on first impressions of this unlikely double act. No, the key words were definitely spoken; a mirror, the reference to another person's charisma and him being drawn to it. The sense of the latter was neither sexual nor did it come across as submissive, I intuited neither of those inferences. There was an increasingly odd flow of energy between them.

The dark guy finally gives up on the rollup, which died at the bulge. His fingers claw a straight out of his friend's proffered packet.

The acolyte leans in to light it.

I really want us to work together, so we can amplify each other.

For fuck's sake.

With this the blond recused himself from any potential kudos. I smile as if reacting to something I had just read although there was little mirth in *The House on the Via Gomito*, the story of a childhood lived under a violent imperious father, yet I had kept with it, rubbernecking the car crash of this family saga over at least four hundred pages leavened by at least three other easier reads, none of which I can remember by name, something contemporary and Japanese and a horror story, yes definitely a horror, a bloody tale soaked in South American tribal curses and witchcraft, the vulnerability of our insides...

The house itself, its rooms and balconies and the close proximity of the people who lived there, is what kept me reading. The way in which they frame our lives, capture us in their memory, as much as we inhabit them in ours. This amplified itself across the books I was reading simultaneously, with their houses of horror and refuge respectively.

The blond guy was now talking up a storm, about a fresh start, things to overcome, hurdles both inside and out, the challenge of setting out on a new path, about his job, the farmers he worked for, how in this valley the opportunities were endless...

All I saw was dirty feet and a shared coffee, sipped from both sides.

Who were these two? Perhaps novices best describes them. Whatever it was they were novices of made them behave like tentative children. They were new to this, to speaking unusual words. Imagine wet clones straight out of the vat in a show like *Star Trek* or *Altered Carbon*, sleeved fully grown yet as naive and innocent – momentarily – as children, slick and fresh from the amniotic sack. What power could either of these two men really possess? One in rags, the other slightly ridiculous. Summer hippies in a mountain village where it is cheap to live, the detritus of the wealthy North freewheeling down to the Mediterranean as they have done for decades. Or had the dark one come up from the South, from Spain, or further, the enclaves of Morocco? Perhaps whatever simmered between them was a clash of the compass rose, a hot sultry Scirocco riding up over a cold blustery Tramontana? A silent yet seductive southern breeze, for I realise he had yet to say a word, communicating only with his eyes and twitches of lips, which are thin – surprisingly not full and sensual – parallel lines like the ridges of a walnut, intricate and mysterious.

Winds of a different temperament.

I lose interest, finish my beer, the last mouthfuls warm and unpleasant as I ponder another, a buzz beginning to build behind my temples, pleasant and familiar. On my way back from the bar I catch...

This is my new home.

Said with a hint of him being profoundly surprised to find himself there. A prosaic turn of conversation. It crossed my mind that perhaps the other's silence was more a lack of comprehension than charisma. If so, the blond was wasting his time, or perhaps indulging his own fantasies, projecting a need in himself onto this relative stranger, who, in his eyes at least, looked the part of something he was looking for.

The blond was not lost, he was too wily to be lost, but he was searching, whether he knew what he was looking for I couldn't tell. It wasn't for me to see it. He was still in the dark, yet confident that he could talk his way into enlightenment. The dark one smiles and listens. He enjoys the chatter without the need to add to it. Oddly, I instinctively trust him. I admire his ability to be quiet yet encourage others to talk, to enjoy that without judgement was a subtle power, a rare strength of personality.

Words are heavy, they weigh us down, what we say implicates us by revelation. Silence is light, mysterious, it soars. Without speaking we can weave spells that strike those below with the surprise and ferocity of an eagle predating a rabbit.

I realise that on some level he is waiting for the blond to talk himself out, like a shrink who listens and speaks rarely, if at all.

That summer I was in the middle of writing a pilot for a TV series set in the world of fantasy wargaming, an almost invisible subculture where the awkward, the nerdy, the misfit, the non-binary (in the broadest sense), the waifs and strays, find a place in which they feel free to express themselves. In a word, to live and have fun just like everybody else. And then this world is discovered. To be monetised/molested for all it is worth and the oddballs become leftovers; half of them are culled, priced out, others make themselves over into cosplay norms, willing victims of the film/TV/game franchise circle jerk that is at the heart of the ludo/entertainment/industrial complex. What's left, the holdouts, radical hardcore nerds, the heroes of my show, have to fight to stay in the shadows as the margins themselves become commodified.

Two waters and one cappuccino.

Wally Hope, another outsider, born on Ibiza, the white island, in a house where his mother kept a locked room full of his father's Nazi paraphernalia. He grew up a different kind of a pagan, an organiser of festivals, happenings, and a seeker of truth through being in the world just like the two men sitting not feet from me. Or was there just one, who invoked the other? Or perhaps none, was I imagining them both? Had I been in the sun too long, had my mind wandered too far? Wally had summoned a snowstorm in midsummer from under his cloak, hastening the tragic end of his life. There are people who will swear that it was so, the snow, his swirling cloak in a summer garden in Essex in the 1970s, and I wanted to believe that, for reasons of romance, but more than that, to fill the void of it not being true.

Had the blond invoked, willed the other into existence to serve him, or – which is more likely – just to provide some company; this lonely outsider, with bare feet and broken toes, thirsty like I was on entering the bar, asking for two glasses of tap water to quench his thirst. The success of his summoning enough to cheer him, like Wally and his snowstorm, manifestation for its own sake, for pleasure.

He pays for the coffee, catches me watching his friend and smiles conspiratorially, as if to say: *you see him too, right?*

A warlock in peacetime.

At the door, just as he is about to step back into the sunlight, the silent one pauses, looking back towards the perilous balcony. His stick sends its shadow slashing across the floor, casting a benign spell, or so I choose to believe and by doing so keeping the peace. For there are many peaces which hold or are broken in every place and at every time, big and small, some visible but many less so, as fragile and quotidian as the things and the people that keep them.

This is mine.

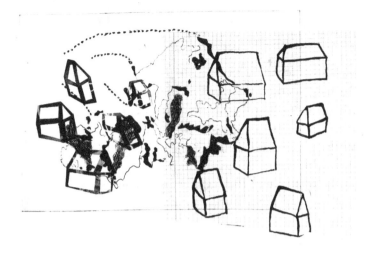

ISTVAN

On the exterior wall of the house, overlooking the valley, is a life-size plaster bust of Istvan's head and shoulders. He has a narrow face with a sharp pointy nose and chin. An eighteenth-century face, suggesting Voltaire perhaps, the outline of his hair reminds me of a periwig. It suited his narrow features but perhaps this was just sloppy casting. Istvan overlooked the terrace for ten or more years until a storm blew it down, leaving a jagged stump, a nub, what was left of his neck and shoulders. This has since fallen away but I remember it more than I can recall his actual likeness.

In the valley a storm can mean the sky emptying a bucket of tennis-ball-size hailstones in the space of minutes, out of the blue – literally out of a blue sky just minutes before – smashing bonnets and roofs like a crazed ball-peen hammer attack, ending abruptly as we exodus our vehicles discombobulated into returning sunshine, the incongruous marbles of ice to be broomed to the sides of roads in banks of slush, flooding the roads an hour or so later. The sort of natural event that is ridiculous, that makes you laugh out loud. Although I suppose one of those stones could kill you, could definitely kill a child, an absurd way to go, the worst of luck, like a coconut falling from a tree in the tropics (which nearly killed Keith Richards, among countless others) or a pane of glass falling onto the pavement in a city, missing passers-by by inches or severing their heads. The odds are long yet getting shorter. If you live *in nature* it is more likely to kill you. *Fire, drought, flood and famine.* Typhoons, for example, catch you out in the open; you run from them or cower in flimsy barns to little avail.

Istvan's self-portrait didn't stand a chance.

Fragments of his work can be found all over the house. I mean the work was fragmentary; he worked in fragments. Primary colours painted on found objects – slashes of yellow on a piece of slate, a hole drilled through a stone, the inside painted a lurid green, white, black stripes, bold circles perfectly cinched around rocks – visitations of colour and form. On the first-floor landing was an old handmade wooden box with many drawers meticulously outlined by a fine brush in red, which feels alpine – red paint on sanded wood – as if from a chalet higher up in the mountains, although I'm not describing it very well. Each drawer – they didn't fit perfectly, swollen by damp, you had to worry each one in and out – was full of small household objects like needles, spools of thread, biros and pencil stubs, faded business cards from local restaurants and taxi firms, shopping lists, a drawer full of nails, another with faded unsent postcards but also a few received, tantalising glimpses into another life in full quotidian flow. Written in German and Hungarian, warped by time; greetings, wish-you-were-heres and see-you-soons.

All unsere Liebe dieses Weihnachten 1986.

Upstairs was a bookshelf full of art books from what looked like the 1970s and '80s, black spots of mould peppering the spines and front edges as if fired from a shotgun. Stiff, crooked volumes propping each other up as the damp worked on them, a collection distilled from a lifetime spent in the art circles of central Europe. Monochrome photographs of mostly naked, hairy men and women, posed in tableaux or as part of an installation or captured in blurry snaps taken at happenings, in basements or warehouses, probably clandestine, performance art that involved the body, paint and big ideas.

The house shares rocks and stones with the mountain it is built into. You can't disentangle the two, they are conjoined twins – house and mountain – sharing the same mother.

Istvan had scribbled this on a postcard – in English, for some reason – I don't know how many languages he spoke, but he was Hungarian by birth and lived in Germany. His paintings that years later I discovered online reflect an ongoing fixation with this entanglement.

I met him at the house for the first and only time to pay the balance of what I owed him. I had already deposited the taxable sum with a lawyer in his office on the coast.

It was Easter, more wet than cold, but I found him sitting in the dark cantina hunched inside a big overcoat. I sat down opposite him at a rickety kitchen table drilled by wood worm. I ran my finger across the braille of it. He stood bolt upright to remove his coat as if I had sat on the other end of a seesaw, my weight somehow displacing his. Under the table I smelt then saw a mangy old Labrador fast asleep. The walls and ceiling were a dingy stained Artex. The cottage-cheese-like appearance was immediately oppressive. It felt like it could drip on us at any moment.

Hello.

A shake of hands. A strong grip, smooth palms, corded arms.

Guten tag. Welcome to casa Istvan.

His hand gestured to the room, perhaps ironically.

This had been a place for animals, cows, sheep or donkeys, who I imagine would have been happy here. He had opened a bottle of wine for us to share before he left. It was half empty and he was already drunk. As he poured me a glass, I noticed a patchwork of old white scars and more recently healed over red nicks on his right hand, wrist and fingers. He could have been a farmer in another life, is what I thought, sitting as we were in a farmer's house, although what would I know about that? His left pouring hand was relatively unscarred but had a slight tremor and the neck of the bottle clinked the glass a little too hard but without chipping it or spilling a drop. An artist, a drinker. The whole place felt like an installation from one of his books. In the corner was an open fire, but I don't recall it being lit. Easter fires were usually smoky, the rain pushing down on the chimney to billow smoke out into the room. A single bulb hung low over the pitted table. Who knew how long he had been sitting there with his dog: a still-life tableau. I don't remember what we talked about. The house, probably. He wasn't the sort of person to give any tips. Definitely not his art, which I only noticed after he had left. He didn't mention it. I assume he wanted to finish the wine, shake hands and take the money. I remember the physicality of the money itself because it was the first year of the Euro. The notes were brash, cartoonish, extra-large and felt like plastic; invented for the performance of exchange. They didn't tear, you couldn't easily rip them. By comparison the pounds in my pocket were old, clipped and fusty, clandestine currency worn down by use and sullied by too many hands. Pounds aged like we did, especially along their folds. These crisp Euro notes in Istvan's hands looked out of place, a prop master's mistake in a low-budget movie, or perhaps the product of a fresh surprising optimism, gifted from a potentially bright future.

How much was it? I have always thought it was twenty thousand Euros. That figure feels right but how would I have given it to him? In a holdall? I have no memory of the mechanics of exchange, just him sitting there a bit withdrawn, dismissive even. If I gave him forty five-hundred-Euro notes, then perhaps this was doable, but again, I have no memory of it or of getting this amount from a bank. I do not know what a five-hundred-Euro note looks like but the house exists; it is ours, and the amount shown on the deeds – sixty thousand Euros – was not the full amount. There was definitely no bank transfer, which, to be frank, would jeopardise the mutual goal of tax evasion. A large amount in whatever denomination would have had to be checked a few times, whirring through the machine, or did the teller pass the notes from one hand into another, right under my nose as it were, fingers licked to count methodically but I remember none of it.

However I came by it, I gave him the money, disappointed that it wasn't bundles of lire. Proper money. I remember them fondly as I do pounds, pesetas and francs, a true union of European lucre. These old lire – like snot rags in your pocket, crumpled up, greasy, ripped, folded origami-tight, bundled with elastic bands – cash that stank, of sweat, of hard work or slick with the adrenalin of easy money pocketed quickly and spent without consequence. Sad single notes or a couple of coins retrieved from the bottom of purses, from deep pockets lined with lint, coins and paper worn from constant use, intimately warm from the desperate passing from hand to hand, or damp, lifeless, sequestered in a shoe box, squirrelled away, perhaps forgotten, acquiring the odour of wherever they had been kept safe, of lavender, a dry linen bag at the back of a drawer, the stink of animals – shit or milk – if hidden in farm sheds or behind rafters in hay lofts, or the acrid smell of old motor oil from being counted into a mechanic's hands or the sweet note of tobacco or biscuit if stashed in a tin – all of this teeming life, the life of money, our life – money in pay packets or freshly printed stacks of notes mustering in a vault, like mint trainers destined to become scuffed, worn and just like us, destined to carry their experiences as they make their way in the world, the scars, the memories running through them and us like liquorice in a stick of rock, money that sticks to some people and not to others.

I would have remembered that.

Euros have no character, only function. Come to think of it, the teller has no reason to lick his fingers before counting, they are designed to separate with ease. Now real money is to be found elsewhere, in India, South America, places like

Kazakhstan, Ghana, Vietnam. Even the mighty dollar has remained unchanged. The last vestiges of proximity to money, our sensual relationship with it. We are just left with the ghost of exchange, ephemeral notes and coins not storied enough to hold out against a cashless future.

My friend Paul arrived at the house, he had gone to get cigarettes from the new machine in the village. So long ago it was a time when we smoked without thinking about cancer, or to be less melodramatic, we smoked without the shadow of mortal thoughts crossing our mind, which is to say we smoked pleasurably, guiltlessly, that's how long ago this was and how young, relatively, we were. He helped us drink off what remained of the wine. Istvan left with his money in an ancient jalopy, which didn't make it further than the first turn on the gravel lane before conking out. We helped him push start the car. Three times it took for the engine to catch, and the car finally lurched forward. The last I ever saw of him was the back of his head and the knuckles of his hand out of the window waving goodbye and the dog sitting up front as the car spluttered its way up onto the tarmac road and off down the hill, on his way, implausibly, to Budapest to visit his brother.

Concrete moments in time, although somehow listless when translated into memory. In the sense of being flat-footed, having lost the anima of the detail they contain, the transient play of light, movement, colour and smell, the conscious expectation and outcome that only occurs once in cosmic time, then dulls, degrades over a lifetime of being just a memory. No longer in the game of life, like money that has changed hands for the last time. How many times can you remember something before the currency of it runs out? The same thing, the same event, either so flattened out as to become rote, with exactly the same details, or the opposite, a shifting series of memories of the same thing but really not the same thing at all, and therefore not fit for the purpose of recollection, downgraded by the vagaries of connotation; a compressed Jpeg, filed away among millions of others to be resuscitated by words, to be used rather than cherished, useful when placed in a story they don't deserve to feature in. And how can one memory ever be discrete from another? They are not inviolate palaces but rather violated prisons, and we the thief, pickpocketing ourselves. Life bleeds, spends itself recklessly, regardless. It is uncontained, we can only imagine it from the debris of recollection.

In that first year – a year of boundless enthusiasm and energy, not to say money – we got rid of the Artex ceiling and pulled up the cream tiles that looked like wet tobacco ends from rollups had been smeared on them. The artworks remained, part of the fabric of the house, subtle details of Istvan's presence until entropy or accident removed them until only one was left, a strange flimsy-looking canopy made from wooden slats wired together like rotten teeth, hanging over the front door protecting a single light bulb that still works to this day, a little miracle.

Cemented into the wall to one side of the door is a piece of slate with the chiselled legend *Istvan Laurer 1984*.

All of this lent a recent hinterland to the house without defining it. The house was inviolate however much we tampered with it. It didn't shrug you off; it was a benign presence. You lived in it, easily. It had never been a blank canvas, nor somewhere that demanded to be filled. Its shape was enough. There was a solidity to it that reassured you: the walls were two feet thick. It had ceiling arches which reminded you of churches, a similar sense of permanence. This was the house, the character you experienced, not the things people had put in it. Things and people were transitory if not irrelevant. In summer the thick walls absorbed heat from the sun, keeping the interior cool. At night they released it, like some kind of battery, the walls were hot to the touch until past sundown. You could feel the pulse of it up to a few feet away. Istvan had felt the pleasure of it and now we did. A small robust memory. Just that, the heat from stones on your hand at night. He took his share of that pleasure with him to Budapest.

I had been to Budapest in 1984. The same year he bought the house and chiselled his name to prove he had done so.

Perhaps Istvan chuckled to himself as he laid those bloody tiles before sunning himself like a pig in shit on the terrace. How many things do we do in our lives, happily oblivious to the fact that somebody else will come along and undo them, replace them, cursing us?

Buda and Pest. A city bifurcated by the Danube, two different places, one medieval, the other nineteenth century. Europe and the Orient, the croissants served in the cafes of one celebrating the defeat of the other. The old town and the new bound by bridges. I remember the stories that spill from this city, spun from other people's memories and served up as entertainment or admonition, along the fault line of story…

Nobody pays the ferryman, the bridge stole his income, an old story already told by another.

The horror of the six-year-old Jewish girl ringing a service bell six floors up from the kitchen to order lemonade and sandwiches, hungry or just for the hell of it, an expression of power and powerlessness. The maid, the servant, ridiculously young or perhaps very old, traipsing up and down the stairs to this unhappy girl's every whim. Oh was she deliriously happy – wielding the power to wear out the soles of another's shoes! – while at the same time being inconsequential, a little girl in a big bad world as 1940 counts down to '44. The servants' hatred or indifference a yardstick of her success or failure. I try to worry meaning from it, circling the story over and over, teasing new details each time as if they would unlock a bigger truth hidden within and the rest would all tumble into place. For what? Insight? Understanding? Of whom? Why else recount it? Am I sick? I imagine this place as a tower, of course, a girl in a tower, the servant feeling dizzy resting halfway up or down the spiral staircase...

The summer of 1984. I was interrailing with my first girlfriend; we roamed all over Europe that summer. Our first communist city, a city without advertising.

In another Hungarian town, Pecs – south near the Croatian border – we met a young Soviet conscript. He wore a military hat with a huge brim, set at such a jaunty angle on his head that it defied the laws of gravity. In a bar we traded stories of growing up in England and Odessa, chased by vodka and beer until finally he took off his shirt to reveal a tattoo of Stalin spread across his pimpled back, the beady eyes and beneficent smile flexed between his shoulder blades. The boy's face was flush with pride as he tasted victory, for what could we show or do to match that? Although I did notice him glancing frequently at my girlfriend's breasts.

I wondered, would he be so happy in thirty years' time on a beach with his grandkids? For me that tattoo was an early intimation that our youth would dissipate. It wouldn't always be like this, but what would it be like? It was right there in front of me, Stalin mocking us for our callowness.

And galloping on horseback across the steppes to Baku, and destiny, to win or lose, live or die, immortal twenty-two…

It kind of killed my buzz back then, on that hot summer afternoon in Hungary. And today – whenever that is for you – I imagine that conscript, now a post-Soviet Ukrainian citizen, middle-aged and under fire, a volunteer, too old to be conscripted, occupied or occupying, dead even, bearing the sigil of another world reclused under his shirt, no longer immortal.

Or perhaps he is sunning himself on the beach, T-shirt on, somewhere out of harm's way, on the Caspian or the Black Sea.

Grandpa, why don't you take your T-shirt off, it's so hot!

A sly smile passing between father and son under the parasol. The son shaking his head.

Or.

At a Ukrainian checkpoint.

Fingers fumbling with sweat and fear, undoing shirt buttons at gunpoint. Fat fingers, sweaty because overweight, out of shape, on the verge of becoming eternal.

My mind circles, I can't help it. Was the tower I imagined the little girl lived in a symbol of destruction? The fallacy of power, like in Tarot decks – which I hardly know anything about – towers like cocks pointing to your doom.

She w/rung the shit out of that bell.

Back then I visited Budapest without the weight of memory, we visited bars in the ghetto, not looking up for any towers, real or imaginary, living our young lives from the perspective of the street and no little wonder. Now I can't wake or move without its hand upon me, not a guiding hand – how could it be that? – but a dead one.

Thirty years later I google Istvan Laurer for the first time. In my mind's eye I remember a Joseph Bueys character – the ex-Luftwaffe pilot artist who had sat in a cage with a wolf – Istvan, whip thin, rolling skinny cigarettes with liquorice paper and pungent tobacco from a grimy leather pouch. He looked old then, in that dingy room, but looking him up he must only have been in his fifties. His hammer and mallet hands and disfigured fingers producing the most perfect of tight rollups.

Et voila.

My age now.

Istvan had bought the house with his German partner who was a banker. Ten years later they split up and eight years after that he sold the house to me. He left here to visit his brother in Budapest.

In that car.

Good luck.

I wonder if he got to see his brother and how long the money lasted. Beuys had survived a plane crash in the Crimea, rescued from the flames by Tartar tribesmen, or so he says. Did Istvan make it home, also in one piece albeit exhausted, with a pocket full of money, to change into Forints and spend as he saw fit, or so I imagined?

Online his photos are very much of a kind. Portraits of a serious mid-century white male European artist staring either into the camera or just off it, smoking intently with his work in soft focus behind him. Scruffy, important-looking studio spaces, full of performative creativity; kinetic spaces in which the artist is busy making. His open face reminding me of Oskar in *The Tin Drum*. In fact, there is a headshot of Istvan as a boy and he is the spit of Oskar, perhaps the go-to face for mid-century middle European children, ripe for AI farming, generating skins for gamers on apps like *Midjourney*, the prompt being:

Malnourished/ war child/high forehead/ blue eyes/twentieth century/Russia/Germany.

A precocious face. Arms crossed over an open book. A prodigy reading a book from a private library. Or was it a professional photographer's prop? A tome made from cheap rag paper. A little cheesy, a little too much Hans Christian Anderson.

White is a default for many of these algorithms so I wouldn't have to prompt that, and if you type *Jewish* (which you might for this look, from this time and place) then this is flagged. As well as Oskar, his stark presence in the photographs reminded me of the boy Flyora in Klimov's *Come and See*, the go to face of mid-century horror.

The paintings are mostly circular, something I don't like, an odd aesthetic. I couldn't tell you the meaning of their content, some figurative representations of animals, birds of prey, tropical birds also, parrots, flamingos, very colourful; a lot of greens, bold colours, kitsch, perhaps not far off early Kate Bush album covers, so a shared '70s sensibility, planet aware, a distrust of human politics, I'm not sure. Tendrils also, the profuse fecundity of nature entwining us, you can see this in his work.

Our house was literally part of the hillside. In the spring and autumn rainwater flowed down the bare rock walls of the stairs until I got somebody to wall it in. The kitchen flooded regularly, water bubbling up randomly, yet in summer and winter it was bone dry. The seasons passed through the house and the house rode the seasons, shrugging off whatever nature threw at it.

As we age, the place we live in stays the same. (If we can afford to stay in the same place, or not afford to move from it.) After a certain time we rarely change things or redecorate, the pictures on the walls stay where they are permanent shapes on the wall; we stop refreshing their arrangement, we hardly notice them, they belong to the house. It's us that change. We no longer live in it in the same way. Things fray at the edges, small jobs go undone, disrepair adds up. The house gains a certain patina. It's second skin perhaps. Physically we make small changes, add extra bannisters to help us get upstairs, perhaps do something in the bathroom, slip mats, handholds, etc., but emotionally the shift is greater; we can't help but haunt our previous life. The house we made love in, had our children in, the patterns of our lives now out of sync (ever so slightly at first, but then...) Hallways we tiptoed down drunk, late at night, the desk where we used to work, the corner we always caught ourselves on, the nub of a nail or carpet staple on the stairs, the same small wound on a wrist, arm or ankle, repeated over years. A house also has many psychological facets, atmospheres, vibes, generated in the dining room or kitchen where we entertained. Memory conspires with the house to suggest our time in it is nearly up. To chide us, and not just for the tiredness of decor, the dust and neglect. Our lives become an intimate study of how time passes in space, our private space observing us more than we notice it, the Hubble telescope of the home.

The tables turn and we become the ghosts of entropy.

Istvan Laurer 1984.

No mention of his partner's name, it was his house. What he left behind seemed so benign I didn't feel the need to find out more about him for twenty years. Perhaps the anniversary of having the house prompted it, or just getting older, like him. I even got a tattoo on my forearm that year.

Forza Agaggio.

Venti Anni.

Which is why I nearly missed it, an archived gallery website of his work on which I found paintings of the house, the shape like a children's drawing framed by the three cypresses on the terrace. An oblong outline, six windows and a front door, exterior side steps to the right and V-shaped roof, the moon behind it. (I have never seen the moon behind the house, it is always in front, traversing usually from left to right and back again at all times of day and night.)

Istvan couldn't stop painting or drawing the house, some date from when he was there but mostly in the years afterwards, from memory and becoming more fantastical, the last dating from 2010.

Archived websites are like houses in which we become archived, nothing is added or taken away or moved around anymore, nothing updated or refreshed, websites that are haunted by our absence, achingly evocative of the more we could have done.

If you stare into the abyss long enough it will stare back at you.

I think a man like Istvan would have read Nietzsche. I haven't, other than a few mis/quotes, like *there ain't nothing Nietzsche couldn't teach ya,* a lyric from somewhere, a song, long ago...

Forest fires are a problem up and down the valley in the summer, and if you make bonfires, you get heavily fined. Istvan must have done this in late autumn, warmed by wine on a cold and starry night. The fire caught, racing up one of the trees like a candle, and they had to come up from the village to put it out and to scold him.

Crazy Istvan. He ran about half-naked up there.

It is the only story I heard about Istvan from Gino, a farmer who has olive trees on terraces below our house of which he was protective, so this is a story he would tell.

The absence of the third, although there is a stump. The two remaining trees identify the house as ours more than the house itself.

I can see him stumbling about the terraces at night, drunk, smoking, howling at nothing, for I have done it myself, a pleasurable release.

His paintings have a decorative style. The perspective is flat and antirealist, kind of like Chagall and Japanese block prints, the innocent framing and bold colour blocks of Gauguin. So the moon, or what represents the moon and gives directionality to the shadows, can be where he wants it and them to be compositionally, without recourse to compass or the natural procession of the sky at night. He chose to place it behind the house, lighting it for us. I don't write about art often so don't know the common terms, but this is what I see: he foregrounds the terrace, which is where we spend most of the time. In real life he extended it; it was his stage, a place from which to scry the world. And it looks exactly like that in the paintings and now I scry the world from there also.

In another painting the house is framed inside an outline of a head, I assume his, with the side steps clearly visible and the moon and stars reflected onto the terrace as if onto a pond or a purely fantastical body of water, a full green moon side by side with a sliver of a silver one. In another the house is drawn inside a geometric projection of a rectangle, which is itself inside a huge head, a block from which he carves his vision of the house, like in the childhood game of *Chipaway*. We have the drawings of the terrace extension, a *Geometer's* plan for the work he went on to carry out. Art and life, his will imposed on the world; the terrace he built is now the centre of your experience of the house, its pleasure, where you survey the valley, the sky and the mountains all at once, and in the summer an inside-outside house.

Yellow is one of his favourite colours. Lemon yellow. It seems to flood his canvases. The reason must be metaphorical, because there is very little actual yellow in the valley that I can think of; a rash of autumn blooming crocus, a lemon tree that grudgingly bears a few lemons, but dry, discoloured nasty ones. Definitely not enough yellow to balance the greens in their many shades and densities throughout the year. Green dominates. Perhaps he chose yellow because it is a hopeful colour, a colour of resistance to the rule of green.

Das Haus Istvan Laurer '83.

Below is – again – a rough translation of what he wrote next to one picture a year before he chiselled the slate on the front wall. He must have been in the manic phase of buying and occupying a new house to write this, the purchase of which empowered him to think differently.

The search for truth was louder both in terms of the pictorial form and the pictorial vocabulary. Those who prefer the more dramatic version may read this as: he lived through the crisis that no artist is spared.

Which probably reads better in German. Is the search for truth a crisis? If so, what are the stakes? And why do artists have to undertake it?

More interesting to me is: what is the story of this house?

In a forgotten folder I find more drawings by Istvan, this time dreams for the house that never materialised. A loggia upstairs, with arches instead of windows open to the elements, also a short bridge from the main house to the derelict buildings behind, which were to be restored. This span creates the beginnings of an alleyway, a shared space between houses, the beginnings of a hamlet. I have seen smaller *Viccoli*, just like this, intimate paths between homes, semi-enclosed by walkways overhead. Were these drawings part of his vision as an artist? His crisis was one of love (which presumably ran out), but also of time and money, which he presumably never had enough of.

I look up at the asbestos roof we have yet to replace for reasons of money. I look at the two derelict sheds behind ours and the upstairs flat yet/never to be converted into a loggia. Not my dream, but these drawings, intricately drawn, coloured and proportioned, had been his. The terrace extension was a beginning, a start to something, a project under way.

In his later works, you find many pared-back line drawings of a male figure, probably himself, reminiscent of Keith Haring; spiky and almost dancing figures as if they were throwing shapes, but overall Istvan painted too many circular canvasses.

I stopped engaging.

I asked Paul what he remembers of meeting Istvan and we mused on why I hadn't googled him before. Paul says I wasn't interested as I just wanted him out of the house as quickly as possible. My house, that I was so eager to take possession of. Charmless if true, but I don't recall that being the case, I hope it wasn't. Perhaps it was exciting to buy a holiday home in my thirties, I was full of myself. Maybe that clouded my behaviour regarding Istvan, distracted me from engaging with him properly. Paul remembers the dog, the wine, the jalopy of a car and push-starting it down the drive and the farewell, standing at the end of our road waiting for him to reappear within minutes, which he didn't do, instead disappearing from our lives forever.

The full stop of that. The symbolic death of him.

Other than Gino, nobody in the village has ever mentioned Istvan to me, but everyone seems to know the house. It's implausible that nobody remembers him in a village which for many years had only one shop, a butcher and a restaurant. He drank, which can lead to notoriety. Perhaps others remember when he burnt down his cypress tree. The drunk up on Via Casoni. Up all hours playing music. The crazy Hungarian artist.

He left us his jukebox, a beaten-up, old and falling apart machine that contained a snapshot of music from another time. *Those were the days my friend, Cuba, Mull of Kintyre, Hanging on the telephone, Life goes on, When you're in love with a beautiful woman*, a softer side, a romantic Istvan, again, somebody I will never know. We cranked up the volume and danced on the terrace to these songs, they became – because they already were – the soundtrack of the house. We became their listeners.

Once upon a time there was a tavern
Where we used to raise a glass or two

Remember how we laughed away the hours
Think of all the great things we would do?

'Yes Istvan, we knew him, he came in here all the time, god he liked to drink, and talk, but we couldn't understand a word of it. An artist? Well, he never mentioned it, but now you tell me, it makes sense, yes, a character for sure.'

A shared smile, a shake of the head at this small collective memory. And perhaps not much more. A disappointment somehow, a letdown, an anticlimax.

But I have yet to hear his name mentioned, and as time passes, I doubt I will.

The house as always, remains silent.

1984.

Tibor was the man who sold us the house and he must have known Istvan! They had a shared heritage. But he's also dead. He was a Hungarian Jew, a man who hated communism. His father had been one of the high-ups in the theatre, a party apparatchik in Budapest, so the rejection of his patrimony might have been familial. In rejecting your father you reject automatically his communism, or the other way around. You grow up hating the system and your father is literally a part of what you hate. How can you disentangle the two? Or you love your father enough to ignore his failings, his complicity in a system you grew up resisting. Or you didn't resist at all, enjoy the privileges of being a child of the nomenklatura, later resenting your father for your own complicity. Tibor couldn't wait to leave his country. I remember he loved speedboats, fancy seafood restaurants on the coast and long winter holidays in Southeast Asia. If that gives any insight into how he might have aggregated his beliefs, the logic of his life and passions. He never mentioned Istvan either; again, I never asked. In retrospect I am shocked by my disinterest.

God knows why.

Budapest was at the confluence of many conflicting passions. This side, that side, East or West, with us or against them, the sword, the crescent, the eagle or the arrow. I remember visiting the Gyorgy Lukacs baths, where old men sit for hours in chest-high water, play chess, smoke and drink tea. Just before heaven or hell, if you believe in such places, you get to spend time here with friends. Tibor played chess. We only played once or twice, he wasn't that friendly or I wasn't. He oversaw the initial building work at the house, with him it was all business, which became no more than a nodding acquaintance over time.

Perhaps the only thing that anchors us is not a house but the dream of one. You can take that with you, you never have to sell it and it never abandons you. That's what you take into exile, all you can rely on: an idea. Which is odd because it is intangible – but perhaps logical for exiles who have nothing – yet I have seen it eat people alive.

Casa Istvan.

I'll stick with that. Am happy with the slight shadow cast by his name, would never think of carving mine, both of which pale next to the certainty of the house and the mountain.

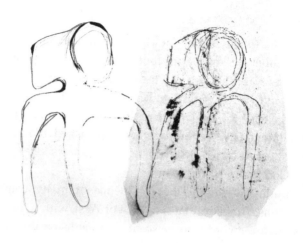

IL TEMPO PASSA

The dreams of youth grow dim where they lie caked with dust on the shelves of patience. Before we know it, the tomb is sealed.

— Sterling Hayden, *The Wanderer*

From the house you can hear two sets of bells, but in twenty years I have only ever seen one church. A very old one. The cliche that people were much smaller in the past – just think how small cars used to be – holds true for this church. It's tiny. A fat priest would have to squeeze through the door, huffing and puffing, definitely not a holy sight. Peasants and workers were mostly slight, plagued by disease and poverty; a poor diet, always hungry, dreaming of food they would rarely, if ever, eat. Feast days celebrated in the shadow of famine.

Every New Year's Eve there is a bonfire in the courtyard. People gather and gaudy presents are handed out to children and everyone drinks hot chocolate or cheap Prosecco. We share the warmth of the fire and contemplate deep orange flames leaping into the sky. Teenagers let off fireworks behind the church. Through a tiny, barred window you can glimpse Midnight Mass, pews packed with worshippers subscribing to a mystery. Outside an old man sits on a bench eating a grape for every chime of the midnight bell.

Chi mangia l'uva per Capodanno, maneggia I quattrini tutto l'anno.

Money, finding one's fortune, superstition, out with the old in with the new. The presence of food and the memory of its absence. Eating lentils for luck, which resemble coins. Pomegranate seeds the same, since Roman times a mouthful of rubies. In an age of tap and pay, the idea of a physical fortune, of filthy lucre, piles of silver and gold coins, the heft of a bag of gemstones, captures our imagination.

Fabulous. The thing itself. The more you eat, the richer you become. A world without metaphor. Transubstantiation.

Accept no substitutes.

The rituals of the service create an armature to protect *the mystery*. A wider folk religion allows *Mass* to exist alongside a much older and diverse set of pagan practices and beliefs. Catholicism is primed by the space it sought to colonise. I mean that war ended a thousand years ago but what came before still haunts the victor. Other cultures held out longer, a few still do, their persistence of self-imagining a thing of wonder.

As an agnostic I don't have any direct experience of this, just an inchoate desire for it to be so. Once in Rome, at night, also in winter, I stepped inside a cavernous candlelit church. Expecting it to be empty, I was surprised to discover a large congregation singing in Latin, in almost perfect unison. On the street it had been silent. The heavy wooden door and the plush ruby velvet curtain behind it accessed another world. I transgressed. This is the trick that bushwhacked me, a sleight of hand that caught me unawares. Soft, flickering gold light, the air redolent with the smell of incense from a swaying censor. A full force gale. I fled down the street. I felt an intimation of having witnessed something not exactly sacred but pretty close. I glimpsed something beyond myself. It felt a little obscene.

I feel nothing other than cold on this New Year's Eve, nothing, not even the comfort of strangers. Meagre enjoyment, I can only analyse from a cold distance, unable to escape the armature of my totalitarian ego.

The house overlooks the valley and sound can appear to come from any direction or distance. You can't trust your ears. Unsighted, sound bounces off the sides of mountains, runs along roads and crosses rivers, obscuring its origins stubbornly. Near or far? Volume is no guarantee of distance. The bass from a midnight rave two valleys over can sound like it's spilling out of the restaurant in the village below. On another night, laugher and mischief from the same restaurant manifests itself from the direction of a derelict house on a promontory baffled by olive groves. As if God were playing ventriloquist.

And so with the bells and the whereabouts of the second church. They start at six a.m., waking the cockerels, which triggers the hunting dogs in their cages howling to be fed, until the last strokes of midnight accompanied occasionally by owls which lull you to sleep. Bar the odd car or motorbike late back from the coast or some other more local assignation, the house is left in silent darkness, unless surprised by the moon which can patrol the valley like a drunken searchlight, for who can predict the appearance and progression of it? Waxing or waning, full, blood, wolf, harvest or sickle, she has many faces and they all shine differently, or not at all.

Framed by a fringe of light pollution from the coast, the valley hunkers down to slumber. In the mountains there is only the night, a single block of unpatrolled time and space bookended by last and first bells. Roman sentries once kept lookout for armies of Goths and Visigoths – names by which to conjure demons – but preferred to warm themselves by the fire, fearing to venture beyond its penumbra.

Night, a nature reserve for time, policed only by imagination – the soft fluttering of wings, a sharp crack of twigs, animal grunts and screeches – a place for spirits, for heavy breathing and silence, goosebumps and night sweats. Night time. In which you gasp awake, dashing hopes of a forgetful sleep, creeping downstairs or not creeping downstairs, because you hear a thud, a creak, a scuttle. Immobilised right there on the top stair. Fight or flight. Adrenalin surges, fine-tuning your every sense, dispensing Olympian doses of courage or fear. Your leg shakes. Night requires luck to survive, misfortune to succumb, a place for left-open doors and creatures in trees, for the subtle interplay between the world out there and your subconscious, one projected onto the other, a recursive loop between the two. I wake up blinded by this overlap, unable to fathom the thing itself rather than its many shadows, groping for my watch on the bedside table, it's radium lume glows the time, as if knowledge of the hour would also secure me in it, so tethered I am to the telling of it. I fear not knowing, and isn't that a pleasure we rarely allow ourselves for long? Reaching as we do for something to fix ourselves back in place.

Night breeds discontent. An unmapped space ripe for misadventure.

*

What are you doing? Discombobulated.

A heavy whisper. *Nothing.*

A low groan. *You woke me up.*

Sorry. A silhouette sits up.

What time is it?

A hand gropes for its phone, knocks over a glass of water. Curses. *Christ!*

It's the middle of the night. Flat, disheartened.

The defensive silhouette replies. *I thought I heard something, sorry.*

Weak phone light spills over the bed.

A grumble, rearranging the duvet.

Silence.

Or on coming back from the toilet, a challenge!

Who's that!

The bedside light switches on.

Whispers.

It's me, who else would it be!

You frightened the life out of me!

I just went to the loo. Sorry.

Christ. Followed swiftly by a gentle snoring.

The mundane sanctity of the conjugal bed, a site of unimaginable terror.

*

Marooned, I toss and turn but can't get back to sleep. My mind races, slows down, speeds up, circling the dilemma of *life so far*. Only incremental levels of ambient light outside offer a clue as to how far *into the night* we have come. My heart sinks, having woken up too soon on a deep space mission, condemned to live out the rest of my life alone before we ever reaching our destination, the planet Dawn.

Six a.m.

Twelve chimes, six from each church, four minutes and twenty seconds apart. The little church has a bell tower but I have never seen the bell itself. Perhaps they are recorded chimes, or are the bells physically struck by some automated mechanism? Why not? How many bells are there, anyway? Recorded or otherwise? I don't need an image of bells being rung by a rota of dedicated bell ringers, or by a lone priest (fat or skinny) stiff in his joints, more than occasionally late to the bells, or indeed by enthusiastic monks flying up and down the bell tower in their cassocks clinging on to the ropes for dear life like in a Mars bar commercial I once saw in a cinema. I imagine there is both danger and humour in vast Quasimodo bells which can drag you up and off the floor as they gain momentum – I remember him from an old black-and-white film leaping from one huge tolling bell to another – or if the swinging gets out of control – like soldiers not breaking step on weak bridges, the bridge collapses – the bells break free of their moorings, careering off the walls of the tower, smashing bricks to powder and crushing anything below in a cloud of apocalyptic dust. This catastrophe has something to do with the law of oscillation or something like that. Like kicking so hard when you're a kid on the swings you reach a point of no return and fly over the top.

I wake up without incident. It's nearly half-past eight. I've missed the dogs howling. I go downstairs and grind some coffee.

Eight thirty. A single toll marks the half hour.

Rather jaunty and light of touch, as if to say *on we go, another half hour gone, top of the hour up next, keep up.*

It chimes in counterpoint to the tolling of the hours, which climax with an imposing set of twenty-four chimes spaced over almost five minutes of time at midday and midnight, straddling the diurnal border as if to sign off; *good night and good luck, you're on your own until six a.m.* The difference in the tone of this half-hour chime is purely in the mind but I swear it sounds different.

I pick up a book from the kitchen table and sit out on the terrace. I think the water in the Gaggia machine is probably hot enough by now, it usually takes ten minutes. I put the book down and go back inside. I pour a cup of coffee, add squirty cream and come back outside. In my absence sunlight has hit the terrace. I get up and open the parasol, swinging it over the table. I put on my sunglasses. I drink the coffee and smoke a cigarette. I pick the book up again. My sunglasses have a peculiar prescription, to read with them I have to hold a book just so, too far away from my body for it to be comfortable. The glasses are also so scratched I usually push them up onto my head and read squinting in the bright sunlight.

The first week of a summer holiday passes in a blur caused by a clash of two currents that cancel each other out, or at least appear to, until the stronger one gains the upper hand and however weakly holds sway. Time always finds *now*, its level ground; the outcome of a conflict between the sense of it you bring with you and the actual time of where you are. A pile-up of City, work, about to go on holiday time, followed by a week of decompression and outbursts of temper as we readjust. The difference in light plays a role in this awkward transition, both the amount of it and its intensity. We are thrown into light. Everything we do or think is seen, observed – by a heightened and frustrating self-awareness – we find ourselves civilians in the constant war between tectonic plates of time and place. Confused by the demands of two places and the rules that pertain to each, we exist in the zero gravity of neither.

Psychic friction.

I feed the dog. She wolfs it down and slumps in the shade under the table on the terrace. I look at my phone and light another cigarette staring at the green hillside opposite. It pulses under the sun, reminding me of the book *Annihilation*.

I anticipate the end of the summer from the middle of it. The tide turns and my mind sets a course for home. Time speeds up, bringing with it an almost chemical melancholy which haunts your remaining days. The last weekend is always already experienced as the memory of *the last weekend*, which is by definition melancholic, self-indulgent, pathetic. Much like the first week where you live under the dissonance of two bells, under heavy manners. Back home you always feel a bit discombobulated for a day or two, experienced as an aftershock of being on holiday unlike the actual *bends* you feel the first week away, the torture of that, a temporary current working against the inevitable tide of *your life.* Holiday time is, in a word, false, creating anxiety, dread, and provoking maudlin thoughts.

Tomorrow I pick up my family from the airport. The holiday as such has yet to begin.

Time for a swim. The dog and I walk down to the river, stopping on the way for a drink at a roadside well and to see the five goldfish who live in it. I take the tin cup that hangs on a piece of string and fill it from the spigot. The water is always bracingly cold, running off as it does from the mountain behind. There are two bright red fish and three silver.

We have the river to ourselves. I lay my towel out on the rocks, sit down and open my book. The dog sits expectantly under a tree overlooking the water. The stones burn my feet. It's already baking hot.

People that travel a lot from a young age never learn the ability, an art really, of settling down anywhere. Not tied to a singular idea of home they are free to develop other habits. You get the 'travel bug', itchy feet you keep for the rest of your lives – or at least the rest of your youth – while you have the energy you spend it wantonly. You live out of a suitcase and experience life as an adventure shared with strangers, making fast and loose friends where you find them. And then move on. I admire these people; they have achieved a certain escape velocity. Before anything can catch up with them, from ennui to bailiffs, or tie you down, jobs, lovers, the comforts of a single place, the claws of sentiment. Hippies, oligarchs, migrants, digital nomads, corporate employees, soldiers, diplomats have this in common, if nothing else.

But how long can it last, and what price do you have to pay for the ride? The older you get, the more like a pinball you feel, bouncing from place to place, gig to gig, posting to posting. You don't have the energy or imagination to stop. The bug is a virus; you caught it from someone and have given it to others, it will get you in the end and when you finally stop, wherever that is and whatever that looks like, all you will be left with is the comedown, the sound of spent energy, a terrible existential tinnitus ringing in your ears.

I put my book down and dive into the water. It feels wonderful, fresh, clarifying. The dog barks and doesn't stop until I get out. We still have the place to ourselves. The bells chime eleven. Too early for lunch, although I think about what to have. I worry my phone. No messages.

The lucky or the damned can roam the earth, find themselves anywhere and fit in. If one house burns down, they find another. Home. Strange smells and habits mark the people we find there, hiding from the world as if in a cave. Alone in the valley, I experience an acute awareness of *being in the world*. I languish in the gaps between bells. On bad days I can't settle. My actual tinnitus screams. I can imagine this becoming intolerable. Some people hear the throb of blood marking time as it pumps through their veins. Proof of the miracle of life or of the inevitable countdown to death. You either love it or hate it.

Lunch time.

Back at the house I open a bottle of ice-cold Moretti to accompany the bread, cheese, tomato and salami I bought at the local shop. I rarely cook for myself when I'm alone and if I do it's just to boil water for pasta and perhaps fry up some Guanciale. I forgot to buy butter and matches to light the stove, so burn my finger using my favourite stubby Bic lighter. It's got Popeye on it. I collect Popeye memorabilia, mostly shit T-shirts and diecast figurines and cigarette lighters. My favourite is a Popeye Toby jug used to hold pens and sunglasses. If only I had his strength. I don't even eat much spinach. All I have to go with the tomatoes are a few soggy-looking spring onions from the bottom of the fridge. I also forgot to get lettuce. For a dressing I mix some dodgy-looking God-knows-how-old balsamic vinegar with congealed olive oil into a pot of mustard with just dry scrapings left in it.

Ding.

I chew off the end of the salami, spitting out the metal toggle. Two drags of a fag and a gulp of metallic beer with the sharp taste of onion on my tongue. I try to focus on my book but the words swim about on the page.

I feel dizzy.

Ding.

It's half two.

I burp onions.

I'm exhausted.

I think of prison time, of the yard, of the cell, of endless minutes, hours, days and years rolling forward. An intense sensual awareness of it that has to be subdued by numbing routine and medication.

I lie down on a deck chair.

Released from prison, having done his time, served his sentence, a man goes into the pub across the road and orders a pint. He knows this pub, has seen it from the window in the prison chapel. His visitors have mentioned it, that's where they go after and occasionally before visiting him, even though they are embarrassed to have the smell of it on them. The pub is familiar although it's his first time. The beer tastes good. He feels born again, expectant, fearful. He is, in this moment, free. Will he luxuriate in this new state or agonise over it? How long will he feel the urge to look over his shoulder like ex-cons do in the movies? Or is that just in movies? He smokes his first cigarette *as a free man*. What is the nature of this pleasure? Inside or outside, how has its meaning changed, the meaning of cigarettes?

The best cigarette, the best beer, the greatest sex, the most amazing meal? The quality of these experiences is essentially determined by how we parse time. The trip of a lifetime. Endless love, one-night stands, all-nighters, three-day benders. The slow, exquisite inhale and release of fresh air, sea air. A quick fag, a long cigar, a four-hour lunch, a bottomless brunch; thick time that gifts each of these moments, usually framed as male bucket list obsessions, but I'm not so sure...

A woman comes out of prison at the end of her sentence. Does she feel like she has wasted her time? Is she bitter, sanguine or mournful? Does she want a drink and a cigarette, to taste her freedom, or does she ache to see her family and – if she has any – her children? Has she been counting the days until her release, chalking them off, or has it come as a surprise, to find herself once again on the outside? Perhaps she is indifferent, her tariff spent.

How long does it take to get used to the wide-open spaces freedom allows but also the small, mean, claustrophobic places you find yourself in everyday life? Is there an old rhythm they fall back into, or did the experience of prison create a break with the past, from who they were before? Lost time, how do they make it up? How do they wean themselves off the metronomy of incarceration? Mix it up, embrace random experiences, surprise others, surprise yourself? What is the day-to-day texture of living on the outside? Do some people re-offend as soon as they can, to get back inside because it's the only way they know how to do time?

A rich man is released from prison, his time regained.

On holiday there is no escape from time. There is no existential freedom, and if there was such a thing who would want it, to be out there dangling at the end of a tether, on an endless spacewalk to nowhere? There are always things that tether us, things we hold in common. Hunger, desire, hope, boredom, contentment, exhaustion, orgasm, indifference, despair. It is only the amount of each that differs.

After two more beers I rally. I change books, shifting my perspective.

Vogliamo Tutto.

We want everything.

Between the ringing of the two bells is a window of opportunity. The temporal equivalent of cinema's golden hour, when the light looks *just so*. Stolen time to be spent frivolously. From the trite close-ups of *Who am I?* to the wide-angled despair of *What the fuck does it all mean?* This soon unravels to the prosaic, the gloriously mundane, the sweeping anamorphic grandeur of *What do you fancy for supper?* And *Is there enough wine?*

Time spent alone is occupied with both subconscious thought and active thinking, in a free-flowing interplay that knocks up the disharmonious polyphonic construct that is 'me' and 'you'. Family, work, plans, money, friends, mistakes, luck, you have time and inclination to riff on and off everything with no particular purpose and in no particular order.

Life is jazz, atonal.

The only music I can tolerate because it demands nothing of me. I am not so slavish as to follow a tune, but I remember coming up to the deep bass and rising tempo of Chicago House. Without drugs I have never been *lost in music*.

Shipwrecked on the other side of ego, an epiphany, passing into the mystic.

Listening to music takes a lot of work.

A lot of work.

To listen to others.

The second bell strikes the hour, breaking the spell.

*

I need to do a huge shop before picking up my family, so will have to write a list. I love these big supermarkets, Carrefour and Conad, wandering endlessly up and down the aisles staring at products, picking up things that catch my eye, noticing new things for sale, for example the novelty of sushi stalls popping up in both of the big supermarkets, staffed by Asian chefs and selling cans of Sapporo – arranged like a wall of beer – in their signature aluminium cans. I have always loved the branding of Terre d'Italia, showcasing delicacies from all regions of the country in the livery of blue gold blue and cream plus the new line of Moretti beers, infused with flavours from Piedmontese, Lucana, Friuliana, Siciliana, Toscana, Pugliese...

Mele, Fiori di Zagara, Mirtillo, alloro e Orzo, fico...

The perseverance of tradition alongside novelty. Now you can buy Moretti beer around the world, it has become commonplace. We move on to Menabrea, Ichnusa and the salty Sicilian Messina, until they too fall to the marketing departments and advertising agencies of their corporate owners. As of writing this I am drinking Forst Sixtus, but also enjoy the new wave of cold filtered and unfiltered craft beers, fiercely regional and as yet unbiddable.

*

Eventually I discover the location of the second church and its bells up on the ridge of the mountain behind us, in a mostly deserted village. How did I miss that? I'm not a huge walker but it's only a half-hour hike up through the olive terraces. When I get to the top I am exhausted, take a long drink from a water fountain, literally quenching my thirst. Sure enough, there is an old derelict church, on a narrow promontory overlooking three valleys. *A place of greater safety*, I think for no reason. You could hold out up here for a long time, or indeed be cut off and starved out. What do I know of such things? I lie down and look up at the spire. I feel giddy but my vision soon focuses on the weathervane and the devil who is riding it, which is odd, to have a devil swim into focus, a black silhouette cut out of a cloudless pale blue sky. There is nobody around, just me, the church and the devil on top.

It's an ill wind that blows nobody any good.

I've never understood what that phrase means. Do other winds blow good fortune?

The other bells now chime from below, you can hear them in the distance. It's four p.m. Four minutes and twenty seconds later and on cue they chime right above me, loud and definitely recorded! The mystery is solved. The door to the church is double locked. Through the rusty iron bars on the door – the glass has been broken – I can see trestle tables and chairs stored inside. Opposite this abandoned church sits its replacement with a big blowsy white and faded peach facade, possibly eighteenth-century, a weather-beaten notice board outside with faded parish notices pinned behind glass.

Between the churches is a turning circle for cars. You can see the grey ash remains of a bonfire here, a burnt circle within a circle. It's so remote and abandoned up here that this feels oddly ritualistic, as does the faceoff between the two churches, with the devil riding the wind manifesting above them.

Symbolism.

Perhaps an ill wind destroys crops, causes shipwrecks, brings pestilence and plagues of locusts.

A good wind may be sweet and gentle, caressing us during a hot summer, cooling the crops so we can harvest them without damage, a wind on which birds migrate. Too much rain ruins crops because they rot, too much heat and they dry up.

To die on the vine.

The false promise of things that don't come to fruition. Perhaps it's that, related to nature, to agriculture, ultimately to survival, seasonal jeopardy that *we* no longer experience directly, despite being buffered by the complexity of global supply chains. For now they remain palatable metaphors.

On the way back down to the house, not through the olive groves but on a narrow road, I google *winds*.

In France the Mistral is a strong cold wind swooping down from the north-west, clearing the air and pushing clouds from the skies of Provence and the Mediterranean, although its dryness promotes fires. The clear light is a gift to painting. The Mistral funnels down the valleys from the Rhone to the Camargue. For centuries peasants have leant into it as they went about their business and trees also bow under its force, growing at an angle like that forever; the wind makes itself visible through them, both immortalised in the paintings of the artists who observe them.

I stumble on some loose shale on the road. Fucking Birkenstocks.

There is the famous Scirocco, a warm humid wind which blows up from Africa, and whips up storms like its sister wind the Libecco, a squally wind that comes out of the south-west – from Libya – after which it is named. A high sea wind in the summer that catches many pleasure boats unawares.

Migrant dinghies upturned, empty, rucksacks, toys, plastic water bottles bobbing up and down, clothes washed up, their owners drowned or saved.

The Mediterranean is their playground.

The Levante joins in the fun, blowing from the east, bringing changeable weather, choppy seas and dead calms. The Tramontana is a winter wind which hails from the north over the Alps, blowing south along the west coast of Italy. A strange wind that also gives us a word for others, the unknown, barbarians, those from over the hills and far away. Although it is a fine weather wind like the Mistral (sometimes they team up), its direction helps launch fishing boats westward into the Mediterranean at dawn, as the wind is strongest just before sunrise.

There is even a Mistral Noir, a rare wind, an evil twin that brings cloud and rain...

It's an ill wind...

Nobody benefits from other people's misfortunes? Is that what it means?

But we do, don't we?

I look down at my watch. I can't believe I still do that. I no longer have a watch, although the memory of it, the weight of it and the way I would shake my wrist to bring its face into view, the noise that made, because it was pleasantly loose, the stainless steel links cool against my skin, this visceral recollection sometimes tricks me into assuming it was still there. I look at my wrist still sporting a phantom Rolex. The Air King I sold in order to pay for last summer's holiday, bought years ago from a shop in Palma Majorca airport on the way home from a shoot. My producer at the time told me I deserved it. All those years on my wrist waiting to be cashed in. Like the two gold earrings worn by pirates – insurance for a decent burial – who knows when you might need the money?

*

On Good Friday the bells fall silent to mark the occasion of Christ risen. In some villages they blew goat or sheep horns so they would still know what time it was. Pagan sound fulfilling a christian duty. Were we so addicted to it even back then? For one day was it not enough for us to just pass from light into dark? What was it that gave time its ascendancy? What were we scared of? Now this arcane practice gives rise to merriment and folk ritual, and the villagers of Mont/alto blow horns and even conch shells to mark the occasion, accompanied by food and wine, an opportunity to celebrate. They cook *Fritelle*, a sort of deep-fried cake without sugar, stuffed with stock fish and accompanied with a glass of Prosecco.

I don't believe it. I don't believe this story. It is unbelievable.

These festivals are false or have become so. Our past provides us with safe entertainment. A catholic makeover of merriment. A calendrical excuse to get drunk, flattening out the richness and absurdity of the original. True carnival is alive in the moment, celebrating the vertigo of being in time. The lusty realism of second sons, Goliards, outsiders, free men, thrown into time itself. With no other choice but...

To see what happens!

Carnival is an intoxication of the corporeal, delivering us back into our visceral selves to experience a good time and celebrate the flow of blood in a druidical sense, a sensibility of time and space that civilisation has stolen from us, burying us under so many clocks and imprecations we forget in which direction to turn.

We are upside the head.

Thrown down into...

A dizzy life of mundane festival, everyday party, inebriation without a sense of bacchanal, nor reason, we become hollow pleasure seekers, surface skaters, sensualists, self-indulgent, frivolous scatterers, bad seedsmen, spendthrifts ignorant of place and of all the intricate workings and aspects of this our forever home.

The tomb is sealed.

UOMO D'OCA

Lasciate ogni speranza o voi che avete fretta. Qui il cibo si prepara al momento e va gustato. In alternativa a San Remo ce il MCDONALD!![1]

When I am away from the house, far away from it, I dream of the valley and the people there as if I had jotted them down but forgotten where and like all dreams my imagination worked up these scant fragments into something grander, whirling around in the centrifuge of my ego; a haphazard subconscious *willed into being,* more dust devil than whirlwind, yet one that made so much sense – a story told with such clarity – before being forgotten almost immediately and the images, feelings, snippets of memory

1   Abandon all hope if you are in a hurry. Here the food is prepared on the spot and should be enjoyed. Alternatively, go to San Remo for McDonald's!!

fall away, the wind snatched from their sails, as they have little or no purchase on the waking mind.

On returning all I bring with me is a sense of familiarity earned only in dreams.

I open my eyes and I see…

Aldo, the chef. A little drunk, a little stoned, one minute up, the next down, flashing a smile or a frown, fluidly moving between kitchen and table, diners and staff, marking his territory, the stations of his cross. Aldo definitely suffered for his art, or indeed just suffered. He had a haunted demeanour albeit a kind one, soft hazel eyes underscored with dark chestnut saddlebags and skin as greasy as the surface of one of his winter soups. Skinny as a rake, with razor clams for muscles, he was held together by his own animus, a preternatural energy.

Roasting, boiling and pan frying, Christ it is hot inside the small kitchen. Waves of heat and tendrils of steam chase him out into the dining room. His character puts you in mind of Harlequin or Pierrot, triggered by the black-and-white check of his stained trousers on which he furiously wiped his hands before vigorously shaking yours. There was no doubt Aldo had a certain style and a firm grip. Sad but funny, quick-witted, definitely not malevolent but carrying a darkness or the memory of one, the remains of something he had experienced. He was somebody who attracted people to him, good and bad, the type of person you recognise right away but can't quite put your finger on what type that is.

Charismatic, sort of, but you also felt sorry for him, a little. Perhaps this was something he lived in the knowledge of. Of having to perform in the shadow of other people's assumptions. People displayed a certain unearned familiarity towards him, to which he reacted in kind. He wasn't exactly familiar, but it didn't feel like it was the first time when you met him for the first time.

Pulling up outside a bar in his beat-up Fiat Panda somebody shouts – You okay Aldo? – assuming he had broken down or needed help with something. People always named him – Hey, Aldo, you wanna earn a little extra cash? That's what I like about you Aldo, always have done – as if it gave them power to know his name and use it. Aldo would brindle at this, light a cigarette, shrug – and you, are you okay? – as if to say fuck you whoever you are, you know nothing about me. It unnerved him, this familiarity. He sits down, a fragile smile on his lips, looking left and right, skittishly tamping down a rising anger.

Perhaps people are drawn to the enigma of him, the volatility of his personality. An emotion containing at its core the possibility of forbidden pleasure not dissimilar to witnessing a car crash or a shipwreck.

Aldo ate on his feet, cheese from the fridge, pinches of mortadella, fatty scraps from plates, titbits from the frying pan, juggling pieces of meat or pasta around his mouth with his tongue to cool them down. Whenever he had a few spare minutes, he would sneak a smoke out on the back steps of the kitchen, by the pots of herbs and a bed of rosemary. Sometimes he smoked while cooking, popping his head out of the kitchen window to exhale or to stub his butt out into an old tin whenever he thought somebody he didn't know was coming through the curtain, theatrically wafting steam from a simmering pan of water or batting away hissing oil and smoke rising from a pan of crispy pancetta, throwing up a smokescreen of obscenities.

Porco Madonna! Pettola a culo!

At the end of the shift he would come outside, light a spliff and stare into space, red eyed, exhausted. He smoked with his staff. They rolled from organic American Spirit pouches that Aldo usually mislaid and they had to search high and low for in an ongoing sequence of mini dramas.

He's that guy, Americans might say.

One evening, after a somewhat erratic service – long waits between courses, forgotten orders and too many broken glasses – Aldo was inconsolable. Grabbing his guitar from behind the bar, he came outside and started to play, his voice off key and the strings out of tune. Like an itinerant minstrel he stomped around the kitchen garden. A waiter came out and left a carafe of wine on the wall without saying a word. The music, if you could call it that, stopped. If he had been singing for his supper, he would have gone hungry. Aldo put the guitar down, slumped on the kitchen step and started drinking. That morning a fox had made off with his goose, leaving behind only a few blood-smeared feathers stuck on the wire of its coop, fox gang signs to mock him, which he now pulled out from his apron pocket. He stared at the feathers and wailed in pain, although the goose had always been destined for the pot, albeit not until Christmas.

Into the goose's imaginary ear, head cradled in his hands, Aldo softly sings an almost lullaby.

'*Se campu vegnu ti viju bella, nda chista terra non ci tornu chjù.*'[2]

These lines in a Calabrese dialect he had learnt from his father, Achille. Snippets of songs heard as a child and on family holidays. A language full of yearning, sung in high-pitched voices.

---

2   If I come and see you beautiful, I won't come back to this land.

'*Partia da casa mia mi mi sdirregnu, e mi ndi vinni a sta terra stranera, ndaju la testa china di penzeri, lu cori chinu di malincunia.*'[3]

Achille would sing as a way of understanding the people and things he encountered. Born in the seaside town of Amantea, he had been a lorry driver, a wholesale grocer, a coffee machine salesman, a locksmith. None of which had made him particularly rich or happy. He loved to cook but had never worked in a restaurant or cafe. His one indulgence had been to fall in love with Cinzia, a girl from Liguria. It was a point of pride that he hadn't come north looking for work *like all the rest*. A bitter pride, but we hang our hats on whatever peg comes to hand.

Aldo dreamed of the world beyond the valley, the experience of being a stranger, unseen, the unknown pleasure of that. Friends who could afford it escaped the slow winter months, to Cuba, America, some even to Russia. To cheer himself, he imagined cooking feasts of many courses. Dishes brought back from his limited travels abroad; Spain, Morocco and once to Thailand. At his most expansive he conjured dishes from these places fused with his home cooking. Wild boar tagine with apricocca, spicy king crab risotto with burnt soy butter, truffled noodles, squid and juniper berry carpaccio, this last dish suggested by a friend who had been lucky enough to visit Tokyo, a destination Aldo held above all others. Japan, the land where cuts of tuna are miraculously divided by strokes of pen and ink on flesh, hundreds of thousands of dollars' worth of fish entrusted to the hand–eye coordination of a master calligrapher, something he learnt from watching a documentary on TV, as he scribbled down

3   I left home, I was dizzy, and I came to this strange land, my head full of thoughts, my heart full of melancholy.

his weekly orders on the back of an envelope, one usually containing an unpaid bill.

In the fish market of San Remo, Aldo would carefully eye up the day's catch, asking one or other of the family-run businesses to show him their wares, each week trying to play one family off against another – there were only seven families and three were related by marriage – amusing and exasperating all of them with this game, which went on for months, back and forth, to very little gain or loss for either side.

Imagine them at family suppers, usually held on a Saturday night, joking about the peculiarities of their customers, the quirks and personality traits of their regulars, gently mocking Aldo as they tuck into a simple rabbit ragu or perhaps slow-cooked *lenticchie e cotechino*, or even *musetto*, meat taken from the pig's muzzle. Anything but fish, the luxurious aroma of herbs and cooking meat temporarily masking the forever smell of the sea.

Today's catch? I didn't make it to the port, but it's fresh, you got it from there today?

Aldo, you never make it to the port.

He points to a fish head accusatorially.

The eyes here are not so bright, like mine, yesterday's eyes. Tell me I'm wrong!

You know we have our own boat, Aldo. Il Brigante, from the sea to you.

This one look, as firm as the breasts of a…

Don't touch the fish, Aldo!

Bravo!

This squid, it smells.

And the colour here along the spine, look.

The scales have fallen from my eyes, these must be frozen!

Aldo, enough!

Madonna!

He doesn't even ask for a discount, he wants us to offer him one, it's just torture, he's crazy!

Exasperated, they would eventually shrug.

Take it or leave it, Aldo!

Perhaps they acted this out at the table, taking parts, remembering the latest exchanges, or perhaps not, nothing so expansive, just a shrug, *well, that's just Aldo, it's the way he is, just like I am the way I am*, with a smile and an expectant look around for another plateful, for second helpings…

Aldo enjoyed watching one of the female fishmongers gut anchovies, which she did methodically with a narrow knife, wiping her hands on her tight apron. He invariably bought from her, regardless of price or quality, mesmerised as he was by a woman wielding a small knife so adroitly.

Basta cosi?

Aldo couldn't help but cook up a storm. His imagination outran that of his regular customers, the farmers and local quarry workers who expected three types of pasta and a stew for lunch, locals who enjoyed nine courses of antipasti at the weekend followed by three or four pasta choices and then a choice of roasted meats (wild boar/lamb/rabbit/beef) and families who expected Friday night pizzas for the kids and ice cream (four flavours) and panna cotta to follow.

It took a while for this audience to embrace crème brûlée with blackberry compote – Aldo enjoyed the theatre of lighting the torch and caramelising the sugar and custard at the table, he lit cigarettes this way also – but they did eventually and how. His mania subsided after a shift where he could see diners trying something new on the menu. He took great pleasure going over who had eaten what with his staff after the shift, poking his finger at the receipts to prove his point. He remembered their habits, what they usually ordered, knew what they like to cook at home, so when he got them to try something different, to take an idea or a new flavour home with them, then he was happy, he had worked his magic.

Mainly he settled for simple dishes, but with his own signature. When he brought fresh fish into the valley, he announced *Entre Mare e Montagna* on the blackboard. Grilled squid, octopus, spada, beef and fish carpaccio (he could still dream), truffles and bottarga, pasta vongole and cozze, deep-fried anchovies with homemade mayonnaise, purple asparagus with crispy-skinned Vietnamese-style seabass, dishes to leaven the dark meats of the valley. He even hit on the idea of serving grilled shellfish with colourful bibs for the diners to wear, again, a little stagecraft, something extra. He made a deal with Andrea, a young man he knew in the seaside village of San Bartolomeo who fished pots from his grandfather's boat. *I'll take all of your lobsters and langoustines up front!*

The restaurants in the village wouldn't buy from Andrea, so for a change it was a deal made in Aldo's favour. Andrea had gone to make his fortune in Genoa and instead ended up in prison. *Who knows what for?* the locals muttered. The prodigal son is just a story but there is nothing more unforgiving than a small fishing village. After every weekend Aldo offered a sliding scale of money and weed as payment, depending on how busy he had been.

This deal worked out until it didn't.

Tourists were greedy, they wanted everything. They craved novelty but also simplicity. They were hungry for the story as much as the food itself. Provenance, authenticity and zero kilometres were their buzzwords. Pasta made from chestnut flour, *farina dolce* was a favourite, something they had read about which channelled, and spoke of, historical poverty. They could almost taste it.

Stoccafisu[4] accompanied by a yarn of war and famine - one garnishing the other - was another,

All the better to eat you with.

But tourists were irregular guests, seasonal trade, albeit a much-needed breath of fresh air and a fillip for Aldo's wilder kitchen fantasies. They traded him tales of holidays, business trips and the places they came from. Food always carries a story and stories have always embraced food, both shared with a compulsive passion; a great night out, here try this, a new restaurant discovery, you must go! Travel, exotic dishes, the taste, colour and smell of far-flung places. The world itself. Cooks find themselves in the eye of this storm whether they like it or not, which perhaps explains a fragility of ego which oscillates from being at the centre of all this attention. Me, my food and I. This is true for chefs in restaurants but more subtly for cooks, bakers and keepers of the home fires. Sex and food attract us in exactly the same fashion, they are both ways of finding satisfaction, of being full, of satisfying our hunger for now, to gain a moment's peace. And this power is magical.

We are storm chasers.

'Bread grows because God has said so!'

The sun, the oven and bread form the corners of a triangle. When the sun rises, so does the bread. The miracle

---

4   Stockfish

of leavening, *Alvadur*, fermentation, being that which gives life. Fire and yeast are the gift of God, itself a recent name for the Sun, both roles latterly stolen by men. Bread baked in the shape of the Sun. Small to start with and rising together they show us their glory. A daily miracle. The oven is also a wolf's mouth, hungry to be fed, or is it a moon, the daughter of bakers, half her face is darker. Possibly also a vagina, a place for phallic loaves and buns in the oven...

The countryside was a wild place of gifts and tributes exchanged with cosmic forces long before being parsed by kings and priests...

Enough.

*

When they were busy, Aldo was alone in the kitchen, his staff rushed off their feet servicing the tables, ferrying dishes, serving drinks and taking orders. When they were quiet, they all sat around awkwardly staring at each other, smoking or looking for their tobacco pouches and then smoking. All the uneaten food spoke of failure, waste, accusing him of not being good enough, his food unloved. When they were busy everything was in motion, a kinetic energy suffused the room. It was a spectacle. A crazy dance. The specials board crossed out with a flourish of chalk, dishes ordered and devoured, washed down with wine, water and beer – praise shouted from the tables towards the kitchen. Aldo was the man to know, to be in with, he worked the room, a few words at each table, asking after the family, the weather, the possibility of a table outside for five on Saturday night?

Cinque? Impossibile!

Let me see what I can do.

Master Carnival, enabler of gluttony, feeder of stomachs, satisfying dreams of fullness.

And then the comedown, an empty restaurant full of chores needing to be done before the next service. A fantasia of unwashed pots and pans lurking behind the curtain to the kitchen.

A sight for sore eyes.

Cazzo.

Where to start? Aldo turned his back to make them go away. But he was no wizard. It would be late the next morning at the earliest, nursing a hangover, fumbling for the kitchen key under a stone on the back step, to find the plates, pots and pans unmoved and unwashed, with flies in attendance to mock him. He would despair, hit rock bottom, light a cigarette, drink an espresso laced with grappa and rise again after having washed them all up by himself, hands sore and with the first sweat of the day on his brow before he even lit the stove, his daily resurrection. By the time the staff arrived he was already cooking. He would rail at them for having left him to do all the dirty work, scraping the pots, the pans, the shit.

Like magic, no? Maybe I should pay the fucking fairies instead of you lazy bastards! Snapping at their legs with a wet towel, he chased them out into the dining room.

Before lunch and after supper he fed his staff, using them as guinea pigs for new dishes at midday and dustbins for leftovers at midnight. He would playfully curse them for ignorant fools when they turned their noses up at something new or asked, God help them, for a pizza. Local kids, sons and daughters of the valley, and occasionally his own back home for the holidays.

The ones who stayed and the others who still came back.

If he was lucky, they would give the pots a desultory scrub before leaving them to soak overnight, before sneaking off back to their own lives and bed.

Sometimes they sit with him drinking leftover wine and smoking and he tells them stories, usually rude and full of swear words, which is probably why they hang around.

Aldo – he tells this in the third person, who knows why? – *Aldo started out as a lonely pot boy, in the kitchen of a hotel in San Remo. You could hardly see him behind the piles of plates and saucepans he had to clean. His hands were raw from wire brushes and scalding water, and constantly under threat of being wedgied up on a coat hook from the elastic of his Y-fronts by the evil, bloody minded sous chef if he ever complained or slacked off. Which, of course, he did, he was sixteen, full of piss and vinegar just like you guys.*

At this point Aldo eyeballs each of his staff.

Now would Aldo ever think of doing that to a member of his team? He shook his head for dramatic effect, pointing at each of them. *No, no, no, no, no!*

By the end of this story they had smiles on their faces and raised their glasses to the boss, toasting him goodnight as he swore at their retreating backs.

Wedged his pants right up his arse crack where the sun don't shine! And his balls, his balls twisted and squashed and pushed right back up inside, it's a wonder he ever had children!

A miracle! He cackled.

They fled in disgust.

Aldo's biggest concession, made under financial duress, was to offer pizza every Thursday and Friday night, but only on the condition – a deal struck with himself – that the pizza chef he hired looked as unhealthy and stupid as the food he cooked. This was his little victory over the heathens, nobody else could care less what the chef looked like as long as he made their favourite pizzas; Carcioffi, Pomodoro e Formaggio, Diavolo, Quattro Stagione, Pepperoni, and the pizza Aldo despised more than any other, a true abomination, Wurstel, German sausage!

The chef he employed was from Triora, which spoke for itself; a place famous for its witch festival. A damp and empty town nobody much liked. Like many people in the valley, he had a narrow ferret-like face, made thinner by a pointy rust-coloured beard which he stroked when thinking. He was thin but with a low-slung beer belly, a sallow complexion and pockmarked skin. He wore black rock T-shirts on rotation. A Rolling Stones tongue lolled over his guts, or sometimes one with a worn, crumbly, silver Twisted Sister logo. He also had a super-faded Meat Loaf tee, sporting the burnished orange legend *Bat Out of Hell*. His name was Eric, and he fired up the pizza oven twice a week to a full house and a queue outside for takeaways. Aldo twitched behind the curtain of his kitchen.

Fast food. There were piles of takeaway boxes everywhere. Aldo kicks one over on his way outside for a cigarette and a glass of wine, pushing past the customers, a stranger in his own restaurant.

Chef? You're not a chef, you just cook fucking pizzas.

This didn't faze Eric at all, he was very genial. Chef or cook, he couldn't care less.

Just think of the money.

They split the profits each Friday night. Pizza was very cheap to make and the margins were excellent.

Aldo eyed the sign that hung above the bar.

Minchia.

Saturday and Sunday were strictly his and each week he plotted his revenge on the pizza eaters.

Eat this.

Freshly harvested bolete mushrooms marinaded in olive oil and vinegar, served with just a sprinkle of sea salt. Fresh mussels and clams for a vongole, salt-and-pepper grilled squid with onion and coriander, stewed apples and pecorino for pudding. For Sunday lunch he was going to put on Kentucky fried rabbit and hot anchovy and garlic dip with vegetables from his kitchen garden, mopped up by fresh bread from Molini, some would say an unforgiving bread (we call it weapon bread, because it was good for throwing at people, becoming hard as rock within hours of being baked), dense and tasteless, but just perfect for absorbing the unctuous sauce of a bubbling bagna cauda.

Achille had either bought or rented Aldo the restaurant when he came out of rehab. It wasn't clear which until later. He would sit out on the terrace, shucking broad beans into a bowl, smoking and talking to the customers. Occasionally he would cook, although his lungs were not up to the stifling heat of the kitchen. But when he did, he would make dishes from home: pasta with anchovies and sardines, or whitebait fritters. Achille still had the energy and wherewithal to look after his only child. He had time on his hands since his wife died. It was what she would have wanted. Besides, he had finally ended up in a restaurant, a place he felt at home in. His eyes would light up when he saw a new item on the menu, a new enthusiasm, his son exhausted after a long day and a busy service, this better life replacing the old one, a life of hard drugs and the city that Aldo had miraculously survived.

When he took over the restaurant, he tore down the maggoty wild boar's head that had hung over the bar for years. He painted the garish yellow walls white and on them wrote witty imprecations to eat and drink in dialect, snippets of doggerel rhyme from popular folklore.

This over the kitchen portico:

And I tell my deeds for everyone,
and then I add a thousand fables.

And on the toilet door, this:

I want you to understand, There alone in an inn
was an ass;
within him he made a sound
so loud you could take it for thunder:
from that Devil wind
was born the stinking Yokel.

Aldo was that guy.

Dialect ran through the valley like an inconsistent seam of silver, each village adding or taking away letters, crushing or stressing vowels, words spoken with subtle inflections and tonalities that pepper the private languages of so many extended families. Dialect spices language, it has fewer consonants; it flows from the mouth, shorthand, slang, but one that also generates song and theatre. Dialect rooted in terroir, like fine wine it speaks of place, of familiarity and repetition. Badalucco becomes *Baaucu*. Pomodoro, Pomate,

Casa, Ca, shortenings, accents, borrowings, itinerant across time and place, phrases picked up who knows where? Dialect supercharging the opportunity for slang, for granular meaning, for autonomy from structure, for fluidity over stasis, for doggerel tongues, bastard speech over what was written down in books, words you can't read. Words in sailors' mouths, migrant words. Different names for the same thing, words for food, for things in kitchens and gardens, on terraces, on the street, or high up in the mountains, extravagant words, mean ones, for men and women and all the ways in which we can exist for each other, evolved and invented words, private words, the intimacies of love and also rhyming words, the joy of nonsense, so much hot air which we love to expel.

Minchia sniggered Aldo one supper time to nobody in particular. Pronounced *miiiinchia*, drawn out to amplify braggadocio, the word was Sicilian slang for *dick*, but meaning *shit, that sucks* and all points in between. *Minchia* a middle finger salute to the vagaries of life and the world at large.

Fuck you.

Suck my dick.

We would dip back into the flow each time we returned. Aldo would update us, and we him. Village gossip, additions to the menu, new staff – *Watch out for these guys!* he would warn them, making us feel good, making us feel like somebody.

Once in Crete on holiday the bar owner shouted 'You guys are tigers!' across the bar as we downed cocktails or beers. We loved it, being only nineteen-year-old streaks of British piss, literal know-it-alls/know-nothings out in the world for the first time, christened by a local, we were Tigers and it was funny but spoke to something deeper – although nothing is deeper than humour – and no less pleasurable now so many years later, watch out for these guys...

How are the kids? What's going on in London? How's business? Where had we been? Were we busy? The easy-going banter of being regular customers which falls somewhat short of being friends. For example, I can never remember his kids' names. He has more luck remembering mine because they were also his customers. For true friendship there has to be something else, an extra step, a more complex entanglement which had yet to and probably never would occur. Sitting with Aldo, smoking cigarettes and drinking long into the night was more of an ephemeral pleasure, a mark of who and where we were in the world, sitting together at his table. We spoke of and from our different lives, voicing our opinions with freedom and without consequence. Food, money, arseholes on the news, other things on TV, life, these were the things we had in common, constituting a level playing field between us. Anthony Bourdain's show *Parts Unknown* was a favourite starting point, and we talked long into the night about him, what it must have been like to be him, all the places he had visited, the food he ate, the people he met, the women, and ultimately like so many others we surmised why he had taken his own life: perhaps a surfeit of empathy for the people he met, leaving little for himself, he was always a guest at somebody else's table, always outside coming in, his own life in free-fall behind the scenes. Aldo had his own take on this, coming from his experience of being in the eye of his own storm, of drinking, of drug addiction, perhaps of women, although we never touched on that.

She sang him a pretty song.

He snorted as if he knew Asia Argento or somebody like her.

Cantatrix cappellana est dyaboli[5].

I didn't know. Somehow it seemed too obvious. I remembered that Asia's father shared a heroin dealer with his producer, or that his producer (Julian?) was also a dealer, or am I getting confused with Vincent Gallo and Abel Ferrara, so probably not Dario Argento at all. Which is kind of the point, gossip never reveals truth, but then again truth is never the goal of gossip, and that is what we were enjoying.

Stronzata.

I never saw Aldo with a woman other than his daughter. I never asked him about a wife or girlfriend, I just assumed he had one, yet he knew my wife, which put me at a disadvantage. The hide and seek of information, of biography, facts, details of lives exchanged, things you find out, truths you offer up, others you conceal and things you are told but forget, only to be told again to forget again. Things that somehow never stick. Perhaps in a rush of Italian he had once mentioned a divorce, that his kids didn't live with him, but maybe I'm imagining it or wrongly translating what he had said. His son (Brando?) once told me he left home when he was sixteen but I didn't know or ask him which home, his mum's or dad's. It wouldn't even have been crossing a line to ask, we were more friendly than that, but perhaps it was unnecessary information, who cares, to what purpose do you need to know these details? Or that the timing was always wrong and again my Italian waxed and waned depending on mood and energy. It could be a

---

5   The singer is the Devil's Chaplain

chore to use it, and I spoke my native tongue so fast and stumbled over my words with a strong accent that using it would equally have been a waste of time.

So we defaulted to silence.

Visitors are inauthentic, superfluous to the places they visit, destined to skate the meniscus of life lived there...

Authenticity? Things that are real, unmediated, people who exist in and of themselves, true to who they are, so much gibberish but we crave it. It is easier to say what is inauthentic: the fake, the copy, ersatz promises, things that are unoriginal but sold freshly minted, an illusion on every level of experience and consumption. In a word: alienation. Perhaps that's what ultimately killed Bourdain (and so many unheralded others). He had everything, which is nothing at all. The gnawing truth of being other than authentic. The nihilism of judging something, especially yourself, as nothing.

Only Aldo was truly there, we were walk-ons. The appearance of equivalence, of being the stars of the show, was misleading; whatever was being weighed, the balance fell in his favour.

Like wearing down the sole of one shoe faster than the other, we hobbled.

He was Goose man after all.

The possibility of being inauthentic in your own life. Luckily something that most of us can live with.

That February – proper winter nights, wearing everything to bed, wood smoke smarting your eyes from fires and stoves, too close too hot, too far too cold, huddling in the sweet spot between the two, bars and restaurants with fogged windows and condensation running down the inside of the glass – Aldo's father Achille died of emphysema. Just like that he was no longer sitting on the terrace, or at his table by the bar. His photos on the wall now memorialising the person he had been but also marking him as one of the dead, erasing him at the same time. Just like that he was gone from the village. A white-haired old man, his rheumy eyes alert behind a glass of red wine and cloud of smoke, happily wheezing away, shucking beans into a red plastic bowl, clinking glasses with guests at the end of an evening.

I am an orphan, cried Aldo, taking centre stage.

This deduction, this taking away, happened many times over the years. Perhaps Achille had experienced this when he went back to Amantea every summer. He was an exile from their story as we were visitors to his. Just like Anthony Bourdain, our presence was always also *authentic*, or gratuitous, our energy somehow other, coming from outside, not unwanted but, in the scheme of their things, irrelevant in this place. By *always also*, I mean we were authentic (how could we not be, being ourselves in the world?!) and inauthentic, one negating the other, leaving us in objective limbo (who am I?), or indeed as self-conscious players of a game. Authentically inauthentic. A gap only possible to close in story, something we can make believe, the fairy tale of fusion…

Aldo pulled himself together and opened a bottle of his father's grappa to toast his memory. We drank quietly, staring past the glass window of the wood pellet burner into the fire.

*

I love the smells of winter – steaming bowls of stew, pasta with sausage, piping hot polenta, piping hot coffee, cigarettes, mulled wine – and walks up in the mountains on crunchy snow in bright sunshine and the wrong shoes. Time congeals in the winter, cold fat in the pan, slowly melting into the present; the past materialises. You sense it in the flames from the fires, stoves and pellet burners in every home, bar and restaurant. The sense of it sustains us. You can smell it and hear it in the sharp cracking of dried olive wood, spitting embers onto the stone floor. Hardwood burns fast, softwood oozes resin. Each wood burns according to its character and seasoning. Wood fizzes, smokes and sputters when wet, snaps and pops when dry, as if more agile. Cherry, ash, oak and birch. The colour of the flame varies from dark orange leaping flames to delicate pale white squibs, cherry wood smells sweet and burns slowly, but not as slow as oak, a lazy burning wood which can keep fires going over night. Fires that lull you to sleep or make you jump, fires that summon each of our pasts with various degrees of clarity. The stage for this scrying set every winter by the cold itself, a solid, three-dimensional being with a life of its own, one you had to respect, for it was an occupying force.

At the end of the second world war the occupying army torched crops and pillaged what it could for a long and ultimately fruitless march home. A blood memory of the hunger to come wormed its way up and down the valleys of Northern Italy, as the coldest winter in living memory scoured the land.

One year, during the Sagra dello Stoccafisso in Badalucco, I think I got the backstory – although the details are a little foggy – from a drunk lothario who cornered me by the partisan statue in the car park where I had gone for a quiet piss. He had a well-oiled beard and moustache and walked like a pimp. I recognised him from the waist up, from the cheap double-breasted suit in a brown heavy check he wore working in the motorway toll booth in Arma Di Taggia. I didn't let on and for sure he didn't recognise me. Under the shadow of two iron men with raised machine guns frozen forever in victory, he presented me with the empty wine glass that hung round his neck from a chain. It was a local custom to go round and get your glass filled up by other revellers. Luckily I had already zipped my fly before filling his glass from a bottle of Ormeasco, a very average local red wine. His face dropped, hoping for something more palatable – a rossese de Dolce Aqua, for example, a much softer and flavourful Ligurian red – but drank his glass off nonetheless. À propos of an introduction, he told me he was a local historian who wrote pamphlets about local history.

Do you know why we celebrate stockfish in the valley?

This in pretty good English, he had tumbled me. I parried with an offhand *Non Perche?* and poured him another glass. You can be a mug in any language.

From the slightly slurred and excited Italian that followed, I understood that in solidarity with the Italian people after the devastation of war, in the winter of 1945, the Finns sent barrels of stockfish to keep people fed until the next harvest, plugging the gap wrought by man in nature's cycle.

Every autumn we celebrate this gift, this, manna from heaven. So, salut!

We drained our glasses and stumbled off into the crowd, looking for something better to drink.

I didn't get his name, nor he mine. Within a year they had automated his job, and now a jaunty prerecorded female voice wishes you good day after paying your toll, instead of his moody silence.

Tales from the war survive by hook or by crook in the villages strung along the river. Twisted out of shape by time and faulty memory, they become gossip. Yet like ivy they bind – friends, relatives, neighbours, enemies and allies alike – swapping endings or reversing the roles of hero and villain depending on where you heard them and from whom. Which bar were you in? Really, well she would say that the old bitch. What street do you live on? On which side of the river? What family did you marry into? How can he afford to drive a car like that? Who joined what party, when? Who were your friends growing up? That one always ran with the wrong crowd. She brought nothing to their marriage. Clean hands or dirty ones? Who stayed aloof and how did they manage that? War grows a long tail and wags many dogs. In villages loyalties divide internally and divide again within families and ultimately bisect each individual conscience. The unreliable dead leave us with the burden of telling their truth. Lives which have folded back into contested memory and soon become fables against a background of slowly fading antagonisms and surprising new ones which aren't new at all, rather a continuation of the exhausting struggle of how to live and what to live for.

During the electrification drive of the late '50s, women from Badalucco protested against a hydroelectric project which would flood the valley by strapping dynamite around themselves and lying across the street. They won.

Neighbours who don't speak to each other ever since – ever since whatever was disputed – generate another source of gossip. A husband who is *cornuto*. The priest with four children, the local butcher who drives a Porsche, behind whose back everyone sniggers, the postman who opens letters and knows everybody's business, a new wife with ideas above her station, as exemplified by the dress she wore to church or to a summer dance.

The visibility of village life. Good, too good to be true, bad, worse, the worst of us, the best of us. Who was who? A universal dilemma but with local characteristics.

*

The day he told us he was being evicted, Aldo left us the key to lock up after we had finished drinking.

Leave it under the pot of rosemary, I got to go to San Remo to pick up some tuna. Tomorrow is going to be sushi night!

Apparently he hadn't paid rent since his father had died and was now also living in the small flat upstairs. Like dirty dishes he ignored it and kept on cooking, but with even greater fervour and imagination, dishes that would make him even less money in whatever time he had left to make them. For Easter Sunday lunch he roasted wild boar in a pit he dug in the kitchen garden. *Korean style!* he called it, although nobody asked. Rubbed down with an oily mixture of sea salt, sesame seeds, soy sauce and a spicy plum preserve he found in a Chinese grocery store in San Remo. Wrapped in banana leaves. Fuck knows where he got them. After a day he dug it up and served with chestnut flour tacos and sides of refried fagioli and a chimichurri spicy sauce. To a packed house and whoops of joy. You should have seen his face. That day was peak Aldo, I'll never forget it.

Miraculously he was still there in the autumn. Perhaps nobody wanted to buy a dilapidated restaurant up in the mountains with no regular income since the quarry had closed? Aldo was defiant, a pig in shit, happy with this ongoing drama. So many pieces of the story were missing.

On our last night, Aldo brought bowls of steaming stockfish stew to the table.

Stoccafissu a Baucogna, Stockfish from Badalucco. Accept no substitutes!

This is not Brandacajun! I am not Genovese, Io Baddaluchese!

As he plonked them down, we toasted him and ourselves for just being there. Aldo started to almost sing his recipe.

Listen to me. No potatoes, no fava beans just this. Dried cod, not fucking salted, this is not fucking Norway, okay? This is not a bacalao! Oil, onion, our olives, *acchuige.*

He looks at me for the word in English

Acchuige, I repeat redundantly.

Anchovy.

He continues, another foreign word mastered.

Anchovy, pinoli, some garlic, Cheriglie di Noci.

He seemed to be sure I knew this last phrase which I guessed was walnuts, or walnut husks.

And now his delivery sped up, no longer lingering on the words.

Some white wine, mushroom salt and pepper e Basta.

And now for the denouement.

In some fancy restaurants and in the homes of tourists they serve the bastard that is Stoccafisso Accomadato. With everything in it, with all the extras, all the recipes in one stew. Cazzo! The whole of Liguria in a dish. But we are not whole, we are all different.

Thank god this man wasn't a fascist, for here he was conjuring a powerful allegorical universe.

We wolfed it down. I mentioned the origins of the stockfish festival. Aldo roared with laughter.

What a load of shit, who told you that?

I described him.

Cornuto! Aldo snorted.

Known as a cuckold, despite in my memory looking more like a *cuckolder*, if there is such a word. How deceptive things can be. How obvious this sleight of hand, when in possession of all the facts, or indeed of more hearsay, gossip, lies. In order to compensate for his wife's infidelities this *Cornuto* dressed and behaved like an adulterer himself, a small act of revenge, an assertion of his depleted manhood, however you will have it.

The habits of men follow a strange logic. A man's love can also manifest as hate, whether it is for a woman or for each other.

Aldo looked at me as if I was an idiot.

This guy is a fool. Un uomo di nulla. Nobody sent us anything after the war, and nobody was starving. The Finns. Haha, he got you good there, tourists so desperate to hear about the war, the fascists, the partisans, cazzo.

Without mentioning it, we shared out bumps of coke and chased them with grappa.

Camaraderie in the face of authority was as close as we came to friendship, I think, because we knew enough of each other's story to comprehend whatever sadness or disappointments lurked behind the exterior, behind all the good times, without having to talk about them. Our behaviour was a refusal to find any of it profound, to bring everything, all of our big ideas about life, down to earth, down to a line of coke and a two-finger salute to the world outside. The rich, bosses, governments, multinationals, globalisation and naturally landlords.

Miiincia.

I didn't ask him shit. Why would he make shit like that up? That's why I am asking you, for verification, you bastard!

He sits down, pulls his bowl towards him and slurps a spoonful of the broth. This is the first and only time I remember seeing Aldo sit down to eat.

Stoccafissu comes from way back, from when the Saracens invaded, when the people moved inland, into the mountains to escape them. They had planted nothing, but took their dried fish with them. The festival was to celebrate this holding out, this resistance to the invader.

So, same story but different invaders.

Ovviamente. He winks and refills my glass.

If it finally happens, where will you go?

Perhaps I will go to Calabria.

We toast this, the romance of returning to his father's home.

Or Cuba Si!

We toast again.

I don't know what to do. Perhaps I will disappear like my goose, just like that a fox will eat me up.

We stood up, he wouldn't take our money. Handshakes and hugs all round, with no final words for a situation that felt very final. Under the harsh light of the restaurant, a table strewn with the detritus of food and wine, not to mention smears of coke, it felt like this was the last of us.

Ciao Aldo!

By the following summer new owners had renamed, redecorated and reopened Aldo's restaurant. They had painted over Aldo's doggerel, refreshing the room with bright colours and tourist friendly trinkets. By the kitchen steps I saw the rusty plum tomato tin he used for cigarette buts. It was empty. I took it back to the house.

Aldo was gone, just like his father had, his slow fade into caricature had already started the night we said goodbye. Nobody knew where he was, people just shrugged when we asked about him, or worse said something about drugs and maybe he had had a relapse, the haters, the ones who disliked him, for having ideas above his station, for coming from Badalucco, of having been an addict.

Remember Aldo? I asked the kids a few years later, having supper in the same restaurant.

Goose man! What a legend! they said.

They had all been there the night of the day the fox killed Aldo's goose. Ten of them in their early twenties staying at the house on holiday by themselves for the first time, cheering Aldo when he came to the table with free carafes of wine and later seeing him cry over his dead goose, they comforted him, young, drunk and high as they all were, shedding a tear in sympathy.

You guys are tigers! he might've said to them.

These were the gestures, the drama and good times he created, this the everyday magic he conjured.

And it was also the last thing he said to me, that he might disappear just like his goose, a trauma then but now symbolic, a touchstone from the past that had become a shared legend.

> *Now here Falcon laments and mews*
> *and takes the moon for a green cheese;*
> *and finds a cask and a mandrake plant*
> *and passes off a boiled chestnut as a date;*
> *would have you believe the arbutus fruit a strawberry;*
> *disguises the barbel, slips when there's no snow*
> *and in and out tells you a tale of cock and bull*
> *a thing, a bagatelle, a berry.*
> From 'Morgante', Luigi Pulci, c.1483

Some years later I found Aldo on Facebook. He was living twenty kilometres away in the city of Imperia, working in somebody else's restaurant on the coast.

I must visit him.

FAVOLE POPULARE

I write so I won't be written.
  — Anon

There's some whores in this house,
  — Cardi B, 'WAP.'

Oh, how thirsty I am! What will become of me? I am the son of a witch and live on top of the mountain, safe in my castle. My name is Babolna. I have only daughters, for I am destined for extinction; the world has become too small for giants. The house won't let me go, I dare not stray from the terrace; I patrol it, unable to settle in one place. I have a nasty burn on my arm, but can't find the cream for it. Perhaps there is some aloe vera in the garden? Back and forth to the fridge for cold beer, looking for cigarettes

behind the sofa, a soft pack I left there at some point I'm
sure of it. Books lie open, face up or down or stacked with
pages folded over, all of them unfinished. Unfinished wine
bottles signpost my frenetic reading. I'm a troll lurking
beneath the bridge but nobody cares to cross it. I hear life
from my eyrie and my fingers crush the toy-sized cars and
bikes driving up and down the valley below. Lucky three,
I am being punished for burning the tree. I sketch all of
this in my head; the house is inside me, yet I am trapped
in it, I have become a superstition…

— Istvan Laurer Notebook 1989 (translated from
the German)

The Welsh cycling fanatic punched out the carpenter right
outside his workshop down by the tennis courts, adamant
that he had made a pass at his wife.

That will teach yer, dirty old git!

The locals split their sides laughing, for the carpenter was
old, married, and besides, was more interested in wine than
women, especially not this English woman, who was mortified
by her husband's jealousy that had only increased since they
had moved to Italy, to a dark and damp house in a dark and
damp hamlet, on the wrong side of the valley where it gets little
sun, hence the cheap price for this new start although there was
nothing new about him punching out whoever he thought had
made eyes at his wife. It was part of who he was, the inevitable
climax to some grotesque stage act he peddled. He'd been
punching guys out since the first few months of their
relationship, the punchline to a – by now – worn out joke.

Now this thin entertainment had come to the village,
who would be next? The mechanic, the baker, or perhaps

one of the migrants, newly lodged in the old hotel? For sure he would see in these young African men rivals for the bed of his raven-haired Mandy.

That first punch was a nailed-on promise of more to come. Violence can be both the start of something or more rarely its ending, woven as it is into so many of our lives, a bloody nose or a turned cheek, or a fact of daily life like a stone in your shoe; *move along, nothing to see here*, or stone towers in which young men live out their lives secluded from the blood lust of vendetta.

But that's elsewhere (yet not so long ago).

Besides, with foreigners there were fewer consequences. In the bigger scheme of things, we were inconsequential. This was the speculation among the men and women of the village, the Greek chorus of humanity who gathered in bars, on the bench by the bus stop, or huddled outside the commune, passing the time while queuing to pay their bills. They gossip in doctors' waiting rooms, places which, however clean, however modern, always stink of the fear of death and provoke darker thoughts, a circumspect nastiness even, about other people not in doctors' waiting rooms.

On the street, stepping out for cigarettes, we conspire over naked flames, formalities to be observed before getting down to business. Faces that flicker in the dusk and at dawn. Gossip spreads as surely as yeast rises.

Laid him out with a single punch. Spark out, he was.
Bet there's more where that came from.
I wonder who's next?
Filthy bitch.
I didn't know he had it in him.

She's a looker alright.
Cornuto!
Skinny as a rake.
English bastard!

A timeless story, one told pleasurably and received with a delicious sense of déjà vu. The village talks. They would force an outcome now the game was afoot.

Every time the husband ran the gauntlet of the street they sniggered and drew back as if in fear, mocking him. He sulked for a while in the cold damp house on the wrong side of the valley.

Even the carpenter's wife was happy to laugh along with the jokes that were partly aimed at her husband – she couldn't deny that – as if he would have the gumption or the desire to have any kind of affair, laughing along despite the implicit poke at her, her waning sexual allure. There is always this undercurrent, the splash-back onto an innocent, we just can't help ourselves in the war of genes between men and women. Our desire, to get one over on another, to literally get a leg over, to conquer, humiliate, tease, refute, even vanquish, to seduce beyond the ability to resist, blood thickening, our shared wickedness dressed up as inevitability, star-crossed attraction Greek in its intensity and careening towards tragedy. Or, more simply put, violence, one man punching another or worse, a man cuckolded by his best friend perhaps the *ne plus ultra* of this phantasmagoria – or beyond that cuckolded by his own father or grandfather, which is indeed beyond, yet I have heard of it – it is the fear of this which leads to, is implicit in, so much male violence towards women.

The farmer had three daughters, each as beautiful as the other, the widowed washerwoman two daughters, one beautiful, the other plain, the king a daughter, sickly and sad. Two kings, the best of friends, one had three sons, the other a daughter of marriageable age. Seven brothers fell out with their father (for he had taken a new wife), many brides had ugly sisters, scheming uncles, jealous brothers, broken hearts, pots of basil, ten commandments mostly broken, unwanted gifts and fortunes squandered, power corrupted, lies spat, mocking oaths taken.

Favourite sons, beautiful of daughters – love beyond measure – literally loved to pieces (a cataclysmic love that destroys its object), for the story is nothing if not metaphor reversed back into life, reanimated horror and violence wrought from the bones of the everyday. Dowries, trousseaus, chattels, arranged marriages, worldly goods, hope chests, laws upheld, custom enforced to be obeyed under dire threat. Remorse hot on the heels of transgression, magically redeemed by the fiat of a second chance. From beyond the grave grisly murders restored to life, victim and perpetrator locked in eternal conflict, love and happiness, forever after. A relentless tumble of life and death, a perverted mirror held up to the reality of human weakness, corruptibility and inconsistency, the comedy of life reflected as the absurd non sequitur it is.

This is the form of the fable, the rules, the original terrain, a language of exchange between people who live in proximity over time and across generations.

I see you. You see me.

Events quickly become part of local folklore, the first pressing of grape or olive, laid down in expectation of nuance, a deeper flavour. (Over)heard and retold, old stories bolstered by fresh ones like this, the fresher the better, topping up a perpetual stew, bouilli for the bouillon. Layer upon layer, mostly snippets… *Twenty Euros for a chicken? No wonder they can afford to drive a car like that!* Embellishments of things you already knew, *worked so hard he would spin the wool off a sheep, and all for what?* Or thought you did, but there were always surprises, we are imaginative in our street talk. The avarice and jealousy surrounding money – yours and other people's – the pleasure in judging others, and to spice it all up, sex, in all its glorious forms and the mockery it makes. (Of what exactly? Life? Yes, and isn't that enough?) All of us stirring the pot, its sediment sticks in our gut, for as we talk/talk too much/can't stop talking, we swallow air and it burbles, farts and repeats where people group together, wherever that is; perhaps by the cigarette machine, one of us banging it hard for change, cursing or waiting for someone to come with the key to open it up to retrieve the packet of cigarettes that wouldn't drop, or gathered in twos or threes by the tailgate of a pickup truck – flatbed full of logs, tightly bound bushels of lavender, or tools, broken bits from two-stroke strimmers, saws, blunt blades – or in the post office, my god the queue for that now opening times have been cut, or outside the bakery, edging forward into the warm fug of the oven, the mystery of rising dough, kneading it to fit the shape of your fecund imagination or parading at *festas* when the village spends time at close quarters, everyone looking at each other as if in group therapy, warily but a place *where we tell each other the story of ourselves and pass it around.* All of this washed down with whatever it is we drink – wine, beer, spritz, grappa – shouting greetings over the din of pop music and floppy plates of fast food: chips, rostelli, links of sausage, bowls of pasta, ragu or burro e salvia, games of cards, football kickabouts, constant chatter and awkward silences, the exuberance of summer picnics by the river, the noise and amplification of the body of water, whispered exchanges on autumnal pilgrimages to holy shrines up in the mountains, saints' days or commemorations of wars, for the village slain, *caduto*, insults shouted and hushed up on late nights on the terrace of the pizza restaurant, spilling out onto the street where it always begins and usually ends up, or in kitchens which perform the same function, ending up in scuffles – usually not more – and quickly the upshot, the outcome, a return of order, balance, happy endings, and a good story to be enjoyed. We raise our own legends from this stuff and nonsense.

Our terroir, which produces *us*.

Yet...

They were all made princes, while I've stayed as poor a soul as ever.

The teller of stories – never her own, which is the power of speaking about others, behind which lies a silence, the mystery of the speaker himself – lurks in the shadows, appearing only fleetingly in the tale told and always this character, ever present in the nooks and crannies of history, man or woman, always sniping at other people's fortune and their own lack of it, the disgruntled observer, dripping ink from a poison pen or venom from a loose tongue and always a sense of biding her time, which makes you flash on *revenge of the storyteller* but what would that look like? Impossible. They have no substance, only the power of their invisibility.

At every party a pooper, at every wedding a mourner, plenty begets hunger, a surfeit of disgruntlement, the story itself offering precious little nourishment other than fleetingly, in the listener's ear.

A few days later the two young people were married. At the wedding banquet they served radish preserves, peeled mice, skinned cats and fried monkeys. They ate that and enough was left over for tomorrow, but nobody thought to say to me so much as 'have a glass of wine!'[6]

The Welsh couple had once been round our house for supper, as the wife had done some cleaning for us, in hindsight a mistake, and no, before you ask...

This supper was an anomaly not least because there was nothing to say about it. Nothing to add to other tales of lust and jealousy in the valley; who is fucking who, who is *Cornuto*, who a prostitute, who impotent. Nothing for the pot, not even a titbit to feed an undertow of sexual prurience, the need to see blood on the sheets, which was literally the lifeblood of a village of less than three hundred souls.

A lock in tower. The man inside was both alive and dead, removed from both his family and enemies. Safe from their obligation to kill him. A frozen vendetta. Food and drink in baskets yanked up by pulley, cigarettes and washing also, everything he needed, a life support system for the living dead. Just so long as he did not venture outside until the blood feud was settled. The door nailed shut, or even bricked up, sealed as proof of the promise made. His life forfeit or the debt cancelled; blood lust suspended in favour of negotiation.

*

A village.

Two bars – a third shuttered – one restaurant, two shops. A baker. An old hotel which is now a hostel for migrants. Butchers (now closed, another story). A river runs through

6   'Invisible Grandfather'. *Fiabe Italiane* Editor: Italo Calvino 1956

it, not much of one for all the silt that slows it, for most of the year it is but a trickle.

Village gossip.

All of this babble is more like a torrent cascading under a bridge, a constant flow of words abrading the hard rocks and pebbles of the riverbed.

Rocce e ciottoli.

Weakness, greed, pride, covetousness, our betters brought down into the gutter. Never swim downstream of a village, for it is full of shit.

She sucked him off in the back of his car, parked right outside her mother's flat. Yes! That car, the blue one. Right under the balcony! Not that she hadn't done the same in her day.

Family.

Things running in families is a common observation. It's in the blood. We always assume agency for ourselves, while denying its possibility in others, we can always change, they can't. Six generations of bakers, three generations of cuckolds, a slut just like her mother. Weak like his father. Simple, too clever by half, scheming, gullible. Even if it skips a generation or two, people will revert to form, a drunk just like his grandfather before him.

If you think he's greedy, you should have seen the prices his father charged during the war.

It's a zero-sum game. Nobody wins.

Being rich, successful, coming out on top, also runs in families all of whom are riding for a fall, just you wait, somebody will cut them down to size however long, however many generations it might take, just you wait and see, what goes around comes around. Luck changes in both directions. No wonder so many folk tales start with a fortune made or lost. The status quo that must be overturned in order to progress the story; a rich farmer, a poor peasant, a wealthy merchant, hapless doctor or a poor knight, and the king in his counting house. To venture from home, to seek one's fortune, or to be expelled for reasons of hunger, honour or rancour, or being ostracised, for being different, for being poorer than the rest, for falling in love with the wrong person's daughter, for not being able to heal the sick wife of a rich man. If you are lucky, you escape with your life to seek your fortune elsewhere; that is to say, the story continues, usually with the blessing or curse of a vast array of supernatural beings bringing to bear their own obscure animus and agenda!

Those that stay, those that leave and those that return. How long has this been going on for, this wheel of (mis) fortune? Powered by a Catholic/pagan sense of fate, morality and just deserts. Revenge is a dish best served cold when not served hot.

After every killing a thirty-day truce, a countdown to the next murder or the fulfilment of the blood feud, the satisfaction of honour. Sometimes a baby in a cradle pulled up into the tower to force a resolution or starve to death. Honour spanning generations, worn like a splendid family coat.

It boils down to this: tell somebody not to do something, it could be anything, just forbid somebody something and lo-and-behold they will do it. And then God forbid.

The whole house is yours to roam but don't, whatever you do, open THAT DOOR. *What happens next*, climaxes in most with a happy ending, however convoluted, implausible and abrupt, a recursive loop back to the beginning, a place of harmony and equilibrium.

For some.

And all were very happy and gay,
But to me who watched they gave no thought nor pay.

You can't help but think these happy endings are false. They are definitely not satisfying. There is always this worm in the night, the grit – autocorrects to *Griot*, which is also correct! – in the oyster of any story. Who is the storyteller? What do they want? Free food and drink in payment for the listeners' pleasure? Surely it can't be just that? No wonder postmodernism loves fairy tales, for they beg the question and are full of remainders, leftovers begging; unconfined connotation, a twisted mirroring of life and metaphor. A sense of lack, of something missing, something always already out of reach. We gravitate towards this absence, in order to worry it. An itch, a sense of unease, unspent energy, constantly pacing up and down, being unable to settle or let things lie? And isn't that what life boils down to?

They will say, smugly.

We are who we are. We live in a stasis of vice, sloth, jealousy, shamed by those who perform acts in good faith. To what end? No good will come of it. *Good money after bad, a leopard doesn't change its spots, bad to the bone that one, it's in the genes.* To make us feel bad for being bad, for being less good than them. *Who do they think they are?* To upset the balance of fortune, to spin the wheel backwards, what good has that ever done? Tempting fate is what it is, a bloody signature for all that we do to each other?

A bloodline of evil stepmothers and seventh sons.

This land has been in our family for over three hundred years.

A sentence begging for denouement. Land there for the taking, for the family to fall, for them to become landless. Taken from them, lost or given away. Lifetimes of diligence followed by a single generation of lassitude; the lottery of inheritance featuring a greedy son, a too beautiful daughter, the dodgy deal, an unforeseen financial crisis, war, an end of empires shredding the precarious status quo, wolves at the door, the inciting incidents of history.

Something evil this way comes.

Our land. Terraces, fields and forests.

The Village Petrol Station
Two farmers. One fills up the tank of a brand-new Toyota Hilux, the other an old rusty Fiat Panda. The poorer man feeds a crumpled twenty-Euro note into the machine. It takes three attempts, smoothing it out on his shirt before it gets taken.

Cazzo.

The other smokes nonchalantly by the pump.

Who put the wire up? one asks, deadpan.

The other shrugs, lights another cigarette.

Tank full, he screws in the cap.

The bastard was in hospital for a month.

If he had only asked permission, paid a little for it, with all the money they make from the mountain bikes, clogging up the roads back and forth all day, ruining terraces, scaring livestock. Thrill seekers, arseholes.

Somebody must have got the hump.

Nodding, they drive off in opposite directions.

The Bar
Three men play cards. One jumps up shouting obscenities. Hushed from behind the bar, he reluctantly sits back down although this has the feel of a regular occurrence, a play even. The barwoman has no lines to speak but shakes her head in mock frustration, her part in the ritual. The other players

snigger and wave for another round of drinks, two vermouths, one with ice, the other straight up and a cold beer for the sore loser.

Let me see those cards again you bastards! Snatching them across the table.

A roar of complaint, hands slapping away hands, Cards gripped and torn, the shaking of heads, a sense of mirth all round, and so it goes.

An Alleyway, by a Lamppost
Two women walk home at night, both older, perhaps widows, definitely friends.

She's all alone up there since he walked out.

Huh. I wonder who visits her?

Madonna! It's only been six weeks.

The other shrugs a sly so what.

They exit the cone of lamplight.

Driving
A son talks animatedly to his father who grips the steering wheel, focused on avoiding potholes. Both crane their necks as they pass the recently resurfaced drive of their neighbour as it joins the main road, a black tongue of smooth tarmac unfurled like a VIP carpet.

Fancy. Must have cost a packet.

It's obvious, isn't it? His daughter works in the commune.

The young man rubs the palms of his hands together signifying job done, nothing to see here.

We pay our taxes, same as them.

His father shrugs.

So what? The tarmac ends right there, before they even get anywhere. We all have to use the same road.

He swears as the car hits another pothole, yanking the wheel from his hands.

Cazzo!

The Street

Outside houses, shops and cafes, old men watch the world go by. A gaze that fixes the things it sees. An old world, of men.

The female gaze is more unpredictable, it probes without seeking to fix. It roves. The possibility of a new world. The demons of fertility were female, don't forget, their power undiminished despite being made over into witches, something that men could burn.

Dabundia, Satia, Diana, Hera, Perchta Wode, Holda, Benzonia, Erodiade.

Say their names. From nativity to epiphany, they fly above us, spreading fecundity. Christianity has become too familiar, it summons our indifference. We search for the mystery elsewhere. Perhaps the rule of man is waning too, the gaze unsteady; it falters, eyes tired and rheumy. The men say women are as bad as we are, if not worse. In this village like any other, issues of class parse into fables of gender and resignation. Asking for help makes you weak, offering it worse, who do they think they are?

In folk tales witches often lie in wait to offer help, intent on gaining more in return. They expedite our quests. A stream full of fish. An empty cottage, a table laden with food and a roaring fire. Upstairs, a soft bed with the finest sheets. Too good to be true. Everything has a catch. Payment in kind. Tasks to be undertaken in order for spells to be broken.

A king has a daughter who doesn't smile, never laughs. She is always unhappy, standing by her window all day wasting away, yet she wants for nothing. Exasperated, he sends out his heralds to proclaim that whoever can make her laugh will have her hand in marriage. Familial love opens the door for a poor man to enter. Love turns the world upside down.

In 1990 in a Balkan village, up to 500,000 people attended a countrywide reconciliation commission, finally ending over one thousand family blood feuds.

As for the rest of us?

Never marry above or below, marry your equal or you will never see the horizon, neither one of you. Who was getting above himself, building another house, how many does that family need? A child off to university, paid for by selling land to foreigners, and us with nowhere to live, the butcher who drives a Porsche and charges seventeen Euros for a chicken, so when misfortune came to his door… A skirt too short, a new coat, a brand-new rifle shown off in the hunting season, it must have cost a packet. Fancy items on the menu of the local restaurant, who does he think he is? And where does he come from? It's too expensive, it's too cheap, their pasta is frozen, the wine so-so, the olives from Spain or Greece, smuggled into the valley at night, fresh sausage, from where? Pizza in cardboard boxes? Soggy. Eleven dishes, six antipasti, two pasta, a choice of meats, rabbit, wild boar, roast beef, including wine. Twenty-five Euros. It's enough.

But lust – for life – always throws a spanner in the works, blinding our judgement, putting its anarchic spell on our reason. This is the heart of it, we leap from one fit of passion to another.

Licentious dissipation before chastity and the rule of law. This is no handmaid's tale. Bawdy and immoderate language vs mealy-mouthed contrition. This has always been the way of the poor because they know what it means to suffer from hunger and so-called justice. Laziness takes centre stage, the swagger of unemployment, the world of work turned on its head like every other aspect.

Into this gap have always leapt mafiosi. The stage has been set for thousands of years. The hard-working – who, at the end of every day, have nothing – watch others who do nothing enjoy everything. So why not take what's offered wherever it comes from? Criminals draw on a rich broth of resistance and opposition, pride in coming from nothing, heritage and honour in the smell of shit. Angels heralded by trumpets, the poor herald themselves with arse trumpets, their trumps in the night a mighty hallelujah.

Buffoons, vagabonds, Sir Carnival, Captain General of all lunatics, the witless. Why not celebrate, make merry, gamble, be brash, scared of no folly, embrace gluttony, drunkenness, elevate the witches' sabbath above all the others. On Twelfth Night beasts can speak to one another, and woe to us. Carnival the dreaded enemy of Lent, the day of the dead, the great return, piping us to the land of Cockaigne, of feast not famine, revel over penitence and all of this pledged by the dead, not the living, the living who make of life a living misery, whereas the dead tease promises of sex and food. Mythical Eden, a journey to islands of plenty, a trip the same as any drug, the natural hallucinogens so important in pagan ritual, the power to survive by escaping, letting ourselves go, experiencing oblivion. *Cogito Ergot sum...*

There is no secret to what makes an earthly paradise.

I believe earthly paradise to be where gentlemen who have money enough to live without having to do a stroke of work.[7]

We would not want for things to do. Lent would be banished or evolve into the exquisite pleasure of mock fasting and self-flagellation heightening even further the joys of spring to follow; a BDSM paradise from winter through spring to summer solstice and the fires of Zoroaster, sessions of delight and all the pleasure that entails.

When somebody fails they shit the bed and we all laugh, but during Lent, we parade our selves wearing shit-stained nightshirts. The Devil's horns are no more than the forks with which we till the earth, turning over the stinking shit of the animals we live with, shit from which springs our food, our abundance, or lack of it.

We are all bellow men. Taking the piss is literally that, celebrating the blood shit piss and cum we are made of, our vital elements with top notes of sugar and spice, (why not?!)

Kitchen humour, farts, spit, burps, roaring ovens from which we are born, rotting meat where we end up, bloated stomachs, arse explosions and belching gases constitute the in-between and have always made us laugh, bringing us down to size, taking the god out of us perhaps, deflating us. Anal wind, ultimately the birth of souls. A pagan exuberance that would have to be made safe in the centuries that followed.

Arse souls.

All things nice.

What little girls are made of.

---

7   Menochio, the wise man of Fruili.

And at a village festa the sound system blares out lyrics that brag of sexual allure, threat, exhortation, mockery and delight, the timeless pleasures of transgression. The beat echoes up and down the valley moving a crowd which has danced to this tune for ever.

There's some whores in this house,

Fairy tales inhabit a fantastic space in which there is constant dialogue between social and imaginary classes, fauna and flora, the quick and the dead in a radical democracy of kings and peasants, fishermen, merchants, thieves and holy women, beggars and princes, bakers, daughters, princesses, witches, demons, sprites, soldiers and spies. Lazy men, businessmen. Everything under the sun and moon interact in these stories. They are fantastic. From cradle to grave we follow the plot. It enchants us. The absurdity of it, bits and pieces of folk memory that lurk in the shadows, motes of dust caught in the light, in the cracks between floorboards, in haylofts on summer days, forests in winter. At night, woken with a start, our minds rediscover these other stories which once meant something, or at certain times of the year when the joy of them feels closer. Always funny, always ridiculous, way beyond (and before) the realism we have become accustomed to and yet and yet…

The twins grew up in a small village. Their father was away a lot for work, but when he came home, they both vied for his attention which was the only thing that the boys ever fought over. When he was away, they shared the same interests: swam in the river, played in the forest setting traps for rabbits, and read the same books full of adventure. Their mother took ill and died suddenly when they were fourteen. The father came home in time to bury his wife and after the funeral took the boys hunting for the first time with the rifle in the locked cupboard, a rifle he had brought back from a war many years before. It was time for them to become men. Jealous to get the first kill, one twin nudged his brother's gun just as he was taking aim, the brother stumbling and shooting his father in the foot. Screaming in pain he bandaged his foot and then set about his son with his belt.

From that day the father walked with a limp. He never took the boys out again. Instead of travelling (as a salesman of household goods, boot polish, detergents, pots and pans and the like) he got a job as a postman which came with a bicycle. Cycling hid the fact that he limped and soon he was off as before delivering letters to the villages and hamlets that dotted the valley.

Soon after this another war came, and their father was one of the first to volunteer. Rejected because of his bad foot, he blamed his sons, cursing the world for giving him twins.

The war dragged on and two years later both sons went away to it. The father took a new wife, for in the valley there were many widows happy even to take a cripple for a husband.

Eventually the war ended but only one son came home. A hero. The father could no longer tell which of his sons stood before him. Was he the boy who nudged the gun, or the one who shot him? They had become strangers and death was the only thing left they had in common.

Fables have no interest in telling us how to live together, or how to go lightly through life. They are the dreams of giants. For that we have to stop dreaming and tell each other smaller stories of who we are and how we live.

A roadside blacksmith in Tripoli, Lebanon, hands black and burnt from cutting and shaping these old chisels, to renew them in the fire, tongs deftly place them for his son to wield the hammer. A rhythm, a synchronicity. The son all muscle, sweat pouring from his brow. The old man, wiry, reduced by heat to sinews and bone, any ounce of fat long since sweated out. Black teeth and a cigarette in the corner of his mouth like a chimney, masking the smell as the red-hot metal plunges into water and an acrid steam engulfs us all. They share coffee brewed on a stove in the street, poured from a brass spout into tiny glass cups, jet black and bitter. The first cup for the father, the second for the son.

Perhaps it is that simple, yet still we dream…

Come hither all you happy-go-lucky, good fellows all. Everyone who hates work, who loves slap-up food and abhors hard times and toil. Stout-hearted men are you all, most certainly not layabouts, though the miserly might call you so. Come hither you all, and let us go to the Land of Cockaigne, where he who sleeps most earns the most.[8]

---

8   The delightful Journey to Cockaigne, Cesena, 1588.

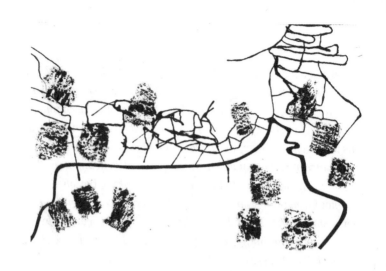

CREPI IL LUPO!

Googling ideas for a treatment for a tv commercial, I come across a time lapse video from Yellowstone Park. In the years before Wi-Fi at the house, the ability to play this video, albeit in stops and starts, was what amounted to a 3G miracle.

A sluggish river meanders through a valley around its many oxbow lakes. The camera angle is high up – not a drone – probably fixed to a tree or some kind of hide, recording over a year in which the river straightens out of its bends and more and more wildlife returns to it to drink, feed, whatever. The riverbed and environment around it transform because they reintroduced wolves to the ecosystem – captions inform us – restoring the balance of nature, which is obviously the point of the video and the reason so many people share it. I can't remember if I shared it, probably a reflexive retweet without comment, but I also don't remember seeing any wolves in the video. The internet celebrates the counterintuitive. Butterfly effects and such like. Bringing back beavers to help tackle flooding is another example of river flow management. Building dams and nests alter how water moves through the landscape. Who knew? Any small win for the environment has become compulsive viewing. *A natural born killer restores harmony in nature.*

That's the headline and I grab it.

Unchecked, deer and elk destroy trees and eat too many plants and vegetables. This happens when your remove the apex predator. Bring them back and they rebalance the equilibrium. They don't just keep the numbers in check. The return of the apex predator starts a chain reaction in the environment. The deer and elk adapt their behaviour to avoid the wolves, allowing a diversity of smaller species and vegetation to return. Wolves also kill coyotes, which means more rabbits. More mice, more eagles, foxes and otters. More bears because they eat the carrion left by the wolves killing the deer and coyotes. Trees grow higher again and populate barren hillsides. Bird species return and thrive. Root and vegetation growth strengthens the earth, stabilising the riverbanks from erosion, deepening the river, which flows faster and eventually straighter. Left unchecked, the deer numbers swamped resources; they relied on eating young willow trees in the winter, which made it difficult for beavers to find material to build nests with. Now these nests and ponds next to the river provide homes for otters, rats and insects and manage the flow of water into it.

Scientists call this a trophic cascade.

All because of thirty-one wolves.

Apex predator theory.

Fuck. My phone rings. I'm five minutes late for the conference call with the advertising agency creative team and their producer in Portland, plus my producer listening in from LA. I stumble up and down terraces to find the best reception; one, two bars, not enough, I keep moving.

Clutched in my sweaty hand is a script for a new hybrid car commercial. In it the vehicle is driving through an American desert scrubland with a river running through it. It is winter, and in the distance we see a pack of wolves as they follow their leader up into the foothills of a mountain range. A family is going on a ski trip. (Boulder Colorado? Mammoth?) The script cuts between the two journeys. Outside it is cold. We deduce this by what they wear, the skis on the roof rack and the snow on the mountains. ThinkAnselm Kiefer in colour. Also, they are happy, expectant, looking forward. There is a voiceover. By inference – we are travelling just like them, with the same grace, the same efficiency of travel, but also the same urgency, we too have somewhere to go – with this car *we* have the agency of a wolf. The wife/mother is driving. The wolf/mother is driving.

Inference and counterpoint are the heavy weapons of advertising, in our War of the Worlds. Electric cars and rising ecological awareness have triggered another trophic cascade, resulting in a new lease of life for people who advertise in the automotive segment. A heady mix, an unholy alliance, of climate crisis, generation-Z feminism and the automotive industrial complex. Show a car travelling quickly and with intent through empty roads against spectacular landscapes. Intercut with wolves. Both scenes embedded in unspoilt nature. Intercut between the woman driving and the leader of the wolf pack. You get the picture. Other activity / cutaways in the car signal she is the alpha here – handing out the snacks that *she* remembered to bring while checking the satnav – the husband happy to play second fiddle. In fact what *is* this fucker doing? Perhaps the suggestion is also that women are more likely to be different, to stake out new ground, to contextualise their decisions in radical sympathy with the planet – I go too far, but to sell electric or hybrid vehicles the commercial focuses on this line of reasoning. To overcome the hesitancy of purchasing an electric car, or a hybrid, they focus on female energy, which channels a blood instinct to protect family. Just like the wolf.

We are both apex predators, although I can't imagine a situation where we would reintroduce humans anywhere, even mothers.

Finally, I get three bars on my phone up in the pergola. I extricate myself from these thoughts as I sit gingerly on a rusty chair and the call comes through…

– Sorry, can you say that again?

I find it hard to focus at the best of times on conference calls – especially if I have to be enthusiastic about fast food or hybrid cars – even talking to people I love, I get distracted. The call goes well until I suggest they look at a video of how wolf packs actually work.

– What was that about wolf packs?

– The leader is always at the back.

The line goes silent. Fuck it, I can't help myself.

The agency producer leaps into the void.

– We're more interested to hear how you would handle the family dynamics in the car, so it doesn't come across forced, it's not a wolf documentary even though the mother is the alpha, in tune with nature and all that, she's still fun to be with, you get that from the script right?

I don't understand the *even though the mother is the alpha* bit. What? Despite being in control, she is still fun? A confused way to sell a car, or am I missing something? I look at the burnt side of one of the remaining cypress trees cursing the drunk Istvan.

– 100 percent. She's the embodiment of fun.

Wolf packs put the old and injured wolves up front, to set the pace, from which I deduce: leave no wolf behind. If they get attacked, these wolves are sacrificed to buy time for the pack to regroup.

– What are your thoughts on casting?

Shoshone cross my mind, one of the last tribes to be kicked out and erased from Yellowstone National Park, where they were planning on shooting the commercial.

I flash on the cost of repairing the terrace.

– Urban, upscale, probably mixed race. I like the idea of them being a fish out of water but finding their chops out in the wild.

Now I was talking their language. I had recalibrated.

Behind the old wolves are five young aggressive males to pick up the pieces. Bringing up the rear is the leader of the pack, who can see everything from all angles. That's how wolves roll.

– In my notes I'll look at all the options, especially how we counterpoint the wolf pack story with our hero car traversing the same landscape, in sync. Having fun. Sorry about the reception. Great, great talking to you, bye...

I manage to open a beer before my producer calls me right back.

He mimics me.

– *The leader of the pack actually leads from behind.* Prick. The whole fucking script is about the wolf mother leading the way, driving into the fucking future or whatever. Traversing the landscape in sync, for fuck's sake. And then to top it all the embodiment of fun, you fucking clown!

We both start laughing, a comfortable laugh we have shared many times before, a healthy laugh. I tell him about all the tribes that got ejected from that fucking park. He said, no shit, you found all of that out from the terrace of your holiday home in the Italian fucking riviera.

Touche.

A good guy, a mensch. Sees things for what they are, says it how it is. No filter. He had just got a new Audi A8 and needed to make his nut on the lease. You do what you can to keep the wolf from the door, right?

Luckily they went with somebody else before I wasted my time doing a treatment, which would have involved rambling on the phone to a treatment writer in LA who typed it all up in a tasteful typeface with some pretty pictures and cost seven hundred bucks. I probably wouldn't have got the gig anyway as I haven't shot enough metal. There weren't any wolves on my reel either. Besides, I had better things to write.

*

Dawn. Two young men return from a successful hunt in the mountains, a Cinghiale strung on a pole between them, rifles slung over their shoulders. They stop in their tracks as they watch soldiers jump down from a truck in the village below.

We open in flashback. Something like this, pared back, timeless: war, mountains, guns, men, soldiers and a freshly killed wild boar. Place, time, jeopardy, but also imbued with a timeless visceral thrill of the hunt, the kill, of meat, the promise of food, a miracle of plenty in a time of death and hunger. Perhaps the very opening of the film could be a gunshot and then cut to a close-up of the death spasm of the boar. This is the sort of thing a director might add, especially one interested in symbolism. The soldiers spy the young men and shout at them to come down. Tension between them as the soldiers gesture to the hunters to gut the boar for them. They were city boys from Hamburg...

I get ahead of myself. Were men allowed to have hunting rifles? It's late in the war, autumn '44, so probably not. At the very least I imagine the soldiers would disarm them. Or was it a case of shoot first and ask questions later?

You can hear the shotguns of hunters from the terrace in the autumn, from the Squadra of men – teams, groups drawn from family and village with now a few outsiders accepted – who teem all over the forest in camo gear with shiny hunting rifles punctuated by the bark of walkie-talkies. Sharp winter cracks, some muffled by foliage. The boar has become a pest, there are too many of them with no apex predator to keep their numbers in check – and us a poor stand-in for that, but there is no other reason for the hunt, no redolence of hunger or fear, just a culling like electric prods in abattoirs really, which makes this tradition a mockery, a just-going-through-the-motions activity, more about the fashion and the shiny guns, the walkie-talkies and impromptu roadblocks, than any confrontation with a primal force. A tradition – albeit not that old, for there had always been wolves to do this job – hunting boar is inextricably linked to a challenged masculinity and territory and a sense of place and continuity more than to hunger or danger. I have yet to see a female hunter.

I keep the two young men behind the tree line, impotently watching the villagers being rousted from their homes onto the street. One of them wears a hunters cap. The majestic boar lying at their feet, blood congealing behind the left ear, irrelevant.

Potent/impotent.

This is the inciting incident, the first plot point of a rising story arc, if I remember the lingo accurately.

Separated by life and fate for sixty years, an exile returns to the village for the funeral of his first love and to be reunited with those he left behind, the friends and enemies he grew up with in a time of war.

They call this high concept, the elevator pitch. I would probably have to add something about the war not being over – some wars never end – or a return which reignites an old enmity, rivals in love, reunited at her funeral and a final boar hunt, a catharsis revealing a shocking truth, something like that. An arc of fifty years between the two hunts; the big idea for a film, the universal hook, an easy-to-recognise riff on one of the six stories ever told if not literally one of them. Hollywood – the machine – fetishises these six stories, as well as the adjacent tropes *Shakespearian* and *Classical*. It loves Joseph Campbell's *The hero with a thousand faces*, rooting the stereotypes it peddles in anthropological observation which turn into manuals for making movies that mine our collective psyche, the mechanics of storytelling scraped from the ages and re-skinned as the explanation for why movies like *Top Gun*/*Mad Max*/*Toy Story*/Marvel Universe/etc. make so much money (sorry, how they connect with so many people around the world), offering you the tools to write your own blockbuster, to climb your own mountain as a writer, for twenty-five dollars a pop from a shelf in Barnes & Noble or in seminars and writing rooms that cost a whole lot more.

I've just watched *The Northman* and if that's not high concept I don't know what is, the Viking version of *You killed my dad, fucked my mum but made the mistake of not killing me because when I grow up I will find you, I will kill you and your family, whatever it takes, however long it takes and I will rescue my mum as well* and probably forgive her. *Or die trying.*

The hero's journey, for nearly three hours.

The heart of my pitch is that these two old men are no longer up to duking it out, they no longer have the physical strength to face off, yet the mind is still willing and in attempting to do so their confrontation tips into parody, waking them up to just how dumb they are a metaphor in microcosm for the pathetic macho shit of all wars, etc. But it also entertains with violence. A sleight of hand that movies excel at. *The End of Violence* being the ne plus ultra of this observation.

I think Danny DeVito was after the same thing in *War of the Roses*, no? The never-ending conflict between men and women, the other war, a tragic comedy.

The climax of *The Northman* is a shield and sword fight between two wounded men in the caldera of an active volcano which spunks fresh ash and lava down on them as they battle. A humourless scene I will rework with humour. *In my telling of the story.*

But first, the setup.

A taxi picks up an old man and his crumpled suitcase from a deserted train station on the coast. His eyes observe a familiar landscape, overlaid by the inevitable memories. An old partisan returning to the mountain valley in which he fought a bitter war. He wears a flat cap redolent of the time of the Partigiani.

The cap suggests he is one of the two young men from the flashback (which we now realise *is* a flashback). Who is he? Where has he been? Where is he going? All questions that engage an audience in the first minutes of a movie. Even in the endgame, set in what is called our dotage – when we become invisible, when we become a burden, locked away in old people's homes or simply ignored, left to starve, to fade or simply to disappear. Only at the end can we remember the beginning. The only two things in life that are both identical and radically different. The in and out points in the edit of our timeline. If you live long enough, you become part of the never-ending story.

Old men who have worked all their lives from dawn to dusk (or thereabouts) now haunt the villages they still live in, walking the streets, smoking and drinking in the bars; short drinks, obscure bitter botanical *aperitivi*. The mysterious pale green of a Genepi or the acid-orange Aperol Spritz, almost childlike, sweet and sickly, a drink served with a straw which they without fail cast aside (for they will be drinking through straws soon enough) – or the mysterious honey orange of a *Bersagliare*, a sharpshooter, which is made from what? You can't google it. A viscous-looking drink with dubious digestive properties, perfect for old men, keeping them regular, probably an obscure vermouth with fizzy water. They drive their old workhorse Pandas or Apes, the high-pitched buzzing from the three-wheelers' small two-strike motorbike engine whining up and down the valley; you could hear them coming, an invasion of the carefree, the bored, the aimless, card players, games as obscure or as persistent as the spirits they drink, farmers become gardeners, now familial child care providers, the Nonno side of the Nanno/Nonno package.

This was the context for my pitch, upending the cliches of old age, which the movie will blow out of the water. Think *Cocoon* on steroids.

You give me the best story you can, the very best according to your ability. It's my job to turn it into the shit people will pay to see, to paraphrase a studio producer I once knew. Your best shot. So jaded are they, they demand total commitment in everything to remind them of their first time. Writers don't get to do it by the numbers, our burden is passion, for whatever dreck we are pushing, we are, perforce, the shock troops of unbridled enthusiasm.

Old men. Yes, sexy! Or at least funny.

You drag out references.

There was a Stallone film where he played an ageing deaf cop, going up against the bad guys one more time, hampered by the challenges thrown up by deafness, as an impediment to *carrying out his duties* but also as a clock ticking down on his virility, being the granularity of that film. Clint Eastwood redefined the cliches of old men in films, as he did with young ones. Polished it into oblivion on schedules as lean and aesthetically pleasing as the films themselves, turning over at nine a.m., breaking for lunch at one p.m. and the last shot of the day leaving enough time for a round of golf, or so they say, crews love him but again don't crews also love overtime, so this could be so much *baloney*, a seemingly quotidian detail regaled as insight from the trenches, deep in the weeds of Hollywood production – the Abby Singer, followed by the Martini shot – followed by a Martini or two and the drive home. This the biz, the money and the shizzle.

Which wasn't what I was after at all. I mean, I was after anything, anything I could get, but not that.

In fact, I pitched this idea years before films like *El Camino*, or the one where Clint saves the young Asian drug dealers, or kills them, that is the one, the same one, they love his car, an old-school muscle car, a shared obsession, a crossover between cultures and generations, also another film where he mules drugs for Hispanic dealers to pay for his plant nursery, one last deal, one last throw down, one last best in show, a busy man still...

The funeral of an old woman. Mourners gather outside a village church. A husband propped up by his middle-aged son stands guard by the church door. The taxi arrives. Two old men embrace, one of them the husband of the dead woman, the other her first love. The returnee enters the church and places his hand on the coffin, tears in his eyes. (Note: On entering the church, he takes his cap off, and it is now in his hand that rests on top of the coffin.)

Timeless ritual is key to this story, how it binds us unthinkingly, we have to go through the emotions before they run out, before we get to the drop, the point from which we have to make it up. For this story this moment of novelty is a hunt, high on the side of a mountain on the day after the funeral, which is also the day of the first snowfall. One ritual of death is over, another one is about to begin. Up here there are no footsteps to follow.

If I had known then about the two clocks, time out of time, the existential anomaly of it, for sure I would have used that as a key metaphor in this pitch, especially as it riffs off For Whom the Bell Tolls, *but this was probably before we bought the house, but perhaps, come to think of it, a couple of years afterwards, but before I noticed the bells at all, because for the first few years I was oblivious to them.*

I mentioned as an influence Lawrence Norfolk's novel *In the shape of a boar* about a Nazi officer being hunted in Greece in the last months of the war and how it resonates with an ancient mythical story of a boar hunt, how the two blur, summon each other somehow, get confused, jumbled up, become inseparably entwined as a single story.

Why not tell that story, one executive said, *you seem so enthralled by it.*

This when they still wanted films with Nazi officers in, with, of course, a twist, hopefully mine.

The boar in my story is also a mythago, a primitive trope, an ever present yet hidden motif, a heartbeat redolent with connotation. Hunting boar goes back into antiquity, a test of human mettle, the promise of feasting; this from *Gawain and the Green Knight*, where Lady Bertilak is attempting to seduce Gawain while her husband hunts for boar. (Over three days and three hunts: deer, boar and fox):

An incredible wild boar charged out there,
Which long since had left the herd through his age,
For he was massive and broad, greatest of all boars,
Terrible when he snorted. Then many were dismayed,
For three men in one rush he threw on their backs,
And made away fast without doing more harm.

Until, like his wife, he closes in for the kill:

The boar charged out, straight at the man,
So that he and the beast were both in a heap
Where the water was swiftest. The other had the worse;
For the man takes aim carefully as the two met.
For the man marked him well as they first met
And set stoutly the sword in the slit of his mouth
So right up to its hilt so that the heart burst open,
And squalling he gave up, and was swept through the water.

So I guess this was what I was thinking for my two main characters, a resonance that transcends them, interwoven as it is with the seduction of Gawain by the Lady, this ancient counterpoint is symbolic of their struggle, behind two warring men is a woman, dead or alive, and the boar mocks them as it ever sought to do. It mocks their sex, their waning virility.

But I don't mention this, I mean...

After the funeral, the two old friends drink long into the night at the bar, sing songs of love and war (in Italian, in dialect, even one in halting Russian, a glimpse of the horror, a return from the front, capitulation...) they entertain the few funeral guests and the tourists who sit in the corners of the room experiencing what they possibly came for in the first place, something authentic.

Who knows what they talk about? Who is still alive and who dead, and the woman they have just buried; she holds the key to their friendship and its undoing. Why did our hero leave the valley? Where did he go? America, as we know, is where people go to start a new life, for Italians it was here or South America, to work on the docks, in restaurants, employed by other Italians, richer ones who stepped off the boat a generation before and were now American. Some came to London, to work as bakers or to wait tables in the big hotels and later to work their way up, to run trattoria of their own, with names like Aldo's, Pan e Vino, Ciao Bella or Versuvio's.

What has been taken from them is the gift of silence that a shared life rewards you with. Old couples sit comfortably in silence. Old men sit around and play cards, happy in the silence that comes after everything that can be said has been said, now the words and rhythms of playing cards speak for them, or to be precise in their stead. Remarks on the luck of the cards, the habits of the players, all of which is in fact as comfortable as silence.

These old friends, have become strangers compelled to talk, and it is uncomfortable, they are not used to it. They have to catch up in order that they can then fully inhabit what it means for them to be old. The heart of the film is this compulsion, which is also the structure of the plot itself. The silence you find in nature versus the noise, the confusion you find in humans, our prattling.

What is unsaid? What will come out? This is what an audience must want to know, we help them to get to the next reel; we manage the information, spoon-feeding them to keep their bums on the seats, this the climax of the first act, at the thirty-minute mark, with a rising impetus, an ascending sequence of events that we can feel coming, the story taking us somewhere as if upon an ineluctable tide, where time passes in the bat of an eye caught up as we are in the action.

The memories stirred up by this return have in a strange way rejuvenated them physically, to match the emotions freshly uncorked inside them. Despite the dismay of the son, the old friends agree to go hunting the next morning and stumble home drunk across the village square under the memorial statue of two heroic young partisans, Tommy guns thrust defiantly up into the sky. The old man throws his hat up in to the night sky in celebration of still being alive.

The son is running to fat, has a desk job at the *commune*, he has never been a hunter. The old men are both still wiry from a lifetime of hard work. We find out what our hero did in America, his job, if he had married or has a family. Perhaps I will make him a merchant sailor, something more exotic. Or he is penniless, an unexpected hook as in most films and books America is the promised land.

The next morning, bright sunlight welcomes them into the hills, but after a few hours, just above the tree line, they tire; out of breath and with aching limbs, they rest up, eating lunch, drinking wine, exchanging tall tales overlooking the valley in which they grew up together. They watch a line of wolves cross a ridgeline through their binoculars, excited as children. After lunch they push on over the top and down into a secluded pine forest, their old hunting grounds. A few small boar cross their path, not worth the killing.

Conjured memories expand into storytelling and laughter, tears, and predictably anger. Tension wells up between them presaging confrontation. Remember, they both have guns and ammo! Which is what Act Two is all about, the middle of the film, the action, the meat, the heart of the matter laced with rising tension, obstacles, twists and yet more obstacles to be overcome.

Obstacle!

A sudden snowstorm descends on the high valley, yet neither of them wants to be the first to call off the hunt. They push on up into the remote crux of the valley.

Nature, the weather, seasons, flora and fauna, all of this is the world in which our struggles take place but also now becomes the antagonist (think *The Revenant*, or *The Thin Red Line*) invoking the struggle of the planet, of nature against us, despite us, oblivious to us. Think *Moby-Dick*, *The Cruel Sea*, *Walkabout*, you get the picture.

Obstacle!

At this point they sight a huge boar and track it back to its lair, a cave. A shot that only wounds, another that misses. Cornered and wounded, the boar counterattacks, knocking one of them to the ground. (Perhaps the boar mortally wounds both of them, and the climax of the movie is a bloody revenge tragedy, a zero-sum game of grisly death.)

Or: The other drags his fellow into an old derelict farmhouse where he builds a fire. This farmhouse is a place they knew from before, with memories of its own. The house of the parents of the dead woman, the wife, the lover. All that backstory...

I have to set up this old ruin as their destination, in symbolic homage to the woman they have lost. Although I love the idea of using the primordial cave as the location where they end up facing each other; I like the schlockiness, the horror of it, but for now will press on with the original idea. So the old farmhouse is just shut up, not derelict, the widow has a key for it. They retreat there after the attack but the house summons other demons...

Do I use flashbacks to tell the story of the house? We have already teased them up front as young men, it just feels a little conventional, which isn't a bad thing. To open the third act in flashback, to feed a little more information to the audience, enough to keep them on the hook for the final denouement. The house, a glass of milk, a German officer, collaboration? (An idea we see later in *Inglourious Basterds*! Replace the milk with grappa, wine or a cold beer on a hot day, the latter a perfect expression of domestic violation, transgressive hospitality. So you see these tropes circulate, there is no ownership of myth or history.)

Are flashbacks from the perspective of the characters or the filmmaker? Or indeed the house itself! The latter two being to all intents and purposes the same. Does this pull back the curtain to reveal our petty machinations? The sad little wizards of Oz we film makers truly are? Perhaps this is why cineastes hate flashbacks.

One reason our exile left after the war is that his girlfriend was pregnant with a German officer's baby. So our characters are: a compromised woman, a disgusted lover, a nazi and the best friend who picks up the pieces. Did the friend think his son was his, or the exile's, or did he know about the German officer?

Note: was it illicit love or was it rape? Why did she keep the baby?

This is the heart of the matter...

Perhaps the better film is her story, perhaps she should be the widow? Then it would be a love story, so similar to others, she is Penelope, which is a good thing!

I'm confused, the pitch flounders. I'm lost on a myriad of paths that lead in and out of what may or may not be a story.

Defeated, all I can write is:

A red mist descends over these two old men, they fight, the house expels them into the night and the snow. The next day the bastard son goes up into the mountains to rescue his father. What does he find?

And here these script notes end, notes for a script I never got to write.

*

I remember giving the pitch in person in a faceless office on San Vicente Boulevard. I was wearing smart cream corduroy shorts, for Hollywood is nothing if not informal. I recall sweaty palms from all the passion I had to summon, leaving in its wake an edgy vibe that stayed with me for the rest of the day, which I killed with vodka tonics.

– For me it is a timeless story of memory and forgetting, of strength and weakness, of ageing and the fear of death, of the lies told because of war and the secrets kept hidden for the sake of peace, the harm that they do and the pointlessness of revenge.

A blank, unreadable face, but one whose eyes have yet to stray to the phone on the desk in front of him, although his hand did automatically readjust a tie, just so.

– All of this set against the immutable backdrop of the

mountains at a time when nature is threatened, a reminder of the power and immutability of the landscape that both nurtures and chides our frail human passion.

A raised eyebrow at the word *chides* (and / or double use of the word *immutable*) and finally a glance down to the phone. I sit forward in my low and deceptively comfortable chair.

– Our heroes are like two old wolves, out of time, out of place, mangy, irrelevant, defanged.

A wry smile. Perhaps prompted by the novelty of hearing fancy words in this context.

– Men puffed up on the bounty of myth and history, and this is its bitter reward.

My last gasp. I've gone too far, transposing the thinly drawn lead characters of my film onto all men, which elicits a cough, a sip from a glass of water, a shrug. Perhaps he thinks I'm talking about him, or he is thinking about himself. He nods vigorously. His phone rings and he grabs it like it was on a timer. Twenty-five minutes had elapsed. Perhaps it was.

– Great, I gotta get this, excuse me.

I escape the chair, wipe my hands on my shorts.

Phone in the crook of his neck, he raises his eyebrows, prods the untouched outline on his desk and mouths *we will be in touch.*

We shake hands.

The pitch has languished, for years, but if I know anything it is that they are always right and you, me and everybody else is wrong, always wrong, until they say yes and then we are right and we are *all right.*

Who was I kidding?

*

A grainy video pops up on Facebook, posted by Fulvio the village mayor and also a big hunter. A shaky clip of a mangy wolf in the valley, a first sighting for many years, picking its way among the stones of a dry riverbed reduced to a trickle of water, running between rock and stone and piles of dumped silt, mud washed down from the mountains into the cleft of the valley, the coat of the wolf filthy with it, as it searches for food, looking more hunted than apex, as if usurped, expelled from her kingdom, her crown stolen, a fish out of water, a freshly minted migrant.

Viva il lupo!

Good luck, wolf!

I click and share it.

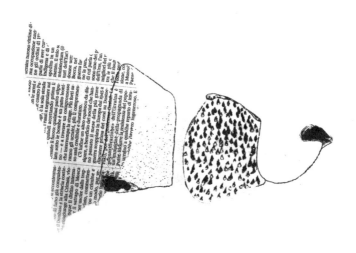

MIGRANTI

Fulvio was standing in the street having a smoke. He called me over.

I've got a good story for you.

It was a hot summer's day, so we sat outside the bar and ordered beers. Fulvio leant across the table in that conspiratorial way he has and started talking in a torrent.

– A migrant, young, from a city, you know, confident, not a country bumpkin, he can speak some Italian, a little English also, he comes into the office to thank me for hosting them in the village, so he's like a spokesman for the others, okay?

Like it was anything to do with me, but I don't say that obviously.

– They are staying in the old hotel, Maurizio's place, it's been empty for eight years, so why not? But that's not the good bit, he then asks me if there is anything they can do to return the favour.

Two beers arrive, along with antipasti, olives, stale bruschetta with anchovy, little rolls of prosciutto with a *picante* cheese paste, all very salty.

– I didn't understand what he meant. I sat there with my mouth open, so he repeated himself thinking his Italian was unintelligible. Checking in his dictionary for clarification. Is there any work that needs doing around the village, to show our appreciation. For free! Now there's a magic word, because nobody in this village has ever offered to do anything for free, never! No wonder I didn't understand him. Well, the cat got my tongue, but I managed to nod and smile like an idiot.

I laugh at his telling of the story, or at least the gist of it, the way he tells it with such relish and good humour. I order us more beers, declining the free snacks, any more of which will ruin supper.

– Malik, he's from Senegal, suggests that for two days a week they are happy to help around the village, whatever needs doing. Odd jobs. I take the smile off my face, this young man is deadly serious, earnest even, worried that I can't understand him, so I pull myself together and offer him my hand and thank him, yes, let me think, my brain gets up to speed, perhaps they can help collect the rubbish, Giacomo is getting old, he could do with some help and we have no money to pay anyone, so I tell him, and that's that. This guy, a fish out of water, not even twenty by the look of him but with a firm handshake and a steady eye...

We raise our glasses.

– *Salut.*

And then he says,

– *Per tutti coloro che vengono da noi dall'altra parte del mare.*[9]

Fulvio has a penchant for melodrama, I think it's how he enjoys what otherwise would be the dull routine of his job. And then I realise he includes me in that too, which I like the romance of, and we down our ice-cold beers, signalling for more.

I had expected some problems with having migrants in the village, some racism, but also interest, especially among the young people, always with their eyes out for something new. I didn't expect this enthusiasm from Fulvio and my spirits rose with a simple love for humanity.

Fulvio frowns, wipes his mouth and continues.

– So I'm thinking, nothing is for free, right? What's the catch here? What do they get out of it? Nothing specific, but this will soften the shock of them turning up, when the word gets around. Clever guy. I scratch your back, you scratch mine, this guy he gets it, like he's already Italian.

Fulvio roars with laughter at the punchline to his story. For him all stories must have punchlines. I never heard him tell a joke. Who needs jokes when we have life, he would say, which is more than funny enough. For Fulvio a story has to have a point, some little piece of wisdom in it we didn't know before and by telling it we all learn something, otherwise it's just gossip.

This attitude makes him a good mayor, I think.

Just as he predicts, the story percolates through the village and as the days go by locals are shaking hands with their new guests, who say *Ciao* in return and little by little life continues with them a part of it. They sit outside the

9   For all those who come to us from come across the sea.

cafes using Wi-Fi to keep in touch with family back home, and two mornings a week they collect rubbish, which progresses to getting paid to work at that summer's Festas. In this fashion they circulate among the local population. After some months, the law changes allowing migrants to legally earn money. The local tradespeople and farmers were more than happy to offer them work if they had it. Malick is a clever young man. New faces, new stories to mix in with what we have left of our own, (mine as well, also from across the sea) to strengthen our connection with an increasingly opaque world and by doing so understand ourselves and it better. Fulvio was captivated by that meeting with Malik, it made him look at life differently, a rare opportunity to think about things that never crossed his mind. These new people, this change, young men coming and going through the village on their way north, a breath of fresh air, a wind from the south.

A few beers in and Fulvio waxes lyrical.

– Like adding something to a weakening concrete, to stiffen it, or something, to stop the rot! I know little about such matters, although isn't that why the bridge collapsed in Genoa?

Our Fulvio was a thinker, the son of a baker, which makes sense as what is more philosophical than bread? In contrast, the mayor in the next commune was a firefighter, who would know the properties of steel and concrete because lives depended on it. Over the next months, Fulvio would get to know Malik's story, his family, where he came from, what his father did, what his culture was like, the words, the food, music, he became almost an expert on everything Senegalese.

– All the years I spent in Stuttgart working in the Mercedes canteen, I was like that young man, but I didn't have to lift a finger without getting paid. I was in a big city and there was work everywhere, overtime, lots of money working the production lines, when the world was going crazy for new cars. And now? What's for them?

We had another beer. It was a day when talking felt good, when it felt like you were active in the world. Fulvio was genuinely shocked and intrigued to recognise not just himself but something universal in this young African man. Fulvio had an older brother in London who was a baker alongside two cousins working at Sainsbury's for the last thirty years, and hardly a word of English between them.

– In the end he's the one who lost out. His wife, the kids, speak English fluently. But not him, nothing. It comes between them, especially the kids, who don't want to speak Italian, and so it goes...

By then it was late afternoon, and some tired-looking migrants got off the last bus. They had been down on the coast, probably selling trinkets on the beach, a hard and shit job to do but one you didn't need papers for, and as they came by a few hellos were exchanged and later they sat outside the hostel and bars and later still went down to the football pitch, where they played among themselves – before attracting the interest of local players, who soon joined in most days after work – but that night Fulvio and I had one more drink, a prosecco, because it was the right time of day for it and we had nothing else to do even though the story had run its course, but we were happy in our shared silence and separate thoughts.

A few years earlier I had been in Rome shooting a documentary about a refugee football team, *Liberi Nantes*, sponsored by A.S. Roma and based in the working-class suburb of Pietralata. Football, like much else, still split along lines of political allegiance, however attenuated. Historically a communist stronghold, a rough neighbourhood built as such and never intended to be anything else. The echoes of the past, aftershocks, were still present. Left wing, right wing, Communist or Fascist, for and against; the poor, the working man, women, gay people, profit, East and West, North and South, fissures that ran deep in Italy as well as globally, a country divided, a civil war waged economically, yet no less savagely, for over more than a century.

Liberi Nantes offered their players guided tours of the city, to get to know their way around but also to understand that their presence in the eternal city was, well, eternal. There was a history of Black lives in the heart of Italy, some as slaves but also those who had earned their freedom and become citizens of Rome. Whatever the details, to arrive in Rome as a refugee and be given a guided tour of the Coliseo where blood of all colours was spilt for the entertainment of thousands must be a trip. Or would they rather be sunning themselves in the villa Borghese, talking to girls to distract them from thinking about the girlfriends and wives they had left behind, or so young that they were looking for their first, an Italian girl, or boy, a Roman one and what would that be like? Or dreaming of making the big time, of being spotted by a big club, football the only stage on which they were visible, much like the coliseum they had just visited.

Two years later and some of the migrants staying at the old hotel had settled in the valley, working, sending money home, making a life for themselves, while others moved north where they had family or simply to try their luck elsewhere. Many more were sent home or returned voluntarily, homesick for mum, dad, children, partners, for the food, the taste and smell of home, for the air, the view from a kitchen window, the sea, the mountains, inchoate reasons that can't be written down, reasons of the senses, perhaps simply living without the weight of being foreign. Home, and with it the problems that haven't gone away. To decide what to do next, to recharge, find the money to go again, to try again to cross the sea or not. To give up on that. To stick or twist. Some have what it takes to make it 'up there', mostly luck and hard work; others don't. Either way, you find out.

Fight, fight, fight.

When south comes north.

*

There are Mexican taco joints in Chicago, offering the taste of home, literally down to village-specific spices; regional specialities recreated with an almost magical alacrity, each taco a miracle – *Christ rises with every loaf of bread* – secret ingredients for broths and sauces like spells, for *mole*, preparations of maize – where there is maize, there is life – techniques, flavours and methods hoarded across generations. Incantations of home. In a word, identity, and the further it has to travel the more precious it becomes, all of this wrapped up with the old religion, where food and worship become indistinguishable.

A hole in the wall specialising in El Pastor taco, passed down by Lebanese immigrants to Puebla in the 1800s, a pork schwarma taco *adobada* to write home about: cloves, garlic, cumin, achiote, bay leaf and cinnamon a communion of flavour, a hot taste of Mexico in cold Chicago, a transubstantiation, one thing becoming another in a mouthful, a moment of stillness in the Windy City.

Migrants are universal, at all times and in all places They carry the taste of us, the daily toil of being human, our simple fables, our world stories.

Third-generation Japanese Brazilian women speaking Portuguese, crafting beer from the fruits of Japan in Brazil. Their cans, bottles, point of sale and beer mats adorned with the silhouette of the steamship that brought their grandparents, one million of them, to the new world.

Silent men wait crouched on their haunches, smoking in bleak car parks of DIY superstores from LA to London, from Eastern Europe to Mexico, Dakkar to Johannesburg. Waiting to be picked up for a day's labour by other men in battered vans with a day's work of their own.

A homeless man in his forties is given an Oyster card to travel around London by the shelter where he is staying. Every day he tries his luck on the streets, picking up odd jobs here and there.

Can I help?

Do you need a hand with that?

The dish washer hasn't shown up, can you do his shift?

Take this package, here's the address, read it back to me, great, come back and there will be something else to do, we're busy, so…

He has the freedom of the city. And at the end of each day he has a warm place to go, some food and the internet. Things could be worse. One day he gets a house-moving job in Walton-on-Thames, a distant suburb. Good money. He takes an early train without realising the Oyster card isn't valid outside of London and gets stopped at the gate.

Ticket please, sir.

He apologises and offers to pay; he has the money, he wasn't trying to cheat, he just didn't know…

The inspector is understanding, polite even, but still issues a fine because that's the rules. He doesn't tell him that if challenges the fine online, he will probably get let off, he doesn't think to offer this information to avoid confusion and the aggravation of a standoff.

The man, let's call him Mahmoud, feels obliged to tell him his story in evidence. He's from Iran, he's been in the UK for twelve years, used to live in Bury - worked as a driver - has only recently moved to London, he can't afford to pay a fine, his papers had been stolen from the last night shelter he had been staying in. He doesn't want trouble with the authorities. The inspector eventually relents, perhaps he's just realised the time, the end of his shift, or lunch and he is hungry, so he allows Mahmoud to pay for the ticket.

Just this once.

But the price Mahmoud really has to pay – and not to the inspector, nor the train company, no, the price is no less than that demanded by fate – is his story. The only currency he has. He has to say that he is an asylum seeker, that he is Iranian. And to apologise. He pays for the ticket with the last of his money and rushes off to his day's work. He passes the cost of the fare plus the fine he didn't have to pay to his Iranian employer, thinking with a smile that Iranians give without ever expecting to get back. Outsiders are trapped within one story after another. Dull, flat, life-sucking stories like this, occasionally spiced with a little rebellion. The bottom line is you either hack it or not. The same explanation, over and over again, bookended by *sorry* and *thank you*.

I write it down here in full ownership of the privilege of not being written about…

*

The following summer my youngest son wanted to play football down by the petrol station. It had become a focal point of the village. I remember dropping him off with his Astros. He watched from the touchline and after five minutes the players gestured to him onto the pitch.

– Where you from?

– London.

– Ah, super Spurs!

– Nooo, Arsenal! Fuck Spurs!

– Sorry, boss…

Laughter, apologies, trading the names of players they like, African players who play in the Premiership the bridge between them, saying those names together, the instant satisfaction of sharing heroes and villains, of disagreeing also, to have your opinion, to declare the name of your club, the easy tribal banter of football. Game after game, week after week, late into the evening, the sun throwing long shadows of players before it sinks behind the mountains.

Let's play!

*

That autumn I had supper with Fulvio, his face full of stubble, for every year he attempts to grow a winter beard. We were eating a casserole of coscia di capretto, sweet and sour onions, rosemary and sweet potatoes.

– Malik is gone now. Sweden, I think. Will he repeat his trick? How will he get on? Perhaps he will write and tell me. I know nothing about Sweden.

Fulvio shrugs, a little miffed.

– A chap like him will thrive anywhere, America, Europe, it doesn't matter. A man who arrives in a new country, sees who he has to deal with, what the situation is, understands what people will assume about him, lazy, Black, trouble, or whatever, maybe even the opposite, maybe they want to patronise him. All he wants is to stand on his own two feet.

I think Fulvio is also talking about himself, his youth in Germany, a nostalgia for that time, that adventure. An excitement he misses even in middle age. Especially in middle age.

He takes a big glug of wine, unusually for him a Barolo, full of cherry and liquorice, exploding on your tongue, a fanfare for the satisfying umami flavour of the slow-cooked meat. I'm still drinking rose, a summer habit that's hard to shake although I regret it now, watching him smack his ruby lips.

– Look at your plate. That's how they stew goat in Dakkar, in a French style, simmered in Dijon mustard and vinegar, a perfect balance to the sweetness of the potato, and today we are eating it like that. Like in a tagine, Malik remembered this same contrast, the sweetness of cinnamon in a pigeon pie he once ate in Marrakesh.

And so it goes, full circle.

And Fulvio full up with food and wine, happy, talking. He scratches his stubbly cheeks as I tell him a version of the following story, something that had preyed on my mind, waiting to be shared, for the context in which to share it to feel right, with few – I hoped – negative consequences, for it carried not a little shame.

That summer, the year of the Grenfell fire, I got a speeding ticket and opted to go on a speed awareness course instead of taking points on my licence. I drove right past the tower crossing the Westway to get to the location at a corporate hotel on Hangar Lane. A black stump, before they shrouded it. I couldn't take my eyes off it. I swerved to avoid a collision with the car in front. Perhaps that's why they covered it up so quickly. It was dangerous. Rubbernecking is what they call it, accidents caused by drivers looking at disasters.

You can't help yourself, you can't not look.

I shared a table with the usual cross-section of London drivers, including a middle-class mum, a young delivery driver, a cabbie and an older orthodox Jewish man who lived near me in Stamford Hill. The man running the course had his shirt tucked in and his mobile phone clipped to his sturdy-looking belt. He led two of these courses a day. After it had finished, I offered the Hasidic guy a lift home as he hadn't driven, so we sat side by side for the best part of an hour. For the sake of conversation, I mentioned I had driven past Grenfell tower, what a tragedy it was, and he replied with a shrug, *I never heard of it, this Grenfell.* He didn't appear to be interested in the slightest. I was shocked and said that lots of people died, at least eighty people I think, it's been all over the news. He said, *I don't watch the news.*

We sat in silence. I was annoyed, I didn't know what to say but thought how ignorant to live in a country, a city, and not be aware of what was going on around you. How sad, how small-minded it was to be such a man, especially a religious and observant one. I also thought this was a very un-Jewish attitude, not to be aware of events in the wider world in which you live. Not to have a suitcase packed in the hall (metaphorical or otherwise), to be blithely unaware of the suffering of others in a world that many Jews know can turn on you at the drop of a hat or in the blink of an eye. How had this man let his guard down, I asked myself? Wasn't this the mistake of assimilation, made by Jews like me but definitively not to be made by somebody so obviously, visibly Jewish like him?

The silence was getting awkward – for me – he didn't seem to mind it, so I broke it.

I read that some families in your community have moved to Canvey Island?

A documentary he probably hadn't seen had been on the telly about it. So I asked.

Why there, why Canvey?

After a reluctant beat or two he replied that young families needed more space, Stamford Hill was getting crowded, not enough outdoor space and not as safe as it was. The plan had been to move to Milton Keynes but that had fallen through, so now some families had moved to Canvey Island.

An advance party, I thought.

A community that lives and moves together must be difficult to organise, to find somewhere new for everybody. They would definitely create a splash in Canvey.

Interesting, I said.

He shrugged. *Let's see what happens.*

A slight downward tightening of the mouth, another slight shrug of the shoulders. He had thin pursed lips, as mobile as a pipe cleaner. He was talking to himself, my presence was irrelevant.

Jews going out into the world, a confident move, forward thinking. I took this as a positive sign, that Orthodox families would choose Canvey Island, a mostly white working-class community in the Thames estuary. Year-round Union Jack bunting, static caravans, pubs, a holdout in some senses against a changing world. An island within an island. A place with a commitment to the past and continuity, of custom, and traditions not unlike that of the Orthodox incomers. You look hard enough you will find a connection, discover similarities. They would also be a novelty, not enough of them to be a threat, economic or otherwise, just enough to be given a chance, for both sides to be judged on merit, a desire to see the outcome of an experiment. There had been a get-to-know-the-neighbours reception party in the community centre. A willingness to understand others. Somebody must have made the first move, held out his or her hand to shake another, to look a stranger in the eye and speak, just like Malik had.

It made great telly.

So why didn't this old guy, with a long flowing white beard, black suit and fedora perched jauntily on his head, a religious man with white *payes* flowing from his head, tattered *tzitzit* from his waist, why didn't he seem to know or care about the Grenfell fire? Why did he just shrug the information off? A towering inferno, fire, houses being torched, pogroms, these elemental things are coextensive, if only viscerally, it must stir up something, some emotion, some empathy on whatever level?

What about the kindness of others? Don't you pass that on, or perhaps nobody had ever been kind to this man. Was that it?

We said nothing more to each other on the trip back to Hackney and I dropped him at the lights at the junction with Seven Sisters Road. He bobbed his head in thanks. What I wanted to say was *Who do you think you are?* There was this huge wall between us, a wall of silence. He looked Jewish, I didn't. He was a minority, and I wasn't. He was living a life the condition of which was a direct result of *The Holocaust*. The migrants in our village criss crossing the world South to North East to West have no holocaust – in our eyes, the cold steel eyes and liberal democratic conditional empathy of the West – no Grenfell tower, just small inflatable boats sporadically sinking on our news feeds; nothing as yet coherent in terms of a capitalised narrative, a Big Compelling Story. Like an engine that splutters into life but then dies, only to try again, a few sharp coughs, a closed cycle of cutting out, sparking to life, cutting out. Migrants, economic or refugee, having to leave home by sea and make a new life for themselves in other countries with other languages, much like that old guy's parents had had to do seventy-odd years ago, and my great-grandparents before that.

For all of those that come to us from across the sea.

Salut.

And I wondered about Malik and all the young men and where their children and grandchildren would end up, what languages would they speak, what jobs would they do? And would they hold tight to their heritage like this old Jewish man and like the Italian bakers, or would they seek to lose it, bit by bit in the desire to fit in and make a new start like my family had? And which was the better course of action, and how could you know, in the moment of deciding, which would be the right one? How long must we remain migrants?

Perhaps the old man was right.

Let's see what happens.

Was all you could ever do.

AUGUSTIN

A stale soft pack of Chesterfields stuffed down the back of the sofa, by some miracle dry, the tobacco crumbles between my fingers like mummies exposed to the air. Chesterfields, a European fag redolent of a vanished, playboy fantasy era.

There are so many cliches involving alcohol and cigarettes it's hard to see the people who smoke and drink as anything more than sketches, manifesting patterns of familiar addictions. They are obscured somehow by metaphor, the lazy tropes of popular entertainment flooding observational reflection with generic connotation. Storytelling leans on them like a sick woman on crutches. Smoking and drinking reverse the polarity between protagonist and the objects she has to hand, like a sorcerer's apprentice playing recklessly with spells over which we have little control. We exhale smoke and stare off camera, we fumble lighters – thumbs rolling flint wheels once, twice, three times – before eventually sparking a flame. We lean in to offer a light. We rip the cellophane off packets of cigarettes, ignobly using our teeth to gain purchase; alternatively we proffer cigarettes delicately held in place by elastic straps in silver cases. Sipping glasses of wine or downing pints of ale, wiping our wet top lips or not bothering to, we perch on bar stools in anticipation of the pouring of shots, stipulating *sotto voce* our preference for neat or over ice, one cube or two, all of this busily suggesting the murky hidden realm of human emotion, thought and instinct. Overflowing ashtrays, stiffeners and nightcaps, lunchtime tipples or all-night sessions, a full *wet bar* or a case of lukewarm beers outside the back door in soggy cardboard, the last half bottle of wine, uncorked in the fridge's door, the very last. Shared rollups outside factory gates, political somehow, clandestine, or cupped timelessly against the wind in calloused hands out on the range or ponced snouts on the street, from anyone, everywhere, shamelessly. These habits are the story itself. We are no more than meat puppets operated by toxins.

These half-thoughts entertain me as I observe the locals while waiting for lunch at a restaurant by the river.

Augustin.

Actually, I don't observe him, for that implies a degree of surreptitious behaviour. I am not a spy as I watch him drinking or fumbling with his cigarettes. Each gesture is expansive, loose-limbed yet intimate, involved, choreographed even. His physical relationship to his chair and table and the things on it which would not be out of place in a modern dance performance. It is an old dance, as old as the hills. He wouldn't notice the audience.

Augustin sits opposite an accomplice who is comparatively sober and therefore not as supple, a little self-conscious. His demeanour is apologetic, aware his friend is making a scene, but also defensive.

It's just August, he's harmless, no?

Or:

So what, he's had a few drinks. Give him a break, and me too while you're at it.

Accomplices enable but also participate often using the other as cover for their own behaviour. He may also be a friend.

Augustin spirals towards the door away from the bottle on the table, an umbilical cord limits the distance he can travel. He oscillates, you can see him pushing the envelope of geometry it allows. A hulk of a man with wild white hair and beard, beleaguered islands of livid flesh in between; it is impossible to ignore him with any confidence. You try knowing you will fail. He eyeballs me, shouts something incomprehensible before spooling back into his chair.

By this time I was drinking a cold half litre of sparkling Vermentino to go with my cheese plate antipasti, served up on an irregular piece of dark slate; Pecorino, Mucca, shards of Parmigiano and a spoonful of fermented ewes' milk *Bruzzu* with a dollop of honey and fig preserve on the side. The latter especially demands to be leavened by the neutral-tasting but absorbent local bread. Pungent and salty *Bruzzu* pairs perfectly with the fizzy white wine, scouring the roof of your mouth. You can't help but smack your lips. This peasant cheese ferments with grappa, named in various dialects *Brus, Bros, Bross.*

Only love is stronger than Bros is a local proverb – apparently, I've never heard it – although you rarely hear proverbs spoken.

We are in an enclosed – by creased transparent PVC sheets – terrace in front of the trattoria. These ugly drapes have popped up everywhere, from down on the coast (where it is windy) to the mountains where it can rain, snow or hail at the drop of a hat. They make me slightly claustrophobic, going inside these spaces always gives me pause, I irrationally feel there won't be enough oxygen inside because they remind me of hazmat protective suits and cordoned off hospital beds in horror films or role-playing games – what lies behind them is blurry and usually dripping in blood, or a handprint smearing the curtain from inside.

These functional terraces are definitely not attractive and adorn no postcards.

One moment Augustin is talking with his friend in a familiar fashion, the next he is shouting and eventually finds himself in a heated argument with somebody else, not present. This escalation – through the gears of intoxication – prompts him up and out of his chair. He regales the invisible interlocutor with scant regard for anybody else. Abruptly his strings go slack, as if cut, his motivation evaporates and Augustin slumps noisily back onto his chair, which creaks but doesn't give way. He clasps his wine glass for dear life. Without missing a beat, he picks up the conversation with his friend.

Booze makes him angry. Trust me, when he's sober he's a totally different person. One glass and he's off, what can you do?

This is how it appears. I don't know him other than by observation and the stories other people have told me.

Up and down, from sober to drunk and back again by degree, or like a switch on or off. You never can tell which Augustin you are going to get.

This sounds more like a generic observation of people who drink too much rather than of the person in front of me drinking. What exercises *him*? Did he have a beef with somebody in particular, or is this a more general world-weariness? Or was he just trying to make sense of things as they came to him? Things he had mostly forgotten, *pushed to the back of his mind*, which every so often ambush him? His past, and his part in it.

Existential anguish generally tortures characters in books rather than those you encounter in real life, so it was probably a slight, somebody must have crossed him at some point, setting him off at a slant. And some people drink to live with this, and the drink feeds it, feeds the shame and the spite of it, growing into a grand injustice – which happens to all of us (mostly men) who see the world in a certain way – life an intricate tally of points won or lost, chased by runs of bad luck, punctuated by moments of relative (but never great) fortune – none of it an excuse but nevertheless constituting a past which colours, and in this case consumes, the present.

Our true weakness, sober or drunk, is this constant tallying. When the story of our lives is mainly behind us, we worry the details silently, or in Augustin's case reanimate them haphazardly into fresh suffering.

He gets louder. I pick up some words but he is mostly speaking dialect which, because of its flow, its soft consonants and unctuous vowels, lends itself to the ruminations of a local drinker. *Dialetto* is full of an unmediated signification of place, a smell almost, a taste, so much the better to talk to yourself with, or am I getting confused – language is by definition mediated – my second half litre of Vermentino fizzing my mind as it does my glass, percolating into a carbonated romance…

His friend turns to my table, smiles, raising his shoulders as if to say (as if to say)

This is what life has made him.

Perhaps we mediate each other.

What life has made of him, what life has made from him. Augustin invoked as a force of nature, a storm, more accurately a flash flood, a localised hailstorm (one of the valley's microclimate effects), and I reply (intentionally) as a man, or (perceived) as a visitor, *no problem*, (as if to say) worldly wise, *I understand, we're all human, this is what life does to us, no?*

The young chef, hands on her hips, comes out onto the terrace and scowls. She has grown up with Augustin and his cronies, is sick of them dragging everyone else down. She says to nobody in particular, to the terrace, to me, *no it's not okay, it's bloody boring, every day he's like this.*

She shouts at him.

Get out Augusto, I can't stand it any longer!

How many times can she stand it no longer? A woman at the end of her tether – who has had enough of men like him and probably men in general – she just wants to do her job, she just wants to cook. Augustin hesitates, looks down at the floor, what she says gives him pause, has somehow got through, and after a beat he wanders off while his friend hunkers down over the last of his food and drink, blending into the scene, a minor character in a different painting.

I take a deep breath.

My pasta arrives, ravioli stuffed with borage and ricotta in a sauce of *burro e salvia*, sprinkled with Parmigiano, savoured best with more mouthfuls of Vermentino and the plate mopped up with rough slices of Pane di Molini – a chef I know serves thick slices of homemade focaccia for the same purpose, to mop up all the juices, to clean the plate with – *Look at that! No need to wash them!* he would gloat at the end of a long service, the bread appearing as *Mopetta* (in italics) on his demotic Haggerston menu.

The friend goes off for a smoke. I watch him through the thick scratchy PVC which filters the world outside so that it appears as a blizzard in a snow globe.

Augustin reappears (stage right) to discover his friend has left a glass of wine. He lurches towards it, so happy to see it he does a small jig by the table, draining it off before sitting down. He looks around, lost. His friend pulls up outside the restaurant in a white Fiat Panda. He gets out of the car and comes back inside, picking up his coat as if he had forgotten it, makes to leave but then sits down again as if defeated by the scene they have created. The play is over but they are loath to leave the stage.

They have been told off. It doesn't sit well with him.

He lights a cigarette and calls into the bar for a refill of wine. An older woman, perhaps the chef's grandmother, it's hard to tell, she has a youthful face made more so by a livid scar running from cheek to chin and dark green eyes, unusual in this valley – a face hard to forget at whatever age. She storms into the room, throws a wet tea towel at him. An intimate, silent rupture. They must know each well and over a period of many years. She whispers something in his ear.

Without a word of complaint, not even catching her eye, Augustin gyrates back out into the street.

This is how the day unravels.

My main course arrives, *cogniglio alla cacciatore* with a side of chips and a carafe of the house red which is only drinkable with the rich oily rabbit. The rosemary and thyme plus the bite of the olives soften the rough tannins of the wine.

I look up to see the young chef – looking closely at her again, her eyes are also green, so they are related – chase after Augustin with a pitcher of water. She throws it in his face and storms back into the restaurant, tearful and shaking with anger, which is actually shame. Her grandmother gives her a quick, compassionate hug and gets back to work.

The two women have curly hair, the older one's is grey and loose, the chef's dark, tight and pulled back under a red bandana. Both are quite tall but not skinny. Big women. I offered a discrete smile and nod of the head to signal compassion but also an apology – I was drinking too but would never be like that, not all men are like that, or at least I hope she could read some of that in my facial expression.

The addition of the cheese and meat boards makes me think she is trying to change up the menu to attract a different crowd. Younger, more mixed, God forbid groups of friends up from the coast for a weekend treat. There is a hardware shop in Taggia that sells these slate platters and they have appeared at all three of the upwardly aspirational restaurants in the valley. Why are slate platters appealing? What do they suggest? Here they are a mark of her ambition, pushing back on the way things have been done for years. Maybe there is no jostling for influence, her family happy to let her take the reins. These platters maybe just the beginning, a shot across the bows, a testing of the water, along with her immaculate cook's apron and the simmering energy implicit in her strong calves, bouncy trainers and youthful complexion.

Slate under which to bury all of life's Augustins...

Oddly, for a moment I thought she had gone after him with a glass of wine; an offering, a bribe – *go on take this, I don't care if you drink yourself to death just fuck off* (he was just about to get into a car) – or even God forbid an apology, as if to say *I give in*, an acquiescence to the regulars and the regular way of doing things, and later alone in the kitchen she would methodically smash the slate platters one by one. What had she been thinking? This bloody place would be theirs until they were all fucking dead.

In winter these characters drink and play cards every night by a wood pellet stove while others stand at a zinc bar top in their hunting clothes. Rotating outside for cigarettes, the change of temperature invigorating them for another round. Cards slap, glasses clink and male voices switch between barks of laughter, bouts of coughing and shouts of momentary anguish to accompany runs of bad luck, this the true language of old men and the younger ones who follow them, bonded by both family and work or the lack of it, the persistence of life over time and an undefeatable sense of *paisa*. A living tableau, the scene reminds you of other paintings and the stories they hide, what shouts, smells, poor fights and everyday despair; the still image shrouds truth like the decency of a sheet thrown over a dead body.

A cafe, a grappa, I walk to my hire car. What pleasure such proximity can bring. I mix up this scene with memories of my own indignities, and those visited upon me. I think about my agent; me listening to all his woes in the pub when he left his wife, downing pints in sympathy and then him persuading me to take what I knew was a shit movie, but I needed the hundred grand and so we agreed silently and probably in bad faith – at least that's how I see it now – to take it. I start the engine and drive home, a little drunk, a little maudlin, up into the hills. Now I'm talking to the car about myself. I know this will subside after the drink has passed, memories compressed back into the sediment of thoughts that churn before settling, like milk into cheese, curdling, my mind a working cesspit, yet remain an ever presence where sober reflection finds them insoluble yet inert, part of the furniture of who I am, literally full of shit, both trapped by and at home in all the stuff that goes to make me up. Hell is definitely not other people. I am a man reflected in – and refracted by – the fortunes of others, as is the case for each and every one of us.

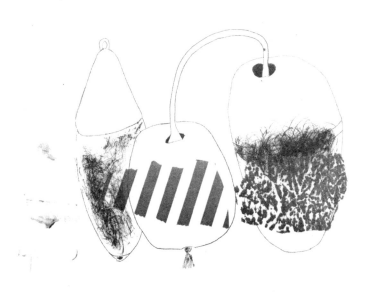

BAGNO AZZURRA

We, people from the plains
Excellent drivers in the city
Are always a little scared of the sea
Because of the idea of too much freedom[10]

At the end of every summer, the house broils, hoarding memories. Our fifteen-year-old pair of fake Versace beach towels survive – faded and tattered – for another year, logo almost as unreadable as a recently discovered Roman fresco. Punctured lurid inflatables litter in forgotten corners, sand in beds and trainers not to mention the plugholes of showers, and between the cushions of sofas, in a word, sand gets everywhere, and our collection of quarter-full and soon to be out-of-date sun cream grows collecting on random shelves, *Black Carrot* the

10   'Gente di Mare'. Sung by Umberto Tozzi and Raf. (Google Translate)

standout favourite of suntan-obsessed teenagers and those old enough to know better. Autumn is long and warm, alas we are not here but have taken our memories with us.

I am a fidget, I can't sit still, you love to sunbathe, as immobile as a seal. I never stop thinking – about nothing in particular – my mind whirrs, while you love to zone out, mind blank. We are neither unhappy nor unduly happy people. We occupy a temperate zone. I have tinnitus which is partially cancelled out by the sound of the sea; you enjoy the sound of silence. We both read, which is something we have in common, although I can't do it on the beach for more than ten minutes at a time. The main pleasure of the beach for me is the sensuality of time suspended: beach time. It feels so present, gravid in the heat, but is worn lightly by those who enjoy it. A pageant of time, I watch it pass. Do you love this aspect of a day at the beach? I must remember to ask you. I know we both love the fierce sun and the stoned feeling you get from a day out in it and the sand that gets everywhere and how later we feel dizzy, drunk after the first few sips of cold wine. We exclaim we are spanked. Spanked by the sun and that is just how it is.

Heading east from San Remo, past its scruffy suburbs, you will find a string of beaches at the bottom of a hill peppered with 1960s apartment blocks and half-finished new holiday developments. A 1930s football stadium sits at the bottom of the hill, luxuriating in a long, slow decline. *Sanremese* fans in the north stand have been cheering on their team since 1904.

L'Irriducibili!

The disused coastal railway line is now a busy cycle path dotted with cafes and deserted stations. There is a rocky public beach followed by a string of sandy private beach clubs and restaurants in various states of disrepair – the vagaries of fortune not spread evenly between them – but enough to go around, keeping them all in business. Just. Coats of paint, of various vintages, fabric awnings likewise with bright to fading colours, concrete decks on a scale between rotting (almost diseased looking) to mint, pate like, geometrically sharp and pleasing, in a word *modern*, being the only outward signs of relative prosperity. Poured concrete has a site-specific resonance, whether it is bodies suspended in the foundations of buildings, a signature despatch, usually underpinning civic developments the contracts for which the victims themselves were implicated in procuring, or revealed in news flashes as poorly mixed in the footage of collapsed infrastructure. Here too at the beach, the quality of concrete varies, and its upkeep or destitution speaks volumes if you care to read them.

Family-run beach clubs go back many years. A little ticket window at the entrance to each, with stamped government licence and tariff legend typed up and pinned under Perspex or cellophane. Each club sports its own livery and colour scheme for its *ombrelloni e Letteni*. Red, yellow, blue, blocks or stripes, mostly pastels, bleached by the sun. Easy to spot from the road – from the scrum of vespas, cars, families and groups of teenagers, trying to park, disgorged from buses, looking for friends – *come and see us, we're on Blue beach!* they text or WhatsApp.

Everybody has a favourite spot they return to day after day, year after year. Whether from loyalty or just animal habit, it's the way these places work, an alchemy of locals and tourists across generations that pertains on beaches around the world. Young and old only see themselves, two moments in time so distinct and each demanding attention, full of selfish drama. The beginning and the end. To enjoy life as much as possible before it runs out, to get the most out of the time you have left, eking it out, or spending it frivolously, each moment an eternity, spoilt as you are by its apparent abundance, unaware of any limit. They both share a rarified sense of time. Middle age lurks between the two. It sulks. Our predicament is amplified. We see ourselves reflected in both directions and for this reason the melancholia of the beach belongs to us. The true value of time weighed on the scales of the everyday. We own it.

Guests pay for their regular spots on the sand months in advance. Families return to the same clubs across generations. You can walk between rows of loungers – usually the two closest to the sea – empty for most of the day, but paid for. Their owners are at lunch or having a siesta in the apartments up on the hill. Some foreign tourists find this off-putting if not rude, but it is what it is: Italian beach club culture. Across the border in France it is far worse and more expensive. Here, somehow, Italians don't add snobbery to the mix, it is just tradition, the reassurance of things paid for.

*

A short walk to the changing room across hot sand as the guy puts up the umbrella. You stuff your pants in the pocket of your shorts which you hang alongside your T-shirt on a hook, attached to the pole of the umbrella. Rubbing sun cream on your face and legs, lying back, taking out your book or magazine, wiping the grease off your hands on the towel between your legs.

You stumble into the sea on what feel like broken feet.

The public beaches – usually rocky bookends at the margins of the clubs or on the groynes that separate them – are free and people put up their own umbrellas anchored with stones, or stake themselves out on the stones to broil in the sun. Not ten feet away on the other side of a cordon is a beach club. For locals coming to the beach after work or at weekends, the public beach is more stylish, more cool. It says: this is our beach, this is ours, this is us. Here we are and there *you* are. To pay looks foolish by comparison, absurd, petit-bourgeois, irrelevant. You park your Vespa on the road under the shade of a tree or a bush if you can find one, come down to the beach via crumbling concrete steps and underpasses sporting exposed and rusting rebar, put down your towel and that's it. You swim or sit around and smoke, chat, their pertains a sexual ease between boy and girl, a playfulness without the restrictions of negotiating privacy. You are free. Perhaps this is why the new beach clubs run by younger generations are more relaxed, less policed, they carry a sense of the public beach over into the private but exhibit less of either culture; being more transactional with less of a hinterland of either tradition or rebellion. Yet as with so many things for young people it is just what it is, a place to meet up: a beach, a bar, the sea, a day off or a few hours after work, to relax, to sunbathe, to feel the heat, and the water on your skin, the sting of salt also on tiny cuts and bitter in your mouth.

*

My boss is a fucking arsehole, the extra shifts I have to take, to cover for that lazy bastard Enzo, and I ask for an afternoon off to come to the beach with my girlfriend who I hardly see and he answers…

– Are you crazy? We're too busy. If we don't finish this job on time there are penalties, I go out of business and you lose your job. When I was your age…

He leaves that hanging there, wanting me to fill in his bullshit story.

– Do you want the extra shifts or not?

Now he's even threatening me.

– Or do I find somebody who needs the work? I pay you, so why the face?

Face? We're on the fucking phone.

– Yes, I get paid, but when do I get to spend it?

– That's a problem?

I turn my phone off.

An old school friend, Patrice, works at the beach bar.

– Hey man, that sounded heavy.

He smiles, I shake my head.

– What do you want?

– Simonetta, Coke?

She nods from the sunbed, her hand shading her eyes, a big smile, still surprised to see me, the number of times I have had to let her down this summer.

I duck under the umbrella, sit down.

– I swear I'm going to get another job. The joke is he won't ever sack me, who the fuck else will do my work, his lazy pig of a son? Let's change the subject, I'm sorry, how was your day, baby?

Through the smoke of her cigarette she takes the Coke and frowns, tucking a loose strand of hair back under her headscarf.

- Don't ask. Let's change the subject!

We both smile and I lean in for a kiss. It's been another shit week.

*

How do you get to own a beach in the first place? Were they once fishermen? Did they push off from it every morning or did they fish at night? Had family members been lost at sea and washed up on the beach; had they paid a blood price for it? Or was it just a good deal made at the right time with the right person? Or just years of hard work, saving and scrimping?

Now these *Stabilimento Bagni* are quaint, written up in travel guides with a list of do's and don'ts, but once they were new and brash, a fashionable solution to the timeless problem of how to make money. Another story that has winners and losers in its pages and all the things that pertain to them. Somebody must have had their nose put out of joint, somebody else missed out, robbed of an opportunity that you took. Smart families and stupid ones, or honest and less honest ones, lucky or less lucky, a lame horse or a racehorse.

Beaches had been fearful sites of invasion, conjuring barbarians new and old but also sightings of monsters and the bounty of shipwrecks, clandestine places frequented at night by pirates and smugglers, lovers and suicides. Beaches were borderlands. The heart beats faster as you scan the horizon, bringing on anxiety, agoraphobia. In a colonial narrative *we* arrive to conquer. It's beyond the beach where the unknown lies, potential danger lurking behind walls of dense green foliage, the tree-line a boundary between you and unspeakable terror.

A conquistador boot print in the sand, quickly flooding with seawater foam, the crazy footsteps of Klaus Kinski weaving along the shoreline as we cower, crouched low behind our shields hidden behind the last row of palm trees.

Peasants, the colour of poverty, cooled down on beaches in the high summer months. For the rest of the year the cold black water of the sea clawed at you as you fought it for something to eat. Now we pedalo on its emerald surface, dive in to cool off and snorkel below to spot colourful fish. The temperature invigorates, enlivens the body. It feels great. For now, for the sea shares an uncertain future with its despoilers.

How many people truly never fidget on the beach? The people who lie on their towels for hours, face up followed by face down, some even prop themselves up halfway to tan those bits in between, like ice-cream sandwiches balanced on their sides. What on earth are they thinking of? I envy them, these alien beings, these animals. I can sunbathe for a few minutes but without warning everyday concerns flood my mind, as well as older, nastier thoughts, that lie in wait for these moments in order to bushwhack me.

Boo!

There was a time when doctors prescribed sea air for its medicinal benefits, which they never do now. I wonder why not? Diseases change as do the remedies. We cure some, discover others. Spas and seaside air offered a cure for those with a nervous disposition, whatever that is, whatever that has become now, also the air helped the lungs, was an amelioration for the symptoms of TB. Wasn't that why the old guy was on the beach in *Death in Venice*? Blood soaking his handkerchief like sea foam in a conquistadors footprints. Or was it his heart?

If you were dying, you went to the beach to delay the inevitable, to live a little longer in that gravid time, to recede from the world painlessly like the tide, resigned if not happy to be taken by it. Pasolini went to the beach for other reasons, as did his killers. Migrants now risk their lives to reach shore and the sea still claims its share, washed up face down in the surf or to disappear without a trace.

I roll over, sit up, lie back down and then nothing for it but to stand up a little off balance and look around for something from which to get my bearings, I squint up and down the shoreline, out to sea, where there are boats and people bobbing, behind me I hear car horns, moped beeps, and turn to see the people behind us, of which there are by now many, and breathe in the smell of two-stroke carried on the breeze from the road. I dive back into the flow of beach time, which dissolves thought with its quotidian bombardment. In these moments, in fact with some effort they upgrade to 'passages of time', I just receive sense impressions and think about them passively without access to the undertow of connotation. Perhaps like the beached-whale bathers? You zap in and out of sensory delights – not even delights, they come unweighted, just things themselves – picking through the day and being floored by small elisions of time, gone before you know it, like so many unnoticed mini strokes. The crunch of squid, a short dip, a stab of pain in your foot from a stone, the sear of hot sand, the tingle of sunburn, the taste of salt, the smell and touch of lotion, the first sip of ice-cold Coke, an almost out-of-body observation of other people, peripheral events – a child's sandcastle being kicked over hundreds of feet away, couples almost making love right behind you! – tiny pieces of eternity.

At one p.m. the beach clubs come into their own. The energy of the street, city, sea and beach collide, infusing the seats and tables with their colours sounds and smells. As if everybody and everything had been secretly preparing for lunch all along. The middle-aged and middle class become less solid/stolid; they elegantly fade into the background with the influx of young tattoos, bodies and laughter. The laid-back take it or leave it attitude, each spot having its own take, vibe, variation on a theme, quirky staff, house rules, different brands of coffee – Elena, Moka, Alfa – and house specials usually cooked up in a tight galley running off a gas bombola on a much worked two-ring hob, from *fritto misto* to *vongole, anelli di calamari* or *polpo griglia*, fresh or frozen, from hamburgers and pizzette to more formal *antipasti, primi e secondi* – the latter usually for the tourist marking up lunches on their holiday scorecards. For the rest a bowl of pasta, a salad, a bottle of light rose or the sturdier pigato, a few beers, *cafe*, a cigarette and back to the beach.

Zap.

I forget what a nightmare it is being on the beach with you. No sooner have you thrown down your towel, you get changed, have a quick dip, come back, drip all over me, dry off, apply sun cream, lie down, then abruptly sit up and ask me what I am reading for at least the third time in as many days. Then, without waiting for an answer, or cutting me off just as I'm trying to tell you, you interject well what now? Time for lunch? For fuck's sake, sit still, stop talking, read your book! I know little of your interior life but it must be as difficult to live with as you are.

Shit.

I improve after a couple of weeks, although we only come back to the beach once or twice in the summer. Somehow it was easier when the kids were with us, distractions. Over lunch, phones narrow the gap between us. Also, the gap between us and everybody else, we become more like them – I imagine – we fit in. This use of phones homogenises us. People scrolling news or social media in the face of 'the life in caps' that is in front of us, and despite how low we may have fallen, how reclused from it we find ourselves, we are still part of. The life of screens is fast becoming LIFE, we fold everything into it.

Zap.

Straw cowboy hat, lots of bangles and a sarong over a bikini combo with a '70s riviera suntan. *Piz Buin*. Just by looking at her you can smell it. Summer. Beach glamour is timeless. There are no seasons. There is no fashion. There appears to be no politics. What I mean is the politics has naturalised itself into the timeless moment of the beach. It's just now and forever the beach. You bathe in the sun, you do not sunbathe. Future-proofed nostalgia. Whatever your age, you were always already here.

Zap.

French bourgeois from across the border enjoying a cheap lunch. Clumsy wealthy young families in low-end designer jeans and dresses, weak-chinned children with great hair, tanned parents, well-maintained teeth. A softened-up middle class, ill-equipped for disappointment or disruption – Houellebecq's people.

Italians own the beach, they wear it. The lifeguards parade up and down in sun-bleached shorts and faded tees like a catwalk for muscles. They never get wet unless for pleasure. To cool off or to perform *Lifeguard: the Musical*. They smoke, flip through magazines, people watch. Pop music blares from behind the bar. They drink Cokes, and in the afternoon, beers. Occasionally they glance up and out to sea where people are swimming or diving from pedalos. They flirt among themselves; the beach is a club for them and their friends.

Thank God I remembered to book a table because the place is always busy at lunchtime. The middle-aged couple who run it don't understand – or have no interest in understanding – my Italian, which is really annoying and makes the words I know stick in my mouth, I mix up my tenses, forget the days of the week, making booking a table way more difficult than it needs to be. So sometimes I don't book in advance because the thought of it makes me anxious, not because I have forgotten. Later on in the summer, if we want to come back, I probably won't book in advance and come early instead and get my wife to book in person in French, which they seem to have no trouble understanding. I only relax when we sit down and the waiter brings out a carafe of Vermentino with some salty breadsticks.

Grazie!

*

A family-run restaurant, nothing fancy but with a great terrace overlooking the beach through huge glass windows. After an age – there are only two people working, a brother and sister in their late twenties I think, probably the children of the owners. A tension between them provides entertainment.

You always wanted to work here, I always wanted to get away, and now here we both are. Dad once told me he had planned to go to Argentina. It was his dream. He showed it to me on a map, so far away, my finger traced a path across the ocean. To do what? I asked him. To be a travelling salesman for an agricultural supplies company in Genoa. I must have been six years old, and I imagined something more romantic, like, well I don't know what, but not that. Grandpa always used to say, this is our beach. They all thought he was crazy to build a pool right by the sea, the only one to do it. Laughing behind his back. Now look at it. Empty. Bathers lie around its ruins. The whole place is falling apart. We patch it up. That's it, we are patch-it-uppers for his dumb ideas. Perhaps we should have gone to Argentina, to be cowboys! You open up every Easter. There are always building works still going on, useless wet cement bags lying around, pipes, guttering, panes of leftover glass, jobs half finished. I can't stand it. Customers step around these to find their spot, to get onto the beach. We must have run-down charm. We are rustics, running a cowboy operation right here. I come home in May to cook, to help Mum in the kitchen, a galley on a ship that sails nowhere. No room to swing a cat, and hot, no place for her, her feet swell up. You and Dad smoke on the terrace, looking out at the sea hatching yet more plans. You think this division of labour is fair? Lunchtime I'm serving fucking tables as well. Every year I say no more but here I am. Fucking hell. It's fucking hell. You dream up themed nights, fireworks, new beach furniture, karaoke, a machine that cost a thousand Euros that, what, we've used how many times? Perhaps while you are both dreaming, what about a new kitchen? Every summer I catch up with old friends and miss my new ones. Each year we have less in common, just the beach, our childhood, the bar, me serving them beer and sandwiches, telling them about the places I have been to, the people I have met, what life is like elsewhere. Fucking hell I'm tired. Perhaps next year I won't come back.

For real this time. Don't smile at me! Fuck you!

Lunch arrives, and we put our phones down after taking a photo of the calamari for our Instagram feeds. Which we never used to do but have succumbed to in recent years. We never refer to this change, complicit as we both are in it. It is painless but I wonder, what is the nature of the pleasure it brings? Or does it simply trigger a chemical reaction in our brain which satisfies, rendering us blameless for the change in our behaviour.

*

People work up and down the beach selling things. African and Indian men with fake watches and shoulder bags full of trinkets. You lie on a sun lounger or on your towel wearing sunglasses and they ask you if you want to buy sunglasses or a new towel. It's a tough hustle. Before I sold it, I would wear my Rolex and somebody would try and sell me a fake one. I didn't tell them that obviously, but... Kids buy colourful woven bracelets for a Euro. Sometimes they give you one so you will buy another. Some women buy scarves. Mostly people blank them or roughly shake their heads, hiding their embarrassment. Others are more polite and apologise.

No, thank you.

Some automatically guard their purses when the sellers approach them, surreptitiously moving their bag closer to them or tucking it under the sun lounger. I have seen this on the streets of London. Middle-class women sitting outside coffee shops placing their hands over purses when a Black man walks past, whether he be tinker, sailor, soldier, spy.

An older Chinese woman offers massages. I have never seen her touch anyone. But she must do, it's her livelihood.

Beaches are open spaces, umbrellas and loungers offer little privacy. People wear swimsuits, bikinis, we are almost naked. Some people are topless. Beaches are like the street but here the difference is we have arrived. To be precise: a street still flows through the beach so it is both a destination but also a place of ultimate transaction. Terminal beach. Where we spend all day in close proximity with others. There is something obscene about this, which is perhaps its attraction. At the very least, it is absurd.

And then there is the coconut seller, straight out of a Fellini/Sorrentino movie – nut brown, squat, bandy legs and a mop of hair like Maradona – with a gruff nasal singsong sales patter and a bell to announce his arrival, or if not a bell a clacker of some sort, heralding his wares; a bright red cool box full of coconuts.

Sound and colour.

Noce di coco! Fresca, naturale!

He criss-crosses the beach, up and down, back and forth, from the road and down to the shoreline, the cool box getting lighter and lighter until he has sold out and has sung himself course.

Similarly, melon and peach trucks ply their trade up and down the valleys, blaring 'Meloni! Peche!' through a loudhailer. A loud, catchy three-chord mnemonic announcing their arrival. It is not just dreaming to draw a line from these itinerant merchants to the medieval hawker, but it is also dreaming. Enervating the everyday goods they sell with personality, so that they vibrate as a single entity. Either way, they put in a lot of hard miles. Melons and coconuts, bracelets and sunglasses. The more things we have to sell, the harder it is for any of them to stand out. The fake Rolex and designer handbag sellers are light years ahead. Even though they also sell only one thing, they don't have a song and their hustle is transparent. It is just beach capitalism. I see watches changing hands for money every time I visit the seaside, but I have never seen inside the red cool box. I have never seen anybody buy a coconut. But they must do, they must. With all my heart I hope so.

*

Click.

I take a photograph.

An old man asleep on the beach, the *Corriere de Sera* spread out over his big stomach, surrounded by people on sun loungers, closely packed. He is oblivious, lost in dreams. A child runs past him obliquely into the frame after a swim, you can see the label sticking out of her costume, a small white rectangle against her dark summer skin. A thunderstorm musters dark clouds above the hills behind them. We used it as the brand image for our new production company in LA.

Restless films.

The contradiction between this old guy and the world around him. Something to aspire to, a time to rest, which by implication wasn't now. *Now was the time to get busy.* A very American thought. *Work hard, play hard* is another one. Or perhaps this was an everyday observation of human travail, as prosaic as a supermarket greeting card. Juxtaposition is a democratically accessible concept. Youth and age, white hair, dark skin, sleeping on a busy beach, oblivious to the storm about to break behind you as a carefree girl runs back to her family.

We signed the wrong directors at the beginning of a recession. Happiness and disappointment, most lives share similarities we can all recognise in each other. We didn't weather the eye of that storm.

*

One summer we found Blue beach deserted. It stood out, either side the beaches were busy, but nobody trespassed over onto the sand of Blue beach. The restaurant shuttered, the door locked. No sign, no note. The awning fluttered sluggishly, and the flag in tatters, left up all winter. The energy had drained out of the place as if the concrete itself had been exsanguinated. Empty, it looked smaller. Had we really spent so much time here? Bereft of sunbeds or umbrellas, it looked very ordinary. An ugly stone groyne, an inconsequential curve of sand.

The following year a few locals were using it again and then, after another year, or perhaps at the end of the same one, it was like a public beach, people brought their own umbrellas, laid out their towels, draped themselves on the rocks on the crumbling concrete, had barbecues by the empty pool. Bagno Azzurra was no more, its signature at first faded, then erased. There were even a few dogs there, forbidden on the private beaches in the summer. Few families trespassed, this was a young single crowd, perhaps a few tourists, northern Europeans are happy with this type of lawbreaking, but mostly it became a beach for young people and at night they partied. The adjacent clubs ignored the loss of one of their fellow beaches. It was a stark warning. You felt them turning their backs on this space. What had happened to them? This family. The daughter who was always at loggerheads with her brother, scowling like he was always pissing her off. She wore a red bandana to keep the sweat out of her face; she had a lot of hair, I think, tied back. Sexy, serious with a faraway look in her eye, distracted. I hope she got to wherever it was she dreamed of going.

Was there a falling out? After the old white-haired man died? Presumably the grandfather, patriarch of Blue beach, always grumpily greeting guests up and down between the sunbeds or taking their money at the kiosk. A contested will? Was the beach club leased? Did they default on it? The family tenure had ended after, what, eighty years? I never asked, it could have been less but the main structures were from the '30s, the glory years of Italian fascism, or seemed to be from the perspective of the *riviera dei fiori*, from Mentone to Genova.

I imagine driving past one day, to find a new beach club, a new owner, perhaps a new name with a different colour scheme for the *ombrelloni*, erasing the aberration of an insurgent public space, of beach as beach, now repurposed as somebody else's private dream with money changing hands, perhaps a bribe, or a debt paid off, a new lease signed and a lot of hard effort to bring it back, to breathe life into Blue beach – why not keep the colour – to make it pay; but that in a nutshell is part of our dreams, of owning something, the sacrifices we make, the pleasure we take in our sacrifice. A time for hard work, good luck and another throw of the dice. It hasn't happened yet, perhaps the pandemic saved the beach from becoming somebody else's living hell.

The last weekend of every summer we visit Gente di Mare, another restaurant on the beach. Thirty-five Euros set menu and the food and wine keep coming. No menu (the holy grail, etc), *Gnocchi all a vongole, Insalatina di mare polpo e carciofi, seppie ripiene, Branzino alla piastra, pesciolini frito, penne fruiti di mare e Piselli, Gamberoni all piastra washed down with carafe after carafe of sparkling…*

As the sun sets, candles are lit and fairy lights come on. Every hour the house lights dim and the speakers blast out the eponymous theme tune and customers join the staff in singing along, high on life, full of food and wine and the ridiculousness of it all.

My mind summons our glorious forebears, Master Lick-Your-Chops, Dame Drooler, Master Muscatel, Master Guzzler, Aunty Greedy Guts; the banquet of Porcolandria, trailblazers for tonight's gluttony, cocking a snoop at this land of hunger.

'Gente di Mare' was the Italian Eurovision song entry for 1987. It placed third and was a hit across Europe, a cheesy song with a rousing chorus you can't help but sway to, lifting your arms, surrendering whatever cool you brought with you. Beyond us, a solitary table keeping the dark sea at bay, the diners' hands in the air singing all the words, this human moment, more like shipwreck survivors than guests, out there on the sand mostly in shadow, a single candle lighting them softly, its precarious flicker under threat of being extinguished at any moment.

People of the sea, who leave it behind
Going to where they like, they don't know where
People dying of nostalgia
But when they go back after one day, they die
of the desire to go away.

*

It's now winter and the beaches are empty. We walk together along it, wrapped up, each as ever lost in their own thoughts. The sea is inhuman; grey and brutal, the waves incessant, synchronising themselves with a strong onshore wind, blowing spray in your face if you get too close. A spit in the eye.

Let's go home, she says.

A time for fires, roasting meat and hot stews. Red foods, red wine, not the oyster white of freshly caught fish on ice or the emerald blue of the sea, colours of another season, the memory of which we assume as a down payment for its return.

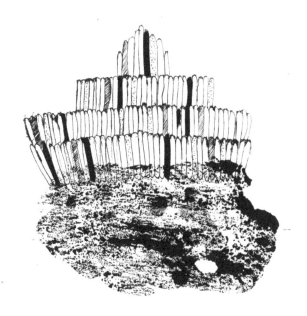

PINO E IL PAPPAGALLO

These are dark years, but the partisan songs insinuate an eternal ardour into me and my heart. What we were, will echo forever and like unstoppable waves, they will devastate and sweep away every obstacle, at least that's how I like to think. I love you, grandfather, thank you.

— Anon comment below YouTube clip 2023.[11]

Credere, Obbedire, Combattere.[12]

I run my fingers over the faded pink Fascist Party membership card I found upstairs at the back of a warped chest of drawers. Fascio di Combattimento, membership card no. 2351556. Stamped and dated 3rd March 1925. A big number. By 1925 they were on a roll. There's quite a few of these on eBay, the more expensive being the low numbered ones – we seem to value first editions as being originals, the real deal – early members of the *fighting bands* made up from veterans of the first war, dispossessed by the Treaty of Versailles.

There is no photo attached – which invalidated it – and no paid dues stamps, just two parallel rows of empty squares, but there is a name, the parents' details and a signature: Antonio Verando, born 10/9/1880 to Gionbatta Verando and Maria Sasso. His father's name written down as *Fu* Gionbatta, meaning *son of the late* Gionbatta. An odd word. I had to look it up.

There was no glue residue or tearing where a photo would have been, it looks like there never had been one, the card unused.

Di Professione: Contadino.

A farmer. No shit. We lived in his house.

Maybe he had been an Arditi, mountain shock troops who fought hand-to-hand combat armed with knives and hand grenades, their emblem a skull with a dagger in its mouth. They killed and were killed by the thousands. Antonio, a farmer, would have been in his late thirties, probably too old. He joined the party at forty-five. That's a fact, but it doesn't add up to a story. Granular detail only enables us to ask questions.

The card in my hand reminds me of my own Communist Party card from the early 1980s, also red, although this one had faded to a softer pink, or more precisely rose, the colour of a single drop of blood diluted in a glass of water. Mine had been vivid but also had no dues stamps or photograph. I had never paid in blood or money.

Half a million Italians died in the First World War only to be sold out at the Treaty of Versailles, for the sake of a lasting peace.

Patria. Famiglia. Dio. Another three-word slogan, how easy it is to stir us.

Casa di Sasso. It was the mother's family house, people in the village still remember that name. Nobody mentions Gionbatta.

Their house, now shared with others.

It's true that the house has a certain agency – the implications of its being in the world – if that makes any sense. It holds your attention, and now I was late for lunch…

*

Visiting with Pino was a clandestine affair, because he expected gifts, tribute of a kind, usually things he wasn't allowed. As I approached, five minutes late and a bit out of breath, a shriek rends the air, familiar but a shriek nonetheless.

Proffesore! Adesso! Proffesore![13]

Pino kept a talking parrot. It spoke mostly Italian, but also a few words in dialect which impressed his neighbours. It was the only parrot in the village. Pino's wife Sylvia worried about having it inside the house because of Pino's asthma, so as soon as it was warm enough, she moved them out onto the balcony, from where they both spied me. The sun was good for Pino's chest and you would find him out in it from late April until deep into the autumn. The parrot shuffled side to side on a wooden perch, preening itself

---

13   Professor! Now! Professor!

smugly. It was a Macaw, the type of parrot pirates keep to entertain themselves on the seven seas, with an evil-looking hooked beak with bright red, blue and yellow feathers the colours of Smurf, strawberry and banana ice cream. You couldn't help but imagine seeing it on somebody's shoulder. At night Sylvia threw an old red blanket over the cage to shut it up. Pino wore dark checked shirts and worn corduroy trousers, usually with a black beret cocked to one side on his head. His face was nut brown, crosshatched with lines. A face that has lived mostly outside. His blue eyes shone with intelligence but were also bloodshot and damp. He constantly patted their corners with a folded handkerchief. Pino wasn't one of the old men who sat in the bar playing cards. He was no longer clubbable, if he ever had been. Instead, he sat on his balcony with his parrot, overlooking his village by the river. He still had a head of thick wiry black hair sprouting from under his beret, so dark you might think he dyed it.

I had been tipped off – by Giacomo the butcher – and had brought a bottle of whisky from London (Johnny Walker black label). Goods like that held cachet among older Italians. Things that in the past you couldn't get in Italy, or were too expensive. For those old enough to know counterfeit, ersatz and ripped-off, the gift of a sealed bottle of scotch. Premium, luxury, the genuine article; a carton of luxury cigarettes, Dunhill or Chesterfields.

At the door, without a word but with a curt smile, Sylvia took the bottle from my hands as I entered the house, like so much contraband and she the customs officer, before leading me out onto the balcony. Pino sat with a blanket across his legs. I think I glimpsed a flash of disappointment cross his face when he saw I was empty-handed. She placed her hand on his shoulder and his hand automatically covered it.

A tricky customer.

– Here's your visitor, the Englishman who bought the house on Via Casoni.

The parrot sidestepped back and forth on his perch, watching me suspiciously, but for now kept its silence. Sylvia poured us both water from a pale green fish-shaped jug that went *glug glug glug* and left us to it.

– Buongiorno Pino. Come estai?

– Salui. bon.

He winks at me. I smile back, my eyes widening.

– Cafe?

– Si. Grazie.

– Sylvia!

She has already made coffee and brings it out to the table; I smile at her, she scowls at me.

– Grazie.

I place the sound recorder on the table between us.

Pino looks over his shoulder back into the house.

I double check the machine is recording, the red light flashing.

– *Da dove vuoi che cominci?*[14]

Years later, long after Pino and Sylvia have died, I get all of our recordings translated – over four visits – from which I write.

*

– Only an hour, Pino gets carried away, so don't encourage him. There's some wine on the table, it tastes awful, like acid, just so you know it's terrible on purpose, so he doesn't

---

14   Where do you want me to begin?

drink too much of it. Don't encourage the parrot she's incorrigible, and definitely no smoking!

We sit silently until we hear the door close, and then wait a few seconds more just in case. Pino gestures for a drink, shaking his hand in front of his face.

A large estate car pulls up outside the shop and a young woman gets out of the driver's seat. She's come round to open the passenger door for an old man (possibly her grandfather). He gets out shielding his eyes, stepping into a hard midday light that bounces off the road and the bodywork of cars that lined the street. They are well-dressed northern European city types, timeless smart casual. From the top pocket of his blazer the old man fumbles a pair of sunglasses onto his face and looks up and down the empty street, orientating himself before approaching the Alimentari. He gestures to the woman that he wants to go inside. She hesitates, asks him a question. He shrugs. She asks another. He replies in a louder voice, adamant. Eventually she offers him her arm – he must be her grandfather, they have the same full, downturned mouth – and as they enter behind the beaded fly curtain, a bell announces them as customers. After a silence which lasts less than a minute, there is a sharp scream and immediately after that the man stumbles out of the shop, back to the car, where he pulls frantically on the door handle which won't open. His granddaughter must have locked it out of habit and she now comes out of the shop, clearly distressed, unlocking the car with the key fob. He gets in immediately but she scans the road first as if to see if there are any witnesses. She gets behind the wheel and drives off at speed. An old woman wearing an apron comes out of the shop wielding a broom and stares down the empty road. There is nobody about. She is shaking, like she has seen a ghost, which in fact she had.

*

Sylvia walks down to the village every morning for supplies, but also to get out of the house. She took a coffee standing at the counter of the shop and then walked back up the hill again. Slowly, because she was also old, although not as old as her husband. Come to think of it, almost none of her generation had married younger men, that would have been unusual somehow. Most of her friends were already widows. Besides, she wanted to give Pino time to enjoy sneaking a cigarette, because she was tired of having to bust his balls about smoking. He would be dead soon, so why bother making a fuss? Also, she understood the pleasure of breaking the rules, the titillation of a moment's transgression, why deny him that? If she caught him smoking, of course she wouldn't stand for it, they would argue, she would put her foot down, so best not to catch him. He knew she knew what he would do the moment she stepped out to the shops. Sometimes she would fuck with him by moving the hidden packet from one drawer to another, adding a little urgency to his duplicity. These hide-and-seek games make up the daily routine of most marriages.

One day at breakfast, the Macaw sold him down the river.

Il fumo uccide! Il fumo uccide! Il fumo uccide![15] she cries, jumping from leg to leg on her perch, such a clever parrot.

Silvia looks at him in such a way – a silent command.

Pino harrumphs and throws the packet of cigarettes he has in his pocket at the parrot.

He shouts at it. *Boccaccia!*[16]

15   Smoking kills! Smoking kills! Smoking kills!
16   Literally, teller of tales.

It squawks back.

Sylvia scowls at the parrot – she also hates sneaks – and storms out ignoring her husband, who grabs the feed bowl and empties it over the balcony. The parrot retreats to its cage.

Sylvia always wore colourful dresses and hats with wide brims in the summer. She was very chic. During the winter you hardly ever saw her; my memory of her is from the summer. Pino no longer drove, Silvia had never learnt how to. His old Toyota sat outside the house. Their son Federico, who lived in Turin, never thought to help them get rid of it. It was no longer insured or taxed; it was just rusting away. In fact, the son didn't offer to help with anything, and they would never ask him. On his rare visits, either in the summer for a few days at Christmas or Easter, they mainly bickered from the trenches of a familial standoff.

– *Dad should be in a home. Okay, maybe not full time, but a few days a week, better for him and would give you a break.*

– *Me? When did you ever care about anyone other than yourself?*

– *Sylvia, you don't mean that, Federico is busy, he has a job, a family.*

– *Family, yes and when do we ever see them, our own grandchildren. Busy? Pfft.*

They both wondered why he rarely brought the grandchildren to visit.

– *They're my kids!* he would say when he ran out of excuses.

As if anybody would challenge that.

He had married late – best not to ask – so the kids were still at school, a boy and a girl, who he didn't bring with him because of the parrot. It scared them.

– Besides, Paolo has asthma, and with your chest, Papa, it's
ridiculous to live with a bird like that!

Neither Pino nor his wife believed this was the reason
and wondered why he used it as an excuse, but again, said
nothing. They had only seen his wife twice since the wedding
for the children's baptisms.

Cold as ice, like most people from Turin.

A bird like that.

A family shame when their neighbours were inundated
by grandchildren during the holidays and Sylvia had to
mutter unconvincing explanations in passing, lightly
delivered, her performance pitch perfect. But the effort to do
this, her responsibility, while Pino sat there with his bloody
parrot...

Their house was in a small hamlet of three or four houses,
fifteen minutes from the village up a steep paved road.
Every day Sylvia would pass the old man who farmed a
parcel of land on a terrace below the houses. You would find
him most mornings bent double over a hoe or a rake or with
a basket on one arm planting vegetables, depending on the
season. A donkey grazed in a field on the other side of the
road, keeping the grass short, like a rough lawn. They
existed in tandem, comfortable in each other's proximity.
Occasionally he gave it a few carrots. The old man has a
rickety old chair and would sit on it when he needed a break,
drinking coffee from a silver thermos flask or when he
wanted to think about what work he had to do next. In the
winter he was less busy and would play cards with the other
old men in the village. The older he got, the more he shrank
inside his extra-large shirts which hung off his shoulders,
reminding me of David Byrne. The shirts were off white

from being boiled clean, with mended collars and patches tightly stitched with rough cotton.

My Popa, a bookie, owned seven shirts in his adult life, handmade from Savile Row; collars replaced every five years, and the sides let out with almost invisible panels as he got fatter. For skinny guys tailors must work in reverse, shirts getting tighter and tighter in anticipation of the winding sheet.

Towards the end the old man would work sitting down, reaching out as far as he could with his rake, throwing it out there like a fishing net. His final stage appearance. One day he wasn't there anymore, but the chair remained to invoke him each time I passed it. I remembered things like the fact he didn't smoke, had no rings on his fingers and that he would feed the donkey bunches of lettuce leaves in the summer which it ate from his hand. Details I didn't know I knew. Then the chair went, probably knocked over in a storm, ending up who knows where, kindling for a fire. The neglected land became unruly within a matter of months. The chair had kept him in this world somehow, a touchstone, a lightning rod of a life lived, to become its cenotaph. Now he was untethered, up, up and away into the thin air of pure memory which isn't much more than imagination, with the power to conjure what it likes and not much use when it comes to remembering an actual person. I never knew his name or heard him speak, things which sometimes can act as organising principles around which to muster the simple facts of a life. Sometime later the donkey also disappeared – from his hand to the donkey's mouth the last link broken – and the grass grew.

Once in a lifetime.

They probably made salami out of her, meat hung then cured in red wine with pepper, nutmeg and cinnamon, sweet tasting from all the grass she ate. There were no vines or tomatoes, just rows of vegetables planted in the earth. I think this old man worked here every day until he died and now the earth is fallow, the planting rows spotted with grass and weeds until somebody works it again. If you don't cut the grass it grows, if you don't work the earth it hardens. Even I know that.

Same as it ever was.

Olive groves are the same, left untended they grow tall and with too many branches that intertwine with each other and the brambles that run wild between them, literally starving the olives and making the trees impossible to harvest. As soon as the price for olive oil went up, the neglected groves on collapsed terraces were brought back to life and productivity. This took a lot of backbreaking work, to pollard the trees, to rebuild the terrace drystone walls, to cut back the branches and brambles, to lay new nets, to irrigate, to treat for disease and finally to harvest the olives, press them and sell for seventeen Euros a litre; the power of money to change a landscape and the fortunes of those who work it. Profit like the wolf, an apex predator. From seven Euros a litre to twenty in the space of twenty years.

*

Pino clears his throat as I fumble with the Zoom H2 Handy sound recorder. Technology always makes me tense, despite it getting cheaper and easier to use. I sniff and shake my head when I get stressed, especially if I want to appear relaxed, and my palms sweat. The directional mic sits on the table between us.

– We controlled the hills, the mountains and forests. They controlled the road and villages. We had a few mortars and would use them to make things awkward, but we didn't want to damage our own homes, so, we had to be careful—

– Am I talking loud enough?

– Yeah, fine. When was this?

– The winter of 1943. To start with they hardly ever came after us, there was a kind of stalemate but without proper weapons what could we do? A cold winter. We survived, that was about it. After the armistice we saw deserters, soldiers with proper training coming to join us. It caused some problems, for we were like sticks compared to them, sticks wearing rags, and who were they in fancy uniforms, who had fought with the fascists? Hard to trust, at least to start with—

A coughing fit, the sound of water being poured and drunk, the coughing dies down replaced by a low volume wheeziness.

– The British started airdrops. It was hard, dangerous work to set up. We had to set two fires, a decoy lower down, near Drago, which the Germans would see and maybe try to do something about and the actual landing zone, on the other side of the ridge, in the old amphitheatre below Mezzaluna. A lot of work, of organisation, stealing copper sulphate from under their noses that was stored at the quarry, to make the signal burn green – a headache to coordinate with only one radio. When the first British officer parachuted in, he spoke to us in Latin.

– What did he say?

– Salve! With his arm out and palm facing up, like some bastard Roman emperor!

Pino chuckles, coughs, hawks and spits – God knows what – out over the balcony.

From inside, Silvia shouts.

– Pino!

– Scusa!

He leans in to continue in a quieter voice. His breathing is louder, with a low rattle. I check the sound levels on the recorder.

– Fuck me, we laughed, all we had were pitchforks, rusty shotguns and a few rifles stashed from the first war. This English prick looked like he was going to shit himself as we loomed out of the dark.

I couldn't help but grin, Pino had a twinkle in his eye, what an old rascal!

– He was the only bastard one of us who spoke Latin. We didn't have a priest, no, no not with us we were against priests. He gestured with his hands for us to put our weapons down, like we were wild animals, I will always remember that gesture and the thought crossed my mind to shoot him. After all this palaver[17] he broke open the crate and handed out boxes of grenades and Sten guns. Now this was what we were after, so we put up with all his airs and graces. He showed us how to use the guns, break them down, how to keep them working. Grenades we knew about. This took some hours and by then it was nearly dawn, we had to go. I can't remember where he went, high on the mountain we were, he must have got away somehow, he had a map – I remember that, but he didn't ask us for help and we didn't offer any. He was an officer, and we had had enough of them for a lifetime. I read later that some survived in the mountains

17   Pino used the word 'chiacchiere'. Palaver is the gist of it I think.

for the duration, hidden by farmers, partisans. But not us. They shot the security guard and two other workers when they discovered the sulphate had been stolen. Everything we did, they paid the price. So it had to be worth it. It was summer of '44 and we thought now we had proper weapons it would soon be over, we would help end the war.

Pino was out of breath and started coughing. Silvia came out with a glass of water, his hand cupping hers as she raised it gently to his lips, before telling me to leave.

– Get out!

*

– She had fallen in love with a soldier, which was going to cause a lot of trouble. Her father was with us up in the hills, a blacksmith, very useful, he shoed the ponies which were the only transport we had. Good news drags its feet but bad news can't arrive quick enough. We couldn't stop him, I mean we could have restrained him but what good would that have done, knock him out, tie him up, for how long? And then what? So we had to let him go, knowing how dangerous it was, let the devil take him not us. He took a pistol and went down to the village that night. He walked straight into a patrol. What a fool to throw his life away like that, without thinking. The soldier went away eventually, with the rest. Not a scratch on him. The girl hung herself six months after the war ended. Erica, she was very beautiful, isn't that right Sylvia?

Sylvia comes out onto the balcony, wiping her hands on her apron. She shrugs.

– What does it matter? Beautiful? We were children.

She doesn't want to talk about this and blames me – I can see it in how her eyes dart between us, linking me to Pino – for getting him worked up, stirring up bad memories. I look away, at the parrot.

– It was so long ago, why would he be interested?

Silence, Pino fidgets, eager not to lose his thread.

She looks at her watch. Her tone lightens.

– I've got to go or I'll miss the bus. There are olives, bread, tomatoes on the kitchen table, help yourself and behave yourselves.

She leaves, bored with men, of old men in particular and today foreigners and their enthusiasms, all of it a burden to her ears.

As soon as she goes, he asks me for a cigarette.

– Sorry, I don't smoke.

The parrot screams.

– *Vietato fumare!*

I jump.

Pinot takes a large gulp of wine. He winces. I decline his offer of a refill; it tasted, true to Sylvia's word, God awful.

– If the blacksmith had used his brain, had got into the village somehow, I have often wondered what he would have done, which of them he would have gone after, his daughter or the enemy? Either would be a reason to kill yourself, I think.

Pino drinks off another glass of wine.

– Either way, they all ended up dead.

Sometimes things go to plan, you research a subject, make them feel at ease, ask the right questions, get it in the can so to speak and move on to the next. This was a different ride.

– Our commander Vito had been in Spain, came back with ideas of the republic, which we implemented right here! I bet you didn't know that did you? They don't tell that story, of our partisan republic, our republic of Pigna.

I had no idea what he was talking about, but I nod, check the recorder, eager for him to continue.

– They came after us that summer, up and down the valley, causing havoc, setting fires, threats, reprisals, trying to turn us each on the other, rub salt in old wounds, in Badalucco, Molini, Triora, to get them to give us up. But we weathered the storm. We were better organised, had our informers, the land was ours, the people our families. The reprisals benefited us, but were terrible to bear. We had to have our victory.

Silence.

– Excuse me. I have to use the bathroom.

Pino points to the recorder. I pause it.

With not a little effort he gets up and shuffles inside, leaving me alone with the parrot. We eye each other. From inside I hear Pino opening and closing cupboards followed by a clink of glasses. He comes out holding the bottle of scotch.

– Well, well, what do we have here?

He unscrews the cap tearing the seal.

Pino pours us both a glass smiling from ear to ear, the cat that got the cream.

I sense trouble.

He drinks his off, pours another. I sip mine. I half expect the parrot to say something about bottles of rum, but it doesn't.

– The future was coming at us a hundred kilometres an hour. Everything would have to be different. None of us wanted to go back to how things had been. I had been born under fascism; it was all I knew. Imagine that! I wanted to speed up into the future, like in the Gordon comics, but our future was right here not in outer space, that was for the birds.[18] Everyone knew it, there would be a day of reckoning. There was no time to waste, in the territory we liberated we would organise ourselves. A republic of the people not for senators, deputies and delegates, whose horse trading sold us out to Mussolini. First, we would clear out the Germans and our own fascists with anyone who would fight with us. This was my understanding of a popular front. Against them. Full stop. But what were we for? A trickier question. For a start, no absentee landlords! Houses for the people who worked the land. To tax ourselves for the common good, each according to his or her ability to pay, yes, this famous line, well it's not just for the books, we wanted it to spread like wildfire. When you liberate somebody from oppression, from hunger, from the invader, this is the moment to seize an opportunity, to open their eyes. Or so we thought. What did I know, I was only sixteen years old.

He pours us both another drink. I rarely drink whisky, don't like the taste, but…

– Two thousand partisans liberated Pigna, down on the coast in late September, cleared the bastards out. What the fascists left behind we redistributed, abolished land tax, organised labour to rebuild the damaged houses, to work the land, we established a newspaper, printing what was really happening in the war from the news we got on our radio. It lasted twenty-one days. The Germans attacked in

---

18   My sense of the phrase Pino used, 'Da imbicelli'.

strength. We held them off in the chibi of Pigna[19] where two men could hold off twenty. Now it's restored, very touristy, bars, restaurants, the views, the Germans especially love it.

He laughs, which quickly becomes a wheeze and then a fit of coughing. Shit! I pat his back and raise my left hand in the air, showing him how to clear his airways. He waves me away, shakes his head. I pour him some water, *glug glug glug*. He drinks it, water ripping down his chin onto his shirt.

Sylvia will kill me.

– The next day they shelled us from Isolabona, driving us back up into the mountains. We regrouped, licked our wounds, took on more recruits. Meanwhile, the first brigade led by Cion attacked the bridges in valle Arroscia to cut the German supply lines. Our first action after Pigna was to break into the jail in Oneglia, freeing all the political prisoners. The trash, the crooks we left behind for their brothers the fascists.

To be honest, by now I was a little drunk, dizzy, that odd whisky drunk that creeps up on you, kind of trippy, which is the reason I don't drink the stuff, but also I had been too passive, had zoned out to be honest, knowing I had it all on tape, to listen to, to translate later. I got the gist of what he was saying; I read him, but some words were unfamiliar or I didn't catch them all in his rush of Italian peppered with dialect. Pino was so animated I followed him, not what he said. I only had him for those few hours, the tape could wait. Also, the whisky softened up my motivation; this was no longer an interview, we had gone past whatever the parameters of that situation were.

---

19   A labyrinth of medieval alleyways.

In a moment of clarity, I tried to get us back on track.

– What was your nom de guerre?

– Me? Parrot. I was a kid, I couldn't stop talking. Our commanders Stalin, Cion and Vito had been in France, Spain, in Russia. They had big ideas. The only thing I commanded was my mouth, but I saw the picture they painted me, they drew me a map I could follow. I did as I was told, that's it, that's how we are at sixteen. I dreamed of a world without war, without bosses, without priests, without having to work yourself to death for somebody else. Like in the wild west comics we read, we were the good guys, that's how I saw it, I read comics the night before combat, I kept them rolled up in my backpack, swapping them with others, we all did, men and boys, they fired us up, Buffalo Bill, Geronimo, Billy the Kid, Sitting Bull. We couldn't read the *fumeti*[20] but we used the pictures to tell our story. But when the fighting finished, so did the dream. The trail to paradise went cold. We had won, but it was back to normal, as if by magic the fascists in the big cities had changed their clothes and become social democrats, sure we killed a few, chased a few more off but the people in charge, the owners of everything were the same as before, just waving a different flag, and everything was now America America America. How many friends do you think I lost to America in those years? More than to the Germans.

Pino found a bent cigarette in the pocket of his jacket, straightened it out. I lit it for him.

– I thought you didn't smoke? he said.

---

20   Speech bubbles, also the word for comics.

Rumbled, I took out my packet and joined him.

– English bastard.

He took a fresh cigarette. We smoked.

– After the war I had no money, so I got a job in the quarry. The war became a fantasy of freedom. Everywhere we went, all over these mountains was home. Looks like the joke was on me. We wanted everything but got nothing.

He coughs and lights another cigarette, holding up his hand before I can say anything. I get up to stretch, perhaps feeling it was time to make a move. I feel dizzy. Discombobulated.

What did I live for?

I didn't ask him this question, but I felt he wanted to answer to it, or repeat it to himself as he must have done over and over again. How could I refuse to listen?

– Relax, she won't be back just yet, it's Monday, market day in Taggia, bus returns…

He looks at his watch.

– …at approximately five twenty-five.

I slump back down on the chair, fumble for the fags and pour myself another drink. Fuck it. Pino, clears his throat, hawks up a greeny over the balcony and, catching me off guard, sings:

We are the mountain rebels,
we live on struggle and suffering,
but the faith walking by our side
will be the law of the time to come.

He stops singing, or the song has ended.

– Cazzo. The law to come was shit.

– *Cazzo! Cazzo!* the parrot finally chimes in.

I don't know what to say. I'm drunk, my focus is gone, suddenly exhausted, as if I had paid too much attention. I had wanted to ask him about Antonio, had his Fascist Party card in my pocket, but it now seemed obscene somehow to mention it, or at least irrelevant. I had become self-conscious, aware of a fakeness in my behaviour. Why I am really here? Pino snaps out of his reverie, picks up the packet, sensing a change in me. For an old man full of rancour, he was well aware of the inconsistency of others.

The comedown.

It was just talk after all. He turns the packet over and stares at the picture of a diseased, swollen heart.

– I read in the paper a man recognised his wife from one of these photographs.

His fingers tease out another cigarette.

– How could he tell it was hers?

He retrieves a copy of the *Corriere della Sera* from under the table, thumbs the pages until he finds the article and reads...

– His lawyer says that the man is seeking a hundred million Euros in compensation.

– No way!

I relax, my dizziness subsides, the moment of dread has passed. Pino reads out the rest.

– The photos came from external contractors who had a budget of six hundred thousand Euros to photograph eight thousand people in ten different EU countries.

He prods the paper, to make a point, as if talking to it.

– But it's a photo of her heart. That's what I fought for. The *Corriere Dei Piccoli*.[21]

He drops it back onto the floor.

Laughing at his own joke he splutters and coughs doubled over. I get up and grab his left arm, pulling it up above his head. This time he doesn't resist, and I realise he must be as drunk if not more so than I am. Fuck. Half the bottle has gone. He's drunk, we are both drunk.

– I should go, Pino.

– On your way out hide this for me, will you. Top it up with water.

He taps his nose, missing the first time. He hands me the bottle of scotch.

– Cupboard below the cooker behind the cornflakes.

I pocket my recorder. Neither of us references the interview, it was as if it had never happened, as if that wasn't the reason we had spent the afternoon together.

We shake hands; he stumbles to the door to see me off.

As I stumble down the hill, I pass Sylvia coming up. I look at her but she ignores me. I look away. I watch her broad back and still handsome legs walk past the turn in the road and disappear. But somehow it was like it was I was no longer visible.

I felt mean and ordinary. I had overstepped the mark, been too familiar, the wine and whisky had propelled me across a boundary, and when I found myself in no man's land Pino had rescued me with the nonsense of that newspaper story, gifting us the dignity of parting on amiable terms.

21   The Correire del Piccoli is the children's comic edition that came with the main paper, the first of its kind in Italy.

I think he died that autumn, although I saw Sylvia occasionally from a distance in her wide-brimmed hats and colourful dresses, until she too disappeared. I never spoke to her again, not even to offer my condolences. I never got to ask her if she knew the old man who worked the field below their house, I never found out his name, if he was a relative or old school friend, something more or less to them than he appeared to me; on nodding terms only. I was a shadow man in all their lives, there or not there, it didn't matter, under licence from my imagination to run amok. I flash on Antonio Verando, a seasoned Arditi home from the war, and can't hate him for all that came next. Another war to end all wars. In 1919 the shame was all ours.

*

I kept the recording of the interview in a folder along with Verando's party card, but only recently had it transcribed. Who knows how much of it is true – although why wouldn't it be – and what does it matter? I remember the song he sang at the end; it had a familiar tune. What was it? Where had I heard it before? This song that had undone me, primed as I was by the whisky? I play it back again, un canto populare, familiar, almost cliched for being so well worn. Songs like much-loved recipes travel the world, adapting yet somehow staying the same. The melody is universal, ancient. I can see it in my mind's eye, a place without words, before them; a feeling, a sense, I'm about to name it for you, it is on the tip of my tongue...

No, it's gone, but I can try and sing it, the melody will return and you can tell me where you have heard it.

Listen.

Siamo I ribelli della montagna
viviam di stenti e di patimenti
ma quella fede che ci accompagna
sarà la legge dell'avenir.[22]

22   We are the rebels of the mountain, / We live rough on the rocks, / But the
beliefs we hold today, / Will be the laws of tomorrow.

BALLA COI LUPI

I am a full blood Ponca Indian. This is all I have to offer.
The sewage of Europe does not run through these veins.
— Clyde Warrior / Ma'He Ska (White Knife), 1961

Sixth Avenue, skyscrapers and everything. Walk a few
blocks and take a shower in people. Men wearing cream or
tan macs over suits, lots of hats – fedoras, pork pies, hard
hats, boaters – giving a sense of direction to this flow, but
seen from above there are threads, weaving eels of colour in
the stream, fresh spoor, clues to a different beat, signs of the
times; splashes of bright orange, acid lemon, deep purple,
loud check, knitwear, brothers in kaftans, hippies in vintage,
hair in all styles, pinned up, let down, all around, corn rows
and afros, women with fur collars, conventional department
store chic and non-conforming styles, occasional flares, cut-

off jackets, glimpses of flesh, all throwing shadows across the street and up walls in this constant churn of a crisp sunny spring morning against the tide of the baseline of ochres, blacks, whites and browns worn with discretion. A burbling of independent personality, a few big fat ties, a splash of polka dots, big hair, pom-poms, crochets even, and accessories, gloves, sunglasses, a man crossing the road twirling a swagger stick. Uptown traffic and at every junction men selling stuff out of suitcases off the kerb, paisley scarves, leather gloves, wallets, people stopping to rummage in the bigger boxes, everyday bargain hunters, knots of momentarily static people, clumps of weed in the stream. Finally overwhelming, you find everyone on these boulevards, all of life's hustle is here jostling past you, and you laugh out loud to find that you too are a part of it, New York City.

A young man catches another's eye. Young man in leather jacket, flat cap, slouched, relaxed. The other, older, suit, tie, mac and a brown Derby, upright and punctual.

– Scusa, you got time?

The young man points at his wrist.

– Sure thing.

The man checks his watch.

– Twenty after eleven.

– Thank you.

– Say, where you from?

– Ligure.

– What country is that?

– Italia.

– Italy? Ha, I was there during the war, weather was great! First time here?

– Si, si, yes.

– Name's Sam Fisher. Yours?

He holds out his hand.

– Nome? Augustino.

They shake vigorously.

– Well, Augustino, welcome to America, son, a big name for a big country.

– Grazie!

*

Welcome to America, son, my god, like a fucking priest in the movies, this place is incredible, I want to check under the table, behind every curtain for the cameras.

It's a shit movie, no?

Not shit but maybe one we've seen before, *It's a wonderful life…*

Over and over and over…

He gets down on his knees, pulls his cap low over his eyes and mimics begging.

– *Mintammicce impizzu mpizzu ca pue largu minne fazzu sule!*[23]

Gloria doubles over with laughter. Gloria, dark, darker eyes, lots of hair tied back with a black band, skinny, a narrow face, the type of person who eats like a horse but looks like a gazelle. Augusto grabs his Nikon and snaps her across the table.

– Fucking America, come on Augusto, this place…

What? I'm joking of course but the handshake, so firm, it's, it's ridiculous, he leans across the table and kisses her,

---

23   Let me in just a little, then I'll make my own way!

like in a black-and-white photo, no? He takes another shot; she sticks her tongue out.

They drink in an East Village dive bar on Mott Street, full of beatnik types, right on hippies, the washed-up '60s, not at all like the man he met on 6th Avenue, who had somehow made it into the '70s without a dent, without a blemish, leapfrogging from the '50s. This man seemed more truly American to Augustine, what he had expected but also fantastical in that he actually existed.

To come here at all, the déjà vu of it, Italians in New York. A real trip.

Counter-culture is always on the back foot, running out of steam, banging its head up against the hard rock of a persistent hegemony, men in macs, and all that lies behind a firm handshake. The turn from peace and love to hard drugs and paranoia came on the spring air, the smell of napalm in the morning. In '73 Black and Puerto Rican gangs attacked hippies on the Lower East Side, smashed up their coffee shops, their nightclubs, beat them in front of their women (a problem in itself), humiliated them out of fear, ornery tribalism, turf war. Violence on the street until the drugs did a more thorough job, heroin and crack the destroyer of worlds.

The sound of the cockcrow that opens Victor Jara's *Poblacion* comes on the stereo. August and Gloria push their chairs back and unsteadily rise to their feet, having chased their beers with whiskey. The high clear female voice kicks in. Propping each other up they dance close.

Quién me iba a decir a mi
Cómo me iba a imaginar
Si yo no tengo un lugar

Si yo no tengo un lugar
Si yo no tengo un lugar
En la tierra?[24]

*

Down into the basement of Wo Hop, a covert restaurant on
a scuzzy street reached by red-walled stairs edged in peeling
gold. Inside, Formica tables, photographs teeming the walls;
faces, stories of meals had and enjoyed, late nights out
covering recent years in colour all the way back to black and
white, a sensory overload of changing fashion and then the
menu unchanged in lurid pictures you read like pictograms.
This is what they wanted, to taste America, to eat *Cibo
Chinese* for the first time on the night before they leave the
city for the wild west.

The place is quiet, so they attract attention and prompt
service.

– My god, taste this!

Gloria tries to pick up a piece of salt-and-pepper squid
with chopsticks, to feed him, but it keeps falling off, August
can't wait, he picks it off the tablecloth and eats it with his
fingers.

– So good, wow.

Bang bang noodles, spicy, hot, meaty, just like ragu,
hand-pulled just like pasta.

– This *brodo* is fantastic, so there was a Marco Polo after
all, spicy pasta!

The chef – in his twenties, same age as Augustin and
Gloria – approaches the table.

24   Who was going to tell me / how could I imagine / If I don't have a place
/ If I don't have a place. / If I don't have a place / On earth?

– Everything good?

They nod their heads.

– Our first Chinese food!

– You like it?

– Amazing!

Gloria has a mouthful of the squid, dabs her face with a napkin, Augustin smiles, he loves eating and watching her eat; it was their thing, a happy thing. She talks through a mouthful of food...

– Fantastic, wow, yes yes. We have squid at home, at the seaside but not like this, we just grill it.

– Where you from?

– Italy, and these noodles, look...

She pulls them up out of the broth with her chopsticks.

He is impressed.

– This is just like the pasta I make at home. Marco Polo brought it back all the way from China to Genova.

August shakes his head.

The chef smiles.

– This is bang bang noodles from Xi'an province. Come, I show you how we make it.

He gestures for her to follow him.

August scowls into his beer, he can't help himself, he hates being left alone.

In the kitchen, small rounds of dough lie on top of a table sprinkled with flour. He shows her how to cut and pull the noodles. Thick belt-like strips. Gloria can't keep her hands to herself. They sink into the dough, and within minutes she is pulling it like an expert, piece by piece.

– This actually makes me *nostalgico*, homesick! Sorry, I don't know the word in Chinese, ma...

She pats her heart.

– *Cuore!*

The chef guesses immediately.

– *Xiang Jia!*

He points to the noodles.

– Xiang Jia.

She mimics perfectly. The chef nods.

– Not so long to cook, it must be *Jin Dao*.

The noodles go into the boiling water for a minute.

Gloria frowns, pulls a strand of pasta out of the pan with a fork, silky smooth. She squashes a piece between her fingers and pops it into her mouth. The chef nods, she smacks her lips.

– Al dente!?

He nods.

– Jin Dao!

They laugh, she ladles the belt-like noodles into a big bowl of the blood-red chilli sauce, garlic and shallots. They eat, faces bathed in steam.

August fidgets, sitting by himself drinking. He hates not being the centre of attention. He enters the kitchen with his camera.

Gloria looks up, holds out her chopsticks.

– *Vuoi provane un po'?*

He shakes his head.

The chef pours three glasses of plum wine. Augusto takes his picture, without asking, just like that.

If there had been a spell cast, it was now broken.

– I'm Gloria. What's your name?

– James Lee Fung.

– This arrogant pig is Augustino.

August smiles. James looks bemused.

Gloria wipes her fingers on a towel and scribbles down his name.

She points to the camera.

– We'll send you a copy of the photo.

The chef nods a little warily and pours three more glasses of wine.

August takes the wine, drinks it.

Cazzo.

He almost chokes.

– So what's going on, James? he finally says.

An awkward moment.

Gloria eyeballs him.

– *Il tuo ubriaco vaffanculo!*

She walks out.

*

The open road, a motorcycle, the horizon, emptiness, occasionally split by a grain silo.

Her hands wrap around August's waist as they fly across the blacktop. Gloria thinks of Piedmont, empty roads straight as an arrow, bisecting fields on either side. And now she thinks of arrows because they are bound for Wounded Knee. A childish association, but boys and girls both grew up on Tex comics in '60s Italy. Graphic, brutal black-and-white panels carved from rock. Tex Willer and his sidekicks Kit Carson and Tiger Jack the Navajo warrior, good guys in complex storylines that recast the tropes of the classic western into a vengeful narrative of ultimate rights and justice, spiced with fantasy, evil wizards, illusionists and dreaded enemies from beyond the grave. For them the wild west represented violent freedom. In post-war Italy freedom came with both compromise and caveat.

Tex was a Texas ranger at odds with himself, fighting against his home state in the civil war, a war which performs the function of *the set of all sets* framing the genre, all of this a comic series with multiple spin-offs, an irresistible concoction of historical fact and Italian imagination involving the Apache Chiricahaus' Chief Cochise and Navajo Red Cloud reimagined as a shaman, subverting stereotypes of both Indian and cowboy that post-war Europe grew up on, with French trappers, Irish navvies, warlocks and mounties, cops, Mexican bandits, all woven intimately together in top-line adventure, subplot and cliffhanger, bristling with passion, revenge, brutality and honour. We cannot get enough of the wild west, we scry ourselves in its tarnished mirror, the truth by definition evasive yet the lies so seductive, in a word we indulge in these comics our addiction to myth, last stands and shootouts, tomahawks, cattle drives and locomotion, Pistoleros, gold miners, coolies, navvies, runaway slaves, generals and outlaws, ranchers, rustlers, six-shooters, braves, bows and arrows…

Gloria will think about anything to avoid thinking about how fast they are going. She hates motorbikes, is scared shitless but can't let this show, has to brave it out, again brave, fuck, playground associations, but if it's another minute without looking down, or up, or indeed anywhere other than the leather of August's back where she buries her face. Always this effort to be confident, to find everything cool, no wonder she is whip thin, the energy she needs, her sheer will must be powered by something. Cooking makes her happy, an extension of eating, wherever she finds herself she likes to cook, to be in a kitchen, it calms her, gently building confidence. Like in the restaurant, until he embarrassed her, his jealousy and temper another thing that stresses her; constantly alert to his mood swings, nails bitten to the quick.

They head for Indian territory, just saying it out loud is unreal, stars in their own comic strip, cross-hatched features, the light and shade of their bone structure up against the wind as they transition from light to dark, into the night or roaring out of inky shadows thrown by mountains, *mesas*, in the late afternoon and under a sinking sun, or reversed from darkness into light, the subtle grades of a western dawn, their own shadows winding out across the landscape, points on a sundial, framed by big sky and distant mountains and slashed by pale blue anamorphic cross panel flares...

Augustin embraces the romance of it. With a camera strapped round his neck he is on his first magazine commission to cover the standoff between the American Indian Movement and the FBI at Wounded Knee. Life made over into storyboard; his mind drew what lies ahead in pen strokes, panels and speech bubbles drenched in the full colour of an American spring, wanted dead or alive.

His mission to tell the real story with his camera. Whatever, this is how he sold it to a gullible newspaper editor in Imperia, himself bored and wanting to mix up their foreign news coverage. This was rock and roll, a tilt at tearing down the big lie, ripping back the curtain, exposing the mythos of the American west right at its source, tracking the poisoned river back to its headwater and devenomising it. The dark heart of Amerikkka, blood and violence its true currency... And yes, this is exactly how macho hotheads like August spoke back then, pure invective and up till now little action.

This is what it's like now, it hasn't gone away, this sore, this cancer, it's not a comic, it's Vietnam.

A selfish romance all about himself. In short, he saw himself as a hip proletarian who took a stance against the man, wherever that was. It was all attitude for him, fuck you. The boss class could never deny him his masculinity, he would never be reduced by his enemies.

She could write the words, he didn't sweat the details, just channelled the energy and hustled the expenses that got the two of them to America, not as emigrants but as visitors, not as supplicants but as witnesses, adventurers, searchers of the real, Cool Hand Lukes of a cultural revolution straight outta Europe. We bring the horror, we bring our revulsion; we who lived through the world at night understand how to undertake the long journey out of it.

It is our duty to meet the dawn, to create a better day. We are not naïve!

They both spoke like this only when confident, high on cheap speed and booze, broken Italian, broken English, words only reached for when high, lyrics more than words, or words made lyrical, top-shelf words they didn't fully understand but Augustin could riff with the best of them – for this was the language of their generation – he just had to get in there to take the shot, his passport to the show being only his realness. In any situation, that's what mattered, being there, wherever that was, and recording it, as if every image was ultimately a self-portrait. *I am the camera!*

At other times he was silent or monosyllabic. Gloria saw it all for what it was, a train wreck in the making, that they would both come off the rails somewhere down the line and she looked for it at every turn, it would not be a surprise, the site of their downfall, the last stand of their hubris, but for sure it was a ride – an escape from the steep-sided valley she had been born in – stifling her as it did the sunshine – her smarting eyes pinned open, absorbing, sensing, archiving her trip of a lifetime, listening, asking, writing it all down, for what she didn't yet know, but instinctively sensed what she would have to do: to leaven the widescreen comic strip story Augusto would illustrate with his camera, to record a quieter truth. This is what her gut told her, as they headed up into the Badlands of South Dakota.

A few minutes later the meeting at Calico ended and the caravan, fifty-four cars long, rolled through the winter night; old people, kids and tough guys and aunts and uncles... Dennis Banks rode in the lead car with Chief Fools Crow, and on arrival at Wounded Knee, a hamlet of around one hundred residents, people from the cars gathered at the mass grave for a prayer with movement spiritual leaders Pete Catches and Leonard Crow Dog...

The graininess of predawn. A front line of sorts, Whiteclay, Dakota. Skid row under fading stars, cold as fuck, ice on the blacktop, a roadblock made up of Indians bundled up in blankets and pickup trucks, small fires started under drive shafts and axles to keep them from seizing, so cold that even drunks looked sober. And there were drunks in Whiteclay, it's what the place was for. A strange place for a standoff. Mean faces, nobody wanting to talk, little eye contact. Fear and boredom followed by jags of adrenalin, confidence, optimism, semi-automatic rifles squeezed off into the sky at random intervals, snatches of songs, a few steps of dance, before subsiding back into cold and still silence. Pine Ridge out there at the end of a road like a world on the end of a stick, a shit stick, a place that exists better in the imagination and for sure comes alive in the fantasy of comic panels and movies more than it ever does in the downtrodden surreality of *the real thing*. The eyes of the world do themselves and the Lakota a disservice; the circus of journalists and the odd liberal arts celebrity in town cars and random rentals dodging FBI checkpoints, making it across to friendly lines, sounds way more interesting and romantic than it is, the everyday jeopardy of life in a reservation amped by guns with everybody suspicious of everyone else. What are you doing here? What do you want? Too much eye contact and always *Who's the rat?* Because there is always a rat.

Finally, Wounded Knee, a place where once upon a time somebody wounded their knee, and still a place that had never stooped to metaphor.

Sunup and August is taking pictures of an old man wrapped in a blanket, Remington rifle across his knees. So far, so cliche. They sit on their haunches sharing cigarettes by the steps of a church, this is the bleakness of Wounded Knee, a landscape that takes no prisoners and gives zero fucks, everywhere you look the imprint in your mind of dead frozen Sioux warriors, women and children dance behind your retinas, almost mocking the sameness of the situation. Spotted Elk, forever sitting up with twisted arms frozen up above the waist, hands broken at unnatural angles, one clawing towards his chest, index fingers pointing to himself, a man surprised at both his own death – you would think – but more so his humiliation, a man forced to accept life and death on the reservation. Spotted Elk watches (over) us.

Gloria fumbles for her biro. Scribbles down: *There are no surprises in places like this. Everything that could happen already has done.* August reloads his Nikon.

Imagine the shame on us for seeing it, how it schools us one picture at a time, and the shame for taking it and his shame of having his photograph taken in death for everybody to see, shame three times over, she thinks, the shared horror of that moment separated by a hundred years but no less shameful. August scouts the camp for his next portraits, unconcerned that they have already been taken.

Click.

Wind on.

Two old snowmen outside the church, naked in the cold scrub, the rest of the snow having retreated, a young scout leaning up against one, shading his eyes and the black and white feathers on the barrel of his semi-automatic blowing in the breeze.

A dog barks off camera.

The old man in a blanket hasn't moved. He smokes, stares out at the horizon, nothing else holds the eye. He talks about broken treaties as if the ink was still wet on them. Made and broken in the same breath. Broken every day since, broken today, breaking right now as we speak and for sure to be broken again tomorrow. Sitting next to him, Gloria follows his eyes, trying to imagine what he sees. He tells her there were more Congressional Medals given out for killing unarmed women and children right here than there were at Iwo Jima against an enemy who fought back. His hand gestures to the flat prairie in front of them. A skinny dark-skinned man, one tooth still standing tall in his mouth, red wing boots on his feet, checked shirt, black tall Indian joe hat (vertical, much like the tooth, she thinks) decorated with a red band, chain smoking rollups.

– I am Oglala Sioux, native American and you wanna know why? Because that's what's written on those damned treaties. Nobody signed shit with indigenous, first nation, nobody. When we sit down to renegotiate all of it, that's who we are. Our tribes and theirs, Red men, white men.

He spits out a thread of tobacco that had caught on his bottom lip.

– You can't write new words on old treaties. You know how tricky lawyers can be when it comes to the details.

Gloria has zoned out somewhere in all the pauses, she couldn't follow his meaning, instead losing herself to the horizon, a projection screen for thoughts and worries with little relation to the present moment. Besides, she was sick of men, wars, treaties. Had a woman ever signed even one of them? Not a one.

This observation surprised her, and she wasn't expecting that, to feel tired of being a woman among men. She got up to take a walk and clear her head. The old man didn't move other than to take his hat off and inspect the band on it, wiping his open palm across it.

August snaps some of the activists. Jangling bracelets, they pass a bottle to keep warm, talking about the war in Vietnam. Hippies from California. Impossible to imagine somewhere further away from the streets of San Francisco than Pine Ridge.

Black rights, Red power, world revolution resolve into a performative standoff that can veer either way, into farce or tragedy. A fighter jet passes overhead, Indians on horseback laughing, shake their rifles at it, ponies rearing up on two legs, just like in the movies, backed by contrails.

Outside, press have to break the cordon and sneak in past the roadblocks. Wounded Knee is surrounded. They hunker down, these few thousand, waiting for the next provocation. In front of the white church a flag is raised; a circle of white tepees against a blood-red ground.

Too many cameras.

Gloria experiences a profound yet acrophobic sense of déjà vu. Resonating between the great plains and her home in a mountain valley, an inverse topology, two ends of a looking glass, one where lives are lived horizontally, the other vertically. Faces here are broad while hers is the narrow *Faccia da furetto*. Men and women ride horses with an easy side-to-side swagger, a timeless gait with which to cross grasslands, scrublands and mesas, to traverse the mountains buttes, rivers and the creeks of history. The literalism of native naming, building a wall of facts, a hinterland of undeniability in the face of genocide.

All you have to do is say their name.

One night Gloria meets a young woman called Jacinta Eagle Deer, they share a beer and Gloria finds her first true subject, a woman, and asks her all the wrong questions: what she thinks will happen at Wounded Knee, about the Federal Marshalls, the reservation police, corruption, the Indian movement, the stand-off, treaties, the history of it all.

Jacinta cuts her off with a growl.

– But will there ever be a peace treaty between men and women?

Gloria understands her in the sense of her own womanhood and her relationship with Augustin. The distance between them evaporates. Instinctively Jacinta knows that this white woman could be an ally – obviously with caveats – but she was a woman. Her bar of trust was set right in the middle. Gloria tries again, groping for the right questions, from growing up on the reservation, to what girls are taught at school, the role of women in the tribe, will it ever be possible to be a modern native American woman, at which Jacinta snorts again.

– Define modern?

*

During the first day of this operation at the roadblocks, there were six FBI agents being attacked and pinned down. McMurtray and Deputy Jim Propotnick (who later became Chief Deputy US Marshal, District of Hawaii) were ordered to repel the attack with an armoured personnel carrier. McMurtray and Propotnick arrived at the roadblock just as a group of the dissidents were about to overrun it. However, with Propotnick driving and McMurtray on top of the armoured personnel carrier firing, they successfully repelled the attack.

Outside, men on both sides cradle guns and when they tire of cradling them, empty them at each other in sporadic gunfire exchanges – as if just to make the burden of carrying them lighter – rounds careening across the prairie, a claustrophobic exchange in which wounds are inflicted almost invisibly, on silhouettes picked out by the light of barrel fires high on the eroded line of buttes and pinnacles. Sporadic raids on checkpoints prompted by nothing more tragic than boredom and the interminable pressure of the standoff itself, men on horseback riding low to the horse's neck or crouched down in the back of pickups, night raids and dawn ambushes along endless strips of tarmac.

Jacinta Eagle Deer grew up on the Brule Lakota Rosebud reservation but left after being raped in the back of a car in '67 while being driven home from babysitting. It pushed her out into the world; well, as far as Iowa. She was drawn back to the reservation in 1975 in order to testify against the man who raped her, but was killed in a hit-and-run accident not long after, probably by men paid to protect him.

Gloria's story was never printed at the time, not until late in the decade when Jacinta's stepmother, Delphine Eagle Deer, was beaten to death on the reservation. She had campaigned for justice for her daughter. An editor at *L'Humanita* dug up the photo Gloria had taken of Jacinta – blurry, a snap taken at the end of their one and only meeting, in a doorway, as she was leaving, so backlit, a woman with long jet-black hair, a flash of teeth and an open smile, in jeans – and ran it along with the original interview.

When will there ever be peace between men and women? was the tagline.

For this, for the rest of her life Gloria was – not unaffectionately – called a communist in a village that had mostly forgotten what that meant.

August came back from a raid, high on whiskey and adrenalin, clumsily and for the last time, wanting sex, silently with the insistence of his body, which Gloria rebuffed. The next day she could barely look him in the eye, seeing him now through Jacinta's.

Increasingly there are reports of people leaving the camp.

Man, they just had enough of being cooped up here, spooked by being cut off, by the heavy armour, the jets flying over and the gunfire.

Word spread and more followed.

The weather was getting warmer, but this had the effect of hastening an ending. Winter had been a fortress, and now its walls had melted. Gloria curses August for not being prepared, for throwing them both into a situation without thinking it through, for not getting the right clothes or supplies, she had begged a coat in the camp which wasn't cool, she wasn't there to be a burden. They slept in a shared tepee, the canvas of which flapped noisily for most of the night. And this made him angry and her silent, resentful, spent. They were the wrong people for this assignment. Foreigners in too many ways. August, who the Americans had taken to calling Augie, the last shred of humour between them, this name, shared with a famous American, now wanted to leave as soon as possible, he had got what he had come for, his rolls of film now stashed in a knapsack. The one thing he had planned was hiding their bike and now he retrieved it from inside a derelict grain silo. They left in the middle of the night, Gloria desperate to get away from him, had to go with him.

Ain't that always the way.

Surprised by searchlights from an armoured personnel carrier at 12.49 a.m., 22 April 1973, Augustin lost control of the bike by Wolf Creek heading east on Highway 18.

*

From her hospital bed, Gloria watched the news and saw footage of US Marshalls raising an American flag outside the church in Wounded Knee. She thought of the old native man and his story of Iwo Jima and she cried, for the first time and because she realised she didn't know his name but that what he'd said was true, simply true. The second time she cried was looking into a hand mirror shortly after waking up. A livid scar ran from temple to jaw, her face a river runs through it. She should have never left New York. She should have stayed in the city by herself, free.

Weeks later at night, following the line of it with her fingertips, her Indian scar guiding her home across the vast Atlantic. Ten days at sea before the boat delivered her back to Genova, time enough to get her story straight before the mountains reclaimed her, folding her back into itself in admonition of the flat world into which Augustin had taken her, the wide-open spaces in which she had nearly died and the horizon on which she had feasted her eyes.

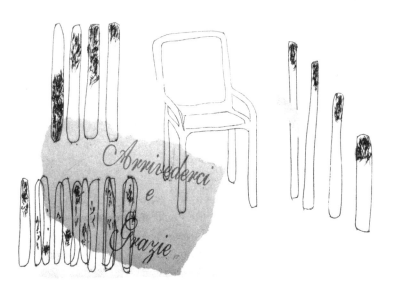

TUTTI LE FESTE DI DOMANI

Bars and restaurants play contemporary Italian and American pop music, peppered with timeless rock classics – the Stones, the Moody Blues, Blue Oyster Cult, Dire Straits, Hall and Oates – a time warp soundtrack of the Mediterranean, now seasoned with the detritus of euro rap and the most cheesy examples of contemporary RnB. This is the diet of most French and Italian radio stations, rotating imported music with homegrown. A mature North American (and to a lesser extent British) pop musical culture dominates, a byproduct perhaps, of the postwar settlement in Europe. We are always welcome to the hotel California and everywhere we turn there are knights in white satin, playing on infinite payola. Indigenous folk music survives on the margins as *subculture, exiled from, yet haunting – however benignly – the national consciousness. Partisan songs are a modern example of this in Italy, Chansons in France, as well as regional musical traditions and song books dating from the late middle ages to the present day. Italian popular understanding of Black American culture is patchy. The misread of both the fashion and politics of rap is but a symptom of a wilful cultural nonalignment manifesting in Italian gang culture as a ridiculous misappropriation, which you can see and hear on shows like Subbura, Romanzo Criminale, and Gomorrah.*

— 'A practice centred reading of popular music and Italian post-war subculture' delivered to symposium on intertextuality and Italian cultural norms 1945–present day, Fondazione Einaudi Torino, 2021.

From the terrace we hear the party, it echoes around the hills and the beat calls us down, up and over to it, bass punctuated by laughter, all of it parsed by the valley itself, amplifying and muting this soundtrack at will.

The *Pro Loco* hold a Schiuma party every summer next to the tennis courts, where the attraction was literally a foam machine which sprayed at intervals over the dance floor. Other villages came up with ideas such as *Cuba Party* where they would sell rum, or more simply *Disco Party*. For people with more fertile imaginations, these *festivi* were disappointing, although they didn't really need to try, everybody went anyway. On the decks were disc jockeys with names like DJ Dave Cox or DJ Snoopy, middle-aged men gone to seed who plied up and down the valleys with their travelling sound systems every summer.

Beers, wine, grappa, rostelli, pasta, Coke, chips you could exchange for tickets bought from a little kiosk. More traditional *festas* are food themed, featuring signature dishes of the towns and villages of the region. Some bands also toured the coast playing traditional music alongside pop standards. Our village held a snail festival every September where they raced snails and ate them. Different snails, obviously. This was an invented tradition, much like the Cuban snail racing lovingly depicted in the classic Guinness commercial 'Bet on black' from the turn of the century.

Like a watering hole in an African plain, these events attracted the good, the bad and the ugly, they all come down to drink and something is always bound to happen, however minor, scuffles of one sort or another guaranteed.

Sabine was a regular in the local bars. Unusually, she shared her custom between them. She would wear delicate antique dresses for her first glass of prosecco, at ten-thirty a.m. A glamourous fifty-something German hippy, she had migrated to the valley in the early '90s to a shack up in the hills above a semi-deserted hamlet, every other dwelling shuttered, a few with forlorn for sale signs with out of service contact numbers. In the summer, Sabine was drawn to the festas. She liked to dance. Skinny, with corded muscles on her deeply tanned arms, she stepped out onto every dance floor. Men were wary of her, I think, they flirted but you got the sense that she knew how to handle herself. She held a glass of wine just so, like in a scene from an old film. A fixture on the street, she was on nodding terms with everyone, with a smile on her face that presided over both an unexpected distance and a razor-sharp presence, somehow she balanced the two – the effort of doing so, of pulling off this feat, flickered behind her eyes. A hippy for sure, but nobody's fool. Far away but always right there.

I do not know what interested her, what she talked about, I never spoke to her.

Sometimes she would arrive in the village with *trombetti* draped behind her ears and braided into her hair – reminding me of cheap alien body jewellery from an old episode of *Star Trek* – usually on the nights when there was a party. Trombetti are courgettes, the size and shape of pagan dildos, and she would dance, alone or with somebody else, and drive home, alone or with somebody else, without these trombetti falling off, as far as I ever noticed, they always stayed exactly in place, worn elegantly, with no sense of being ridiculous, carried off as if on a catwalk, or in a scene from another movie. Over the years, they became a thing, we all looked for them behind her ears on high summer nights, approaching legend, Sabine and her trombetti.

She had been young during the Swinging Sixties in Hamburg, or perhaps Stuttgart, bourgeois or bohemian, probably both, involved with protests, drugs and music. The only predictable thing about her was when she drank too much, her mask fell off – rather than slipped – the more shocking for being cool to start with, and everybody took the piss out of her as if they had been waiting for this opportunity to switch. Inebriation distracted her from policing the unruly pieces of her herself, which took the opportunity to rejoin their civil war.

Instead of saying she changed, became a nightmare, or a worse version of herself, all the cliches used to describe people, especially women, when they are drunk, I choose this more circumspect observation, which is neither here nor there because *in the eyes of her audience,* the street the village, the valley, she took on another role when in this condition. *Just like that she was* made over into a sad joke, a clown to be pitied, especially by those she had rejected, Sabine and her trombetti took on the darker, reproving tone of a moral fable. Crowds can be cruel, or just so intoxicated by their collective pleasure there is little room for individual sympathy. Things go too far. One hundred people sprayed with foam were just such a crowd, goading Sabine on as she spun around and around, the courgettes flying from behind her ears, trampled underfoot and Heidi stumbling, drinking whatever she could pick up, her dress soaking wet from too much foam and her hair bedraggled much to the amusement of everyone else to a soundtrack of generic euro house. Teenagers pointed and laughed from the shadows, too cool to dance, too bored to stay away, drinking beer and eating chips, unimpressed by what it meant to be grown up.

One such night, Sabine got stopped for reckless driving. She got out of the car drunk, waving about an open penknife. The police cuffed her over the bonnet of her Suzuki Jimny. It seems far-fetched somehow, Sabine in chains. Instead of arresting her they took her home, and soon after that she disappeared. Her father had been a big industrialist, an old Nazi who had bought her the house here to keep her from embarrassing the family.

Apparently.

But if somebody was that wealthy, why buy a shithole like that, it's not much more than a shack, he could have sent her further away, Brazil, Argentina with all the other fucking Germans. Why come here?

The cops must have found contact details – shaking their heads at the state of her home – when they deposited her onto the bed, by this time exhausted, sleepy, apologetic.

Her sister came to pick her up. They knew where she was, all those years they knew, letting her live in a place like that, with all their money.

Her departure caused more of a stir than her presence, for more than a few years she had become part of the furniture, the date of her arrival unspecific. Her acquaintances missed her briefly, others who might have been more intimate kept it to themselves. That's how it goes, our guest appearances in the lives of others.

Other hippies live up in the hills. Occasionally you see them down on *dog beach*, where the fitter ones come to kite surf. They are usually older, the same generation as Sabine, on the run from post-war settlements that unsettled them. I imagine a few phantoms from the darkest of all worlds. German hippies go hard – a few old Red Army Faction types – gun and drug runners, overspill from excessive idealism, nihilism by way of self-hatred, but also more benign back-to-nature hippies who build tiny pieces of paradise, toilets you pour water into before flushing – a jug left to the side, filled daily from the river – natural cesspits built into terrace walls, badly rigged-up solar panels trailing cables, midnight tokers turning their back on the modern world they eke out a living in eight-hundred-year-old shepherds' huts and broken-down houses hidden up among terraces of weed. Some are carpenters, others work iron or stone, but slowly, and rarely to order. You see them stocking up on canned goods at Aldi, prepping for nothing. While others escaped to the beaches of the Far East, these hippies preferred the seclusion of the mountains. Compelled to stay close to home, unable to achieve escape velocity. They descend to drink and to buy jumbo-size cigarette papers and pouches of tobacco with which to roll joints. They keep to themselves, the German, the Dutch, until they drink or smoke too much and either draw attention by dancing wildly or fall out with each other over money or things borrowed but not returned – usually tools like grass strimmers, hand saws, wood planes – or scuffle among themselves just for the hell of it. Old-school heads who still read scrappy passed-around copies of Heinrich Boll novels or by the other guy who killed himself. Locals found them mostly amusing, they spent what they had in the bars and shops, and mostly kept to themselves.

Chic Italian hippies populate a semi-derelict village half destroyed by an earthquake in the '50s, now a magnet for artists and tourists, with restaurants, art galleries, antique shops and a cactus garden leading up to the *pigna*, which hosts a bar of sorts, a throwback to the '90s – which reads as a throwback to the '80s or even earlier somehow, as if we have all lived lives way longer than natural, which we can relive, re-inhabit at will – this bar is a product of this compression of time. Overlooking two valleys and a motorway, a Dutch ex-vice cop holds sway over his own autonomous non-stop party. Bare swollen lobster feet and blistered legs, fists like hams, broken nails, ruined T-shirt riding above a bulging stomach, sour booze and cigarette breath, a human earthquake of a man who drawls in Flemish, or Dutch – I confuse the two – they have the same thick-tongued *cha cha* sound, a drunk German perhaps, not a consonant clipped, but a rolling tongue spitting heavily accented English, he welcomes you to his bar with a warm bottle of Heineken, Amstel or rotgut wine. *On the house.*

A man who took more drugs than he ever took off the streets. Drugs he used or sold, hard drugs, speed, coke, smack and got busted out of the force, ran out-of-town up into these hills, a two-a-penny drama where both good and bad guys are after him, their motives lost in the cat's cradle of his mind addled by propping up too many bars, downing too many cheap and expensive brandies – depending on who's paying – for decades on the take, his world populated by – as the story goes – a fraternity of pimps, snitches, whores and stone cold killers. Trusty protector turned rotten apple. Innocence ruined by experience... My imagination sparking off the guy crushing my hand in his, bloodshot eyes smiling in a broken-veined open face that celebrated ruin. I must have read too many crime novels because it was like we had met before.

Willem! I'm Willem, welkom, this is my place, enjoy it!

Every day the party begins again, life at the end of a broken rainbow, a timeless milieu of bad sex and hangovers and the trading of petty favours. Every night Willem cooks frozen or donated pizzas or sausage links on the barbeque and the beer flows, you pay what you like and share what you fancy, sitting on the terrace overlooking olive groves running down to the sea backed by a huge cemetery on the other side of the valley. The place is always busy with tourists, mostly other northern Europeans, as well as a few fellow exiles, kindred spirits come to sit it out. A brain squint makes you feel that this could be at the centre of something, a valid place from which to see and experience the world, but on reflection it isn't, not really. Italian hippies avoid it, sticking to the hole-in-the-wall art galleries and antique shops arranged in the alleyways below. They rarely make it up here. Like in the derelict streets of Viriconium, or more prosaically the alleyways leading up to a castle in *Game of Thrones*, they adorn the approaches – characters that populate side quests in fantasy computer games, exotic in their own way, manifesting at the epicentre of a Venn diagram which includes Versace jeans, yin and yang tattoos, designer weaves and sophisticated eye makeup. Literally hippies after a fashion, cigarettes twirled by manicured fingers, nails painted with elaborate varnish. A wonderful Italian contradiction. Delicate ankle bracelets, second-hand Elena Ferrante novels, pierced navels, cowboy boots, late nights strumming three-string guitars on the public beach, illegal bonfires and at midnight, naked swims.

Those who make it to the top – to the eyrie – come in all ages, but are mostly older from the time when the '70s bled into the '80s and kept on bleeding. A Tower of Babel manifesting in this Dutch ex-cop's bar, the name of which I cannot recall or refuse to remember, a dissonant carnival of a place in which I wouldn't like to take ketamine or any hallucinogen, or be out of control of the senses needed to navigate it.

*

Some friends are staying with us at the house and one of them complained when I took a work call at supper. She dropped some snide line *soto voce*, of which I heard:

—*always on his phone, how can you ever relax if*—

Delivered with a reproving smile that only a middle-class woman can deliver (in my observation). Fuck you, I thought, how the fuck do you think I paid for this place and your free fucking holiday without this fucking phone, as if I wanted to be on it, or indeed to talk about work, always some pointless project (for me) that seemed the be all and end all for whatever group of American/Eastern European/Italian Advertising creatives I was on a conference call with, that I couldn't give two flying fucks about any more than I can about your opinion of me...

I said nothing, but she had jarred me back into my everyday way of being, my ability to relax now retarded even further by her snarky observation. Fuck you for raining on my parade, for killing my buzz, for puncturing my balloon, deflating my prose, ejecting me from Eden, delivering me back into the hands of the mundane, the crass, the vulgar, exchanging the fuck-yous of everyday life, contemplating my faltering career, damaged self-esteem and all that jazz. A path littered with hard rocks and sharp stones, each one a compromise, mortal wounds on the road to a life compromised and all that jazz.

Fucking witch.

My partner gave me a wry smile. I poured myself a beer, a salty Messina, perfect with some mortadella on hot toast, fat melting into the butter.

Our kids were still young enough to enjoy Halloween, so later we piled into a minivan, to take us up the hill to Triora. I have never liked it, a husk of a town, empty of the thousands who had lived there hundreds of years before, featuring a prince's palace perfectly restored by UNESCO, for what? The purposes of a lacklustre tourism. The dark and damp of that town would always repel visitors, eventually. An odd atmosphere, a feeling of absence as if people were needed to soak up all the moisture and to light our way with candles. I have never been in a haunted house, but I imagine they are a bit like this. A friend who grew up in upstate New York told me about an empty hospital his friends dared each other to stay overnight in when they were kids. Worse than a house, I guess, when it comes to being haunted. Anyway, he's not a spiritual guy, doesn't believe in shit like that at all, he's a down-to-earth sales rep in advertising, a rational guy who knew the price of things, but what he told me had happened to him, what he saw when he stayed there overnight, was inexplicable.

I mean he must have been trippin'.

Triora was the opposite. It was haunted by the absence of ghosts, if that makes sense. The place itself was dead. A bar, an overpriced shop selling fancy wood-burning stoves for over a grand plus what the locals called city fridges: large and presumptuous. A so-so restaurant and a bank of concrete holiday apartments built in the '70s, metal-shuttered for nine months of the year. The whole town busy for a few weeks in the summer, around the witch festival following hot on the heels of a cowboy-themed wild west festival. Stranger, yet equally cheesy. Then came Halloween, a reprise of its major theme: ghosts, folk magic, and all-round medieval spookiness. It had a witch museum open all year round. Of some interest was the story that German soldiers had thrown grenades into the houses of those thought to be helping the partisans. A style of reprisal familiar from films and books. The families to be punished had their doors chalked up with a mark (like a plague house, this connotation is – and was then – unavoidable). I don't know what this mark was. Perhaps the whole story was rubbish but there were overlapping WW marks in white paint daubed on walls in Triora and other villages, worn but still visible, which may have had something to do with the war – the Waffen SS – all of that. The sign of the beast. Witches also made the beast with two backs with the Devil himself, but again I have never bothered verifying this, why would you if it's something you are happy to believe in, take at face value? Witches also cursed men's penises, and if not burnt then taken to court for it, which would go some way towards explaining *our* sexual insecurity and obsession with cuckolds.

Revellers swarm the steep road or jam themselves into minibuses, everyone in fancy dress, witches and demons, sexy vampires and trolls, porn elves, and let's not forget to mention lots of teenage goths with purple lipstick, ripped tights and cobweb makeup. The dispossessed. Sexualised, cheap and gaudy, representing an eclectic profusion of cultural references from *American Horror Story* to *The Addams Family*, from heavy metal to Italian gothic and at a stretch films like *Suspiria* and '70s schlock horror.

In our van, bodies flung from side to side at every bend, kids screaming, the driver, fag parked in the corner of his mouth, oblivious to the can of sardines he was driving, he threw us round every corner gears screaming, brakes whining, depositing us in the car park outside Triora, into a crowd of the same, revellers, kids, parents, locals, tourists, expensive stalls selling food and handicrafts, fireworks going off everywhere, warm beer and wine served in plastic cups which when discarded littered the street. By the time we got up to this hellhole a little punch drunk and desperate for a drink, I'm still annoyed. I couldn't shake it off. Why am I so fragile, why do I find it so easy to slip between worlds, states of being, to lose equanimity *at the drop of a hat*; to reach out for anger and find it so close to hand? Is this what Thomas Covenant felt – I flash on a book from another life, one in which I read fantasy fiction – the memory and knowledge of it flood back, as if I have accessed a hitherto forgotten hard drive. Thomas Covenant, a (literal) leper in our world, could reach for power unlocked by his anger and then wreak havoc in another one. I can't remember the book's title, just this character, an ordinary man, whose anger at being disabled, his shame of being a lesser man allowed him to become something much more than everyone else. I see myself in him, the prosaic version of him, all anger, shame, powerless as so many of us are. Thomas Covenant was an everyman, if that's what you were looking for. Doubting Thomas – hence his name – who took a leap of faith. To reach for something extra. I loved fantasy in a literal sense. I wanted adventures, epic battles, vast imagined worlds, a stab at the infinite, story for its own sake not ours. I still do.

> *Women were burnt as witches to explain famine, accused of poisoning livestock and ruining crops. There had to be an explanation, and men found it in the poor and single women who lived in the poorest quarters of town, independent women, some herbalists who had failed to cure somebody's loved one, or perhaps spurned lovers, their names being known, their cards marked. The vulnerable. The terror of famine and no godly explanation, so they found an ungodly one.*
> — 'Narratives of Italian witchcraft from heresy to tourism', University of Bologna Press PHD thesis, 1976

Badalucco has a two-day summer wine festival, literally an *Invito al vino*. Trestle tables and benches are set up in the main square and the local restaurants compete with mobile food and wine trucks to serve the hundreds of people who descend on the piazza. The local commune *pro loco* pays for the entertainment. Usually this was so-so. But for three years, they miraculously raised enough money to pay for The Shary Band. A five-piece band, two female singers, two guitars backing a male lead delivering high-energy dance moves, covers plus original songs accompanied by multiple costume changes and a synchronised-to-the-max light show. High camp, these guys knew how to party and whipped the crowd up into a frenzy. From Italian classics to disco, rock covers, from Abba to the Rolling Stones.

Hands up in the air!

Mani mani mani mani!

All the hits, delivered like a live version of Stars on 45. 'What is Love?' 'Rivers of Babylon', 'Sugar Sugar', 'More Than I Can Say', 'Jump!', 'You Are the Only One', 'Video Killed the Radio Star', 'The Rhythm of the Might', 'YMCA', 'I Got a Feeling', ramped-up full-throttle beats per minute. Kids on shoulders, everyone pushing to the front to soak up the energy as it poured off the stage, the three main performers mesmerising the crowd and at the apex of this energy, as if channelling through him was the lead singer Shary himself. Spiky dyed-blond hair, with coloured highlights (one year green, the next black), huge sunglasses, fake tan, the smarts of a minstrel singing for his supper, the swagger of a clown milking the crowd of whatever joy we had inside us, in another register gurning his way through banter with his band, with us. Making us feel special.

He was the jester, we were his kings.

Fluorescent lights raked the scene, colour-coded with the costumes, the valley had never seen the like. Taking his sunglasses off and ageing fifteen years under layers of pancake, a Mephisto of dance, the girls, big breasts in bustiers, slashed dresses, high heels, thigh boots, swapping out for Egyptian goddess masks, posed on prop catafalques born by roadies. Shiny jewellery, outrageous costumes, poses and suggestive dancing, shaking their bums, thighs, heads, hands, singing, making eye contact with the crowd provoking waves of laughter and applause, and flights of pure dance energy.

A storm in the valley.

Nossa, nossa
Assim você me mata
Ai, se eu te pego
Ai, ai se eu te pego
Delícia, delícia
Assim você me mata
Ai, se eu te pego
Ai, ai, se eu te pego[25]

What the fuck are they singing about? Fade to black, intro, beat, lights up and costume change, as the band slides seamlessly into 'Walk Like an Egyptian' and we sing ourselves hoarse, full spectrum entertainment, a modern-day Bacchanal.

25   Wow, wow / You're gonna kill me that way / Ah when I get my hands on you, (poor you) / Ah when I get my hands on you, (poor you) / Delicious, delicious / You're gonna kill me that way / Ah when I get my hands on you, (poor you) / Ah when I get my hands on you, (poor you)

This was a blip, since then *Invito al Vino* has reverted to popular music of the worse kind; a female singer fronting tacky backing tracks, or perhaps the most basic of 'bands' plugged into workmanlike sound equipment, featuring badly balanced mics and out-of-tune instruments. This music drew on no heritage of Italian popular music or folk culture, taking its cue instead from the fallout of American cultural imperialism that had died out in the late '70s but still haunted us every summer into 'the modern era' – surface skaters on a low tide of history plying derivative plastic pop covers to (small) crowds of increasingly drunk villagers and occasional tourists. Deeper into the valley and things got both worse and better, drunken if not orgiastic mountain village raves that went on all night, waves of bass and the high-pitched squeals of mopeds reverberating up and down the valley roads until dawn.

*

There are two brothers, musicians from the same village, who have grown up playing in the same band. One plays the accordion, the other tambourine, like a drum, to provide percussion. I am fascinated by his floppy hand slapping faster and faster on the drum skin. It mesmerises me. They play on the local folk circuit, in bars, at *festas* and also more cultural events organised by regional government agencies. They discover there is good money to be had playing weddings, birthdays and office parties, so they do that, recording their first CD in a studio with the proceeds, selling them from a little table at gigs and in the local bar of their village. But as things develop it so happens that one brother becomes more famous than the other. Even in this small world, jealousy and ambition can work their black magic. Somebody, a friend, a wannabe manager, a girlfriend, pours poison in their ear – sweet poison.

What a voice you have, but this music, it's for old people, who can't even play the CD you just spent the time and money making. Not your idea, I know, but bad none the less. Let's change it up, find a keyboard player, a proper drummer, or a machine, we can go on the road, to the city… solo, make some real money!

The brothers part ways, the tambourine player finds himself another band, but misses the back-and-forth exchange of verses traded with his brother, the challenge of going higher in tone, faster, one on the heel of the other: jousting voices. This was the thing itself, timeless, beautiful. He never understood this in words until now, singing by himself with people he hardly knew. He thinks words are a pointless substitute for feeling. He soon gave it up, went back to college to become a mechanic, a passion for cars he also shared with his brother, who meanwhile gets a recording contract and shoots a music video featuring a Lamborghini. One brother under the bonnet, the other slouched against one, singing pop songs. I should say now that they are twins, from Calabria, both as handsome or as plain as the other. Fate has shown them to be as different in character as they are identical in appearance. Calabrians sing of violence as part of a world where violence has always been a part of life, and it is this life that they sang about. Part of which is violent. How to disentangle the one from the other? A local boss has a party, his daughter's wedding, let's say. A band or a singer is hired and they sing folk ballads derived from the nineteenth century concerning outsiders, brigands, men of honour from the past. Do the modern gangsters feel good about this, does it justify them, is what they do normalised by history, by an oral tradition steeped in who and where they are?

Probably/perhaps.

Singers for hire.

YouTube clips and Instagram feeds of musicians being ushered into a wedding party and having to be shepherded over to the bride's table, to sing first for them. Bored and tired from the weekly grind of entertaining, or, indeed, having to release videos assuring their audience that they don't glorify or endorse the Mafia, since local councils ban what they see as the cultural expression at the root of Mafia life, an easy target for them in their mostly phony war against criminal gangs. Writers and filmmakers the world over are more guilty of this than wedding singers, who themselves appear in these movies serenading gangsters since the 1920s, minstrels for any party.

*

When possible we stay after the summer has passed, for when September comes and beyond, late autumn festivals have a different character. Smaller, more intimate now the tourists have gone. An impromptu setup of laptop and speakers outside a bar. Background noise of pop music for a few hours and then, when they played an old song, a folk song, the atmosphere changed and people danced together, two steps, a little tango, half-remembered steps. As soon as the pop music came back on again everyone sat down a little deflated, or carried on talking, ignoring the music with a resignation which shrugs *this is what the kids want now*, although they didn't seem to enjoy it either, except the tiny children who also love watching *Frozen* on iPads. These shifts in atmosphere are on a microscale the essence of what change is as a lived experience.

Most gatherings are not even festive, they just happen, a bar plays music outside because it's a warm evening, people meet, dance in the street, women walk up and down with their babies, people are delighted by them. They appear miraculous. Young couples respond to this with their own dreams. Some shy away, not wanting this future for themselves. The drudgery of having children. Dogs lie under plastic tables. Old ladies dance together and with their partners. Everything is copacetic, all the moving parts of life appear well oiled. A sudden downpour and some rush inside, others embrace the rain, one man dances in it in homage to the film, people laugh at this, clap, remembering the movie, others twirl umbrellas they must have retrieved from the bar. On this last day of warm weather, of warm rain, I see two people kiss, by the monument to the village dead, I kid you not. I don't enjoy watching people kiss, I usually turn away, but just this once, how was I to know it would be this kiss that chose me as its witness, of all the bad luck, what mocking twist of fate for it to pick me? This kiss revealed itself behind a passing truck, driven by an old rascal I knew, an old truck driven by a German hippy, well known to all because he farmed and ate guinea pigs, which people thought eccentric. He reminded me of the roadkill-eating judge in Carl Hiaasen novels, dark, crazy horror film hair, low-slung jeans with a belt that takes a shortcut across his back flab and in front disappears under his guts, but with shiny intelligent eyes and this cool beat-up old truck. The sound of its engine drew my eye, revealing the kiss behind.

An intense kiss, a compression of lips, as serious as the docking of a space station, critical, urgent, lip contact that contains the whole history of kissing, that is a descendant of this history, its latest iteration but is also the future of kissing. This kiss was its own child. Beyond sex, sex immaterial to the power of this kiss, a kiss for all time. Tongues like the dark hard chocolate inside an ice cream, hard sweet tongues, feasting, gorging themselves like aliens sequestered in our mouths. A kiss that has no place in the pages of a book like this, no place at all, a kiss that will crush books and the lies about kissing that books tell, compress them like the rubbish they are and everything else like them, songs, poems, gossip, compressing, I repeat this word, an imperative, because from this kiss will gush oil, or spew diamonds, or any other thing that is created by having such pressure placed on it in this world. A kiss to haunt dreams, to ruin them with pleasure, the unobtainable kiss, but one we know exists in the most ordinary of mouths, one that only needs igniting by another, despite all our complex beliefs and patchy understanding of science, we know this to be true because we learn it on days like this, unexpected lessons in love found on the simplest of streets.

High days of unexpected celebration.

A contradiction sounds in these my words: but you, I know, are sensible and wise and can by intuition read my mind and my true thoughts.

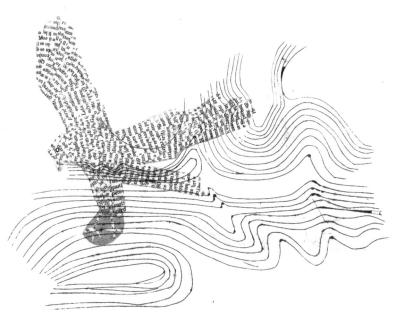

LA LUNA STORTA

Ravioli, tagliatelle, ragu o burro salvia, cinghiale ragù, coniglio arrosto con olive e pinoli, capra fagioli…

Basta!

Two voices mimic the slow, deep-voiced owner of the restaurant where they had eaten earlier. Two men nurse their bloated stomachs. A messy hotel room, clothes spilling out of an open suitcase, empty bottles of beer and wine on the table, cigarettes spilling out of an ashtray stubbed out at different lengths, one man laid out on the floor pleading to the gods.

– No more fucking food! Crazy fucking goat? You would die, literally explode into piles of shit and fat and who knows what before making it to their signature dish!

– When she brought over the snails, take me now!

Creased up with laughter, they are suffering.

– Stop, stop, it hurts.

Chris slumps on a tired, lumpy sofa and lets off a series of bottom notes, bass-heavy farts.

– You're fired, I'm sending you home, that's crossing the line my friend.

Shouts/laughs the skinny guy on the floor.

– I can't help it. It has to come out.

More laughter, groans.

– Come on, you must have room left, just a little goat, some beans, come on, you're a man, perhaps one more glass, yes? Grappa to help with digestion…

The guy on the floor flails his arms like a spider crab.

Eventually Chris gets up and stumbles to the door.

– Right, I gotta go, tomorrow's call time is eight a.m., better get some sleep.

Tony coils himself up from the floor. He's tall, lanky, loose-limbed and not just from the booze, it's how he rolls. Watching him get up, you experience how precarious it must be for him to stay on his feet is at this moment.

– What a good little boy you are, Chris. What's the word, *diligent*, no, that's not it. *Conscientious*, that's it, very conscientious.

Tony chuckles.

Chris's eyes light up.

– Night Tony.

Tony smiles back, nods his head, bows from the waist.

– *Buonanotte e Grazie*, Tony replies in the same deep voice, shutting the door.

He stumbles out onto the small balcony of his hotel room and in a moment of vertigo grabs the wonky guardrail to steady himself, sitting down suddenly on a chair. Rubbing his hand over his face he lights one last cigarette and looks out at a heavy, nearly full moon against an array of stars framed by a dark velvet crown of mountains. He stares at it through watery eyes, a blur of silver bruises.

Che fai tu, luna, in ciel, dimmi, che fai?[26]

And the quiet, he breathes it in. After some time, he jots down in a notebook:

A pair of golden eagles ride the thermals, looking for rabbits.

The pen hovers over the page, before crossing out *looking,* writing above it *silhouettes hunting.*

*

Day, high on the side of the mountain shaped like a half-moon. The moon itself, a crescent, is still visible in the sky, reflecting sunlight, pairing the mountain. Between them a pair of golden eagles ride thermals. The sharp tang of two-stroke rides the crisp air as a cloud of dust chases a dirt bike along the spine of *Mezaluna.* A trike with a cameraman strapped onto the back follows it. Tony slams on the rear brakes, spins the bike to a standstill, showering the crew in dirt. He pulls off his helmet takes a bow grinning like a Cheshire cat/laughing like a hyena. The crew laps it up.

A walking simile for many, Tony was born to run.

The trike pulls up, from the back of which jumps Chris, his cameraman, usually full of piss and vinegar, but right now pretty green to the gills from the night before.

Tony catches his eye, searching for an answer.

Regaining a little colour, Chris hunches over a small monitor with the director checking the footage, looks up at Tony, flashes him a triumphant thumbs up.

26   What are you doing moon, in the sky, tell me, what are you doing? – Giacomo Leopardi.

– Got it all, baby, the bike, the cloud of dirt, all of it framed by the mountains. Normal speed, fifty frames and a little spurt of extreme slow mo.

Tony pushes out his lower lip, impressed.

– You want a beer?

– Nope.

Tony smiles, turns to the director.

– So what's next?

*

Tony shares a cigarette with a young, tanned shepherd in a checked shirt and jeans, sitting on an upturned bucket outside a Portakabin overlooking the crux of three valleys.

The camera assistant translates, mostly the odd word of Italian, but they also communicate with bits of English, gestures, faces. Two muscular black dogs saunter over, one slurps water from a bowl.

– *Hold the roll!* says the sound woman.

The dog stops drinking, wanders back to his master.

– *Sound!*

The camera rolls with a nod from Chris.

– Great dogs.

Who knew if Tony liked dogs or not.

The shepherd takes him at his word.

– The dogs are for company. I round up the sheep with the bike. Not really sheep dogs, perhaps for wolves. But this is better.

He picks up a shotgun. Sniggers.

Tony digs this.

– No shit, you get wolves up here?

He nods and pours them glasses of a white spirit.

Tony sips, winces and downs the rest.

– Juniper, right? Wow.

– Yes.

– I know my spirits. So where are the sheep?

We notice for the first time that there are no sheep around, just twists of their wool on the wire of empty pens.

– Anybody see any sheep?

Tony smiles into the camera.

– There.

The shepherd passes Tony a pair of binoculars, points high up the mountainside.

– So how do you round them up?

– Simple. I have my bike and a bag of salt. Sheep will follow salt off the side of a cliff.

– Wow, who knew?

From inside the shepherds shack a radio is playing a Sex Pistols song.

Tony gets a kick out of hearing it.

– Are you kidding me the fucking Sex Pistols?

The shepherd shrugs his shoulders, grunts.

– Inglese.

– Yes, they are definitely English.

The shepherd reaches for the bottle of Ginepro, refills their glasses.

– *God save the queen!*

They toast.

Tony looks round to the director, a big smile on his face.

We can't use this crap, thinks the director.

Chris instinctively looks over his shoulder as she calls *cut*.

– Yeah yeah, you've got no soul, you know that right?

An awkward moment, perhaps unintentional, possibly bullying, but definitely throwing a darker shade. The fixer is busy on his phone arranging times for the next locations.

– We got to pick it up Tony, okay? complains the director.

The bored flat tone has got under his skin. The director isn't falling for his shtick, not at all. The shepherd picks up on this, but can't understand what the problem could be. Underwhelmed by all of it he just wants the rest of the day to himself, just like they do.

– Just get a clean link to the cheese and we're good.

Tony scowls at her, nods to Chris.

– *Rolling*, the director barks.

– End slate, let's go.

Tony rolls his eyes.

– So those sheep, what are they for, cheese, milk or the pot? The shepherd's finger makes a circle in the air.

– *Tutti.*

He gets up and goes inside the cabin.

Tony smokes.

– *Cut. Moving on*, the director shouts.

Chris, his assistant and Tony huddle.

– After the fucking cheese shots how about we shoot rounding up the sheep on the bikes, you down with that?

Chris looks up the mountain.

– Come on!

– Out on that edge? No fucking way. That fucking trike is a death trap. You know how many people die on those things?

– Yeah, but it's usually famous people, right?

– Fuck you.

– You came up on it, for Christ's sake.

– I ain't going up there though.

– Pretty please.

Chris shakes his head, it's a game they play all round the world.

– No fucking way Tony.

Tony winks at Giulia, the camera assistant. She shakes her head.

– You got a long lens? This pussy ain't budging. Shoot that shit from here.

Giulia waves a long lens in a soft pouch.

– *Come on guys, let's shoot the fucking cheese*, shouts the director.

Tony turns back to his host, who has brought out a plate of cheese, honey and some bread.

Chris focuses.

– Rolling.

– And… action.

First up is a sweet fresh pecorino. Then the shepherd brings out a small bucket covered in cloth, which he removes and they can all smell what's inside.

The cheese is soft, and Tony spreads it on the bread with a knife. Chris moves in for a closeup. Bruzzu.

– This one is super strong, oh yes, fermented straight from the ewe, with spices I think, perhaps chilli?

The shepherd nods, he likes it spicy.

Tony spreads another slab of bread.

– Almost wrong but soo good. As hard to get this into the US as cocaine, scrap that, harder.

– *Tony!* the director shouts from the trike where she is staring into the monitor. He eyeballs her through the lens.

– You feel close to the moon up here?

The shepherd is caught off guard and worries the crucifix at his neck.

– They love it.

– Who?

– The sheep. Sora luna. Their big sister.

– Wow, that's cool. Shepherd in the sky, sort of right? You wanna go round them up?

– Si, certo.

They shake hands.

– Cut! Tony! Great link!

– She speaks! I need a cigarette.

Tony and Chris chuckle. A director on this show has little power or indeed input. She lets them get on with it, within reason, patrolling the perimeter of what will be useable in an edit. An edit she will not be involved in. Guns for hire can go off for this reason but not this one, she knows what she signed on for. It's a machine. She's there to earn money, add to her CV and move on up to another, hopefully better, gig. Few shoot over three episodes consecutively, they only ship for short tours as the crew likes to say. Pirates always prefer the cook to the captain.

– Let's get a move on, enough already with the shepherd.

Tony crashes an unlit cigarette under his boot.

– So cruel. You ever see *La Terra Trema*?

– That the one about fishing?

– Really?

– Sophomore year film studies Tony. Neo realism, and the post-war blah blah in Italian cinema.

– Wow, kids these days. My bad.

She flips him the finger, but with a smile on her face. *Fuck it, in two weeks' time I'll be on the beach in Waikiki.*

The shepherd is oblivious to everyone but Tony.

– You ready to go?

– Fuck yeah, let's do it.

Tony kicks-starts the Kawasaki, Chris screws on the long lens and the shepherd and Tony burn rubber up onto the mountain. The director shrugs her shoulders, walks over to the Portakabin and tries some of the cheese and a shot of Ginepro.

*

The crew walk back to base along the tree line. Bright sunshine, but then as soon as they cross into shade, thigh deep in snow. A bifurcated landscape. The fixer shushes the crew, gestures them to get down and follow him silently. There is something he wants to show them, just up ahead. They crawl forward towards the edge of a tree line. Tony is in a great mood, throwing himself into the moment which is a kind of his trademark, his attitude on and off camera. On a good day. As they crest the grassy ridge, a huge natural bowl opens up below them. It's full of marmots, cartoonlike oversize rodents sniffing the air and not liking what they smell. They shoot down into their burrows in the blink of an eye; the crew getting up, running down the steep incline for the sheer hell of it. The fixer lopes down to the centre of the natural bowl and points out a carved horizontal stone table. He runs his fingers along a runnel gouged into both sides of the raised stone plinth, opens a bottle of water, pouring it onto the stone, and they watch it run off through the ancient carved channel.

– Per il sangue, he says.

– Cool.

Tony lies down on the altar, plays dead. Above him, the golden eagles circle.

I am a rabbit, he thinks.

Back in the sun, they eat lunch. Hot chocolate from a thermos, Focaccia Rosso e Sardinara, fresh wild boar salami, ruby red, soft tomatoes, local pecorino and bottles of Moretti. Tony hands the first one to the director, Mandy. They clink bottles.

– Not so bad, right?

She nods. *What a dick.*

Later, the van twists and turns its way back down to the village.

A tired Tony looks at his schedule and eyeballs the fixer.

– So what's next? Says here the local olive oil blight. Are you kidding me? Come on already, I mean, who cares? Show me the bones of this place. Like that fucking Neolithic altar, the fucking menhir, the hunters, let's find that on a plate.

The fixer looks around for support. The director is on her phone, texting the East Coast, her family are up.

A researcher's voice, young, she didn't even get out of the van, working her laptop, printing out schedules...

– Tomorrow we have a cooking segment, local resto, cool old cook with a story, farinata, think chickpea pizza, and then Saturday a local group of boar hunters, says here Second World War backstory, yada yadda, starvation, charcuterie and an illicit love story...

But Tony has already fallen asleep wrapped up to the eyeballs in his very warm Canada Goose parka.

*

1. Wide Establishing shot of Tony entering restaurant by the curve of a river. (Music cue TBD/Sex Pistols?)
2. Wood smoke trails into the sky against mountains.
3. Mid shot: A heavy plastic awning covers the outside terrace where old men and sit, drink, smoke and gossip.

*

Later, on the balcony of the hotel room, just him and Chris, wrapped up, drinking. Tony in a reflective mood.

– Wow, nobody told me about the old chick with the scar. She came to New York to be a model, hung out on the Lower East Side, what must have been early '70s, went to CBGB's when it was a biker bar for fuck's sake, had a motorbike crash, well her boyfriend crashed their bike on a trip upstate, after she got out of the hospital she came home and that's all she wrote.

– She tell you all that?

– Who the fuck else would tell me that?

– I mean why tell a stranger the tragedy of your life just like that.

Tony shrugs, he expects the story of people's lives – he collects them.

– Fucking boyfriend escaped without a scratch.

– I had this friend – he had a thing for disabled girls, always wanted to go out with somebody with one leg, so he could wheel her around you know, I mean he didn't just want to fuck her, but be like her knight in shining armour...

– Where's this going, arsehole?

– I mean, you got a thing for…
– You, my friend, are a fucking pig.

*

The crew cram into the kitchen.

4. Wide shot of interior.
5. Handheld mid shots (various) of cook (Gloria) – the story of farinata.
6. Cutaways of people/location/animated sequence of map/pirate raids.

– Don't worry I prepared some yesterday. She smiles, pulling another bowl out of the fridge.

– From Genoa to the world. In Punta del Este, in San Paolo, from Buenos Aires to Caracas, you will find our poor *faine*, food of the poor, of migrants, the dispossessed, which first came to us from Africa.

– Yeah, I had the chickpea fritters in Algeria, Libya, you getting this Chris?

As if he wasn't. Chris smiles.

– The story goes that after a big battle, captive rowers and victorious Genovese sailors were caught out in a storm. Sacks of chickpeas got soaked and a barrel of oil spilt in the same hold. The storm passed, the wind died, becalmed, friend and foe alike, all they had to eat was this mush of salty chickpea paste and oil. Left in the sun to bake, they discovered an unexpected delicacy and also survived to tell the tale.

– Wow! Can't wait to taste some!

– Nice! The origin story of farinata. *Love it!* shouts Mandy from the monitor out on the terrace. Tony pulls a surprised face into camera and turns back to Gloria, who pours the mixture into a copper pan spitting with oil, and pushes this into the fire, carefully levelling the pan with chips of wood.

– This smell, burning wood and baking chickpea, is ancient, you can find it anywhere in the world.

– And cut!

– Ten minutes, time for a cigarette, you want one? Gloria nods. They step outside, Gloria unaffected by the crew, or indeed by Tony, anyone.

– You like Chinese food? she asks him.

– Hell yes, I love it.

– Here in Italy it is shit, I don't know why, perhaps not enough people like it? Which is why I make it, I make it, hand-pulled noodles and a spicy broth, the same as pasta, don't get me started, the same things, the same food, different spices, from Genoa to the world and back…

– Oh my god, that is so true, I once took a jar of pesto with me up the Mekong Delta, I'm not shitting you, just to prove the same thing, we boiled the noodles, added the pesto, and it tasted exactly the same as right here.

*

Gloria takes the farinata out of the oven, slightly crispy on top – the smell of the rosemary and onion floods the room – they pick it with their fingers, blowing on them and eating straight from the *testo*, the copper pan. Tony dives in.

– Gloria, this is glorious.

She smiles, watches Tony eating, eating with such passion and attention to what it is he is eating, lost in the moment of eating.

– Now we make it with whatever we like, for flavour, for surprise, rosemary, onions, we can make what you like, sausage, gorgonzola, white fish, here in the fire, out of our very own Sciamadda!

– So freaking delicious, I'm thirsty.

She gestures for everyone to help themselves and the crew tuck into the big pan of farinata, her middle-aged son Giovanni brings out carafes of wine. They sit at the small bar. It's like she can't leave him be. It's not flirting, but close, he has sparked her memories of America, a memory that soon curdles.

– My granddaughter Elizabeth now uses tuna, nduja, aschuigi, for the tourists in the summer, come back when the whole valley is busy, six, seven restaurants, in fact why you come here now in the winter? For what? Authenticity? For the chestnuts, Madonna!

*

On the balcony it's cold, but the two of them can't seem to rouse themselves enough to turn it in.

– She's great, should have her own show, and what about that scar? You're just a heathen, the romance of this valley, it's right there on her face.

Tony looks over at Chris, who has nodded off.

*

– Let's start with something simple. How about walking shots? I can look interested left and right, here's a cafe blah blah, an old Roman bridge bada bing, perhaps slow mo, then I literally have to do nothing other than walk, super slow mo, even less so...

The crew were on edge, sometimes Tony got mean like this. Like a comedown from the high he gets from the people he meets, he's jonesing for his next fix. A change in weather. It's cold and wet on the streets of the village. A slow day to shoot pick-ups and get on each other's nerves. Mandy has retreated back into her WhatsApp reverie, the shoot runs on nervy auto. Chris stays behind the camera, leaving it to the producer to wrangle Tony, who stands in the middle of the road staring at his phone like he's going to crush it. Nobody interrupts him, the crew look down at their phones as if there's been a sudden gold rush online. After a few hours of this Tony's had enough. They break for lunch, the crew piling into the van to take them to a restaurant down on the coast.

– First things first, cigarettes.

He goes to the machine and feeds it. Nothing. It's eaten his money. He pushes the refund button. Nope. Slams the side of it like a pinball machine. Nada. Tony kicks it, walks away.

– Fuckin' shithole, he mumbles.

Tony goes into what looks like a closed-up restaurant, pulling the door hard to open it. Inside Aldo is smoking.

– Hey, you got any cigarettes?

Tony gestures outside.

– The fucking machine ate my fucking money.

He mimes kicking the shit out of it. Aldo laughs, offers him the pack on the table.

– Giusto!

– You speak English?

– Yes, sure.

Aldo eyes him up, reads him.

– You want a drink?

– Fuck yes.

Aldo lights him.

Tony pulls up a stool at the bar.

– Smoking indoors. Heaven.

Aldo looks out of the window at the van full of people.

– They with you?

– Nope.

– Huh. You hungry?

– You got a free table?

Aldo looks around the empty room, pulls a face.

– You're in luck, it's early.

– What's on the menu?

– It's cold outside. summers finished, you like Bollito? I cooked enough for...

Tony loves Bollito: brisket, tongue, potatoes and a fucking sharp salsa verde to cut through it.

Aldo eyes the window, the van outside.

Tony weighs the situation up. He's been here many times before.

He knows who I am, right? Wants the whole crew to eat at his restaurant, make some money, and why not? Wants us to maybe film him, have our photo taken together so he can put it up on the fucking wall, like Willy Wonka's golden ticket, or am I being unfair? I fucking came in here, because of my stupid bad mood. For fuck's sake, I don't know up from down anymore.

Tony goes to the door and whistles his crew inside.

*

The room is busy, the crew at the back, a table of workers from the quarry and regulars popping in to see what all the fuss is about – *this TV guy Anthony Bourdain, what the fuck is he doing here? Is he Italian or what?*

Tony is back on form and Aldo is in his element, furtively calling his staff to get at least one of them to come in – *there's a lunchtime rush on, here! Where else, you fucking moron, a film crew yes, Americans* – cuffing them round the head for gawping when they turn up, hurrying them out into the dining room with the orders. All the food he was going to have to throw away, because it's been another slow, shit week, now it's going to be eaten.

First up and bowls of steaming ravioli, chestnut and pumpkin.

– *Oh, my god. That's good.*

With a nod from Mandy, Chris and his assistant go out to the van to get the camera and a directional microphone. He knows the routine: when Tony finds something not on the schedule, he has to film it – *This is the real stuff, off the cuff, life happening ad hoc, in the moment, fuck the schedule, look at this guy, it's just what the show needs, the unexpected, a chef in his empty restaurant, what could be more poignant than that? See him? This Aldo guy, that's me. We're filming it.*

Tony doesn't need to say it. That's his power.

The fixer arrives. He argues with Mandy. *Why are you here, this place is a shithole.*

He stares at his watch.

My brother-in-law opened especially for us, it's arranged.

Ask the boss, she says, she has surrendered, two more days and then home.

Tony blanks him. The door bursts open and Augustin appears, momentarily warming himself by the pellet burner before stumbling between the table to sit down right opposite Anthony Bourdain. He still has a nose for what's going on, when sober enough to use it.

Oh no, who's this guy, somebody thinks.

One of your oldest fans, Tony, thinks another.

Are there any women in this fucking village or what?

Here we go…

My cousin is going to kill me…

A beat of pregnant silence, Augustin gathers himself before roaring with booze and memory twice removed.

– I was in America!

This guy looks like Grizzly fucking Adams.

– Oh yeah, what did you think?

– A place full of arseholes.

– That's a lot of arseholes my friend.

Cheers go up all around, led by Tony, drinks poured into proffered glasses. Augustin smiles, takes his glass and wanders off to sit by himself. Satisfied, he doesn't say another word.

Aldo brings out the first steaming dish of Bollito. More applause, Tony and his crew are in their comfort zone, they film, they eat.

The fixer whispers to the director.

– How can you use this rubbish on television? There's no view, nothing, just…

– Voiceover and cutaways, every time.

She chuckles pours them both some wine.

Tony steps outside with Aldo.

Aldo stamps his feet, Tony doesn't react to the cold.

– You know in the summer I like to make sushi, fish tacos, grill lobsters.

– For the tourists, right?

– No, for me, they order it for sure but fuck them, I make what I like. I used to travel…

– Before you had a restaurant.

– Certo. I think about all the things I could make.

Tony shrugs.

– I used to have a restaurant and now I travel. I don't miss it.

– You still enjoy cooking?

Tony shakes his head.

– Nope. Sometimes I miss the people, being in the kitchen, but not the hours and making thirty plates of the same fucking thing, no. I don't miss that at all.

Aldo smiles.

– I love cooking. Being by myself in the kitchen. People get on my fucking nerves.

– I hear that.

– You should have met my father. He loved cooking but never once in his life worked in a restaurant. He would sit right there and *fagioli sgusciati*, you know, take the beans out of their skin.

– The dream.

– But you get to visit so many places, amazing no?

– Oh, I've been everywhere.

– And?

– And what? If I stop, I'll die.

Aldo tries to place this phrase.

– *Se mi fermo morirò.*

The penny drops.

– Ah si, Richard Pryor!

He mimics the Black American comedian running down the street with his hair on fire.

They sit on the step by the kitchen. Aldo gestures with his chin, as if taking in all of existence. He lights another cigarette.

Tony digs this, he really digs it.

Aldo pours them both a glass from a bottle in his apron pocket.

– *Minchiia*.

Back inside and the pirates have taken over, another ship to board and ransack, from which to wring every pleasure, every drop. It's late afternoon and a few local girls arrive and out of nowhere it's a party. This happens *when the crew turn up* all over the world, two hundred days a year. They expect it to happen, or at the very least don't miss a beat every time it does. They take their pleasure where they find it. Lunchtime, evening, Mondays even, each time no different from another, but with a scrolling backdrop. For the locals it is a one-off, the world visits them, and they indulge it, hungry for the novelty, and nothing wrong with the money being spent either.

But always somebody with their nose out of joint, which if you think about it must add up...

Hai La Luna Storta.[27]

They sat down and ate and drank their fill, while here I am dying of thirst.

Aldo and Tony are now talking music, arguing what to play on the stereo next, Ramones, the Stones or MC5. They both share the same predictable taste in music.

---

27   To carry round a crooked moon / to be in a foul mood.

New York, just like I pictured it. Skyscrapers and everything.

Everybody else just fades away.

Nobody noticed us leave the restaurant. Me, the van driver, wardrobe girl and grip, already drunk. What would I say to my brother-in-law, opening his restaurant for us out of season? Who would pay for the fish? The fucking director doesn't listen to me. We go back to the hotel, drink a few more beers and grappas in the empty bar. I was only on board for a few weeks, I should have just been happy to take the money. I think Tony shook my hand when he got off the plane before he and his cameraman jumped into a cab to go for supper with an old friend, they would see me in San Remo for the preproduction meeting the next morning. Bastards. Nice to meet you too.

They were as happy as happy could be,
While here I sit grinding my teeth.

Nobody likes to be left out, to feel superfluous to what is going on, to have no influence, to just pick up the pieces after them, the bosses. Somehow I must have made a bad impression, or perhaps no impression at all. I didn't say anything interesting, so decided from that moment on to say very little at all. I wished them all to hell. Inside, I know I would have turned on a coin to wish them every happiness if only I could have been part of it, one small part of their story, for somebody to say, 'thanks for a great shoot and amazing locations at good prices, because of your hard work we had a great time in Liguria.'

Nobody wants nothing.

They had a big feast. I was there, under the table. They threw me a bone, which hit me on the nose and stuck for good.

Perhaps I made myself a fool, but a fool I felt nonetheless. It still rankles, my face flushes with the memory of it. My humiliation which should have been my triumph, fixer for an episode of the famous CNN show Parts Unknown. *Of all the places to come in Italy, why here? Nothing to see here. You wasted your time. I should have said that, right at the end, all paid up and fuck you very much.*

But I kept that to myself.

My wife tells me I am too sensitive, that I shouldn't let things wind me up. Work is work, just accept it for what it is. To move on and not take offence. Instead, I feel every new slight as one too many, one on top of another, the exquisite pain of wound inflicted on wound, skin peeled back and salted. I can't help it. Every funny look, or overheard exchange I only catch the end of, laughter I had no part in making, the film set a trap in which to catch and flay me. I was paid well, made sure of that, wouldn't let the stingy producers screw me over, but in the great division of life (one of many swords that hang over our heads before falling remorselessly time and time again) I am one of its losers.

Their life was happy and long;
But we, poor we, sing another song.

I hated Tony for not liking me, pathetic I know. How was I to know then that this was what we truly had in common? If only I could have shared with him that which I hid – like he did – that I too was suffering, that every change of schedule – a schedule I had spent weeks preparing – on which I wasn't consulted, at every joke that wasn't shared, every meal that went on long into the night with people he had just met and to which I was not invited. Two weeks alone with the truth of myself.

My youth has gone to the ends of the earth to die in the silence of the truth.

I had hate inside me, a terrible desire to wreak havoc and revenge on those who had no part in making me feel like this and I

*knew that for the truth in the moment of hating them – ruining
even that pleasure – but still riding the lie of it, unable to let go of
the fantasy of how much better than (all of) them I was, cleverer,
kinder, funnier, how could they be so blind not to see me for who I
really was.*

**The truth is an endless death agony. The truth is death.
You have to choose: death or lies.**[28]

*But perhaps I hadn't hidden well enough my sickness, my
weakness in the face of failure, my inability to get up, brush myself
down and go again like so many others. My need to be liked (do I
blame my parents for this, my childhood?) If I was somebody else,
I would shy away from me.*

*The truth of who I am eats me alive. It is a living purgatory and
I don't even have the strength to ask myself why this is the case,
how did I come to be me?*

*Tony burned through his life until there was nothing left, while
I still burn endlessly with shame. Now he's dead and I'm not, so
fuck him.*

---

28   Journey to the End of Night, Céline.

TEMPESTA

When he had spoken, he reversed his trident and struck
the hollow mountain on the side: and the winds formed
ranks,
rushed out by the door he'd made and whirled across the
earth.
— Virgil, *Aeneid*, Book 1

Usually when we go to bed at night, we assume that nothing drastic will happen to the world in our absence. In the morning when we pull back the curtains, open the window and look out, there should be no surprises. Life may fray at the edges, the day-to-day squabbles of romance, work, childcare, the annoyances of city life, of bins not being emptied on their allotted days, cars scratched, post delayed, colleagues off sick. Minor grievances are all part of the granularity of life however you live it. When we rush out to work in the morning, slamming the front door behind us, or hastily (because we are running late) prod, prod, prod the call button for the lift, mostly *it's all still there and it all still works.* The lift may be out of order, if so you take the stairs. You run for the bus, catch it just in time or get the next one. There are always options. The noise, the bustle, the changing moods and random behaviour of people living together, presents itself as one immutable whole. *The eternal city, the city that never sleeps* implies continuity and we are a part of that. This is the comfort of living in a city. This assumption is obviously a privilege, but it is also a powerful illusion, not dissimilar to the trick played by movie cameras running at twenty-five frames per second.

Verisimilitude, seamless movement.

In the countryside the seasons bring both surprise and predictability. Farmers take a gamble on what crops to plant, what animals to rear. Planting and harvesting proceed rhythmically but also contain the possibility of unexpected outcomes: bumper crops or unexpected blight, fluctuating prices, uncontrollable costs that either bring fat or squeeze margins thereby determining fortunes. Have we made enough profit to buy that new tractor, do we just about keep our heads above water for another year, or finally, after so many years of hard work, sink without a trace?

Chance is immutable, from strangers on a train to Heisenberg's principle of uncertainty. You just never know.

Yet we persist.

For more than twenty summers I have spent a lot of time at a river which is a ten-minute walk from our house. The rocks form a natural pool, eight feet deep in places, upstream from the village. There had been a medieval or perhaps Roman bridge across the river, and you can dive from the ruins of one of its towers. From blurred Kodak colour snaps of small children splashing about in inflatable armbands, through sharper and sharper digital photos of youngsters swimming and jumping in, to slow-motion videos of teenagers sunbathing, diving, bombs and other dares, mini home movies edited at first by me, to whatever soundtrack we listened to that summer ('When September Comes' by Green Day being one that comes to mind, 'Someone like you' by Adele another).

Videos we would share each Christmas, including latterly underwater shots and rolling movie titles. The river marked the passage of our lives. Children, parents, grandparents and friends sunning ourselves on rocks, picnics of cheese, bread, tomatoes and salami from the local *alimentari* and cold beers retrieved from string bags in the water, stomachs big and small, haircuts long and short, balding men and greying women; this place held our record. Each visit layered on top of the last in our memory, experienced through the continuity and permanence suggested by déjà vu, which grows stronger with the passing of the years. Hundreds of photos taken from similar angles and vantage points, of the same returning cast of characters doing the same things as they themselves change. The sort of maudlin sequences now edited by an iPhoto algorithm set to music which pops up 'for you' on your home screen. High tech prompting low melancholy. Before you die, it won't be your life that flashes before your eyes but a curated version of it set to music, bittersweet, a rotten apple, a gift for which we traded our lives, leasing ourselves, outsourcing our memory.

We showed the kids how to dam the river when the water level dropped in high summer. We took shelter under the branches of trees during flash thunderstorms, the surface of the water strafed by machine-gun fire at which we would laugh uncontrollably, such a ridiculous downpour, and then it stopped just like that and you could hear the respite in the trees. The water regained its composure; the air reclaimed its territory, an atmosphere of tentative calm prevailed, as if stepping onto the field of battle not knowing if the fighting was really over.

We shared the space with locals and other visitors, reading and talking, bathing ourselves on hot slabs of rock by the pool, communication was bits and pieces of English, Italian, German, French and Dutch, adequate for genial conversation, exchanges of pleasantries, from extracting restaurant recommendations from locals, simple questions and answers worked out with or without recourse to pocket dictionaries (or, latterly, Google Translate), to *where are you from, ah Londra!* and all that comes of that, the name of your home but also a world city, one visited long ago or to be visited in the future.

'I want to come to London,' said one of the Libere Nantes refugee footballers years before, and I didn't question that at all, didn't put him off or criticise London itself, didn't say it was expensive, that there were few good jobs, the economy is shit. For I lived there, I had a home, a job (of sorts), why put a downer on this young man's dream? Why wouldn't somebody want to come here to seek asylum if not their fortune? What did they have to lose, surely that was their choice to make, to weigh up the pros and cons, not anyone else's, certainly not mine.

Across the river was a steep forested hillside, although I have never set foot there. I stayed by the water, dipping in and out, a sun worshipper of sorts, albeit a fidgety one, gazing up at the sun when it passed behind the scant clouds, eventually releasing me when it sank behind the hillside, no clock told the time better than the sun.

Upstream from habitation the water ran clean, although once some Danish tourists showered in the river leaving dirty shampoo bubbles behind, eddies of scum gathered in rocky crags, catching water skaters and spiders unaware. Later, walking back up to the house, we passed their caravan, piled high with mountain bikes and kayaks. I wished it would roll away down the hill. It didn't budge. They had parked by the water fountain in which the goldfish lived. If the Danes fucked with them, I would set their van on fire.

Our dog Stella enjoyed barking anxiously every time any of us ventured near the water, a habit that never abated over the sixteen years of her lifetime. Infuriating but also exactly what it means to have a dog, the responsibility of it, of the bond it creates, bigger than the both of you.

Let's go river.

The demotic of youth.

And so the valley, the river, the house and terrace with its Cinemascope framing, the permanent shape and outline of the mountain opposite; a sleeping dragon slouched across rock, shedding its coat every winter, or perhaps a dinosaur, a huge benign herbivore, changing with the seasons but with immutable bones, the shape of the world, became over time cardinal points of my horizon. Wherever else in the world I go, they come with me and I go back to them, borrowed and renewed like books or films from a library, sound and image without the characteristics of *memories* – which get all silted up the older they get, ox-bow lakes that meander to no good purpose – instead they are an anchor, around which the world flows, an anchor which holds fast.

*

The storm when it came was predictably out of the blue. A deus ex machina, a blessed relief from the pandemic, then in its first year.

Two full days without mobile reception and then suddenly the phones that still had a charge – newer models with better batteries – started pinging one after the other, resuming their role as our focus of attention. But we remarked on their absence, reminding ourselves of what life had been like. The spell was broken, but then quickly recast. It was like 9/11 all over again, time suspended, then restarted, and the outside world, whatever remained of it, flooded back, announcing itself shrilly.

The moment we landed everybody turned on their phones in what felt like unison, a symphony of pings and a cacophony of vibration heralding our miraculous arrival, delivering us the news while making news ourselves.

These sounds even if from just a couple of phones has always at some level triggered pieces of this memory.

Each of us has a ping (imagine we are icebergs, and the ping is just the bit you can hear), signposting a chorus of alarm, what lies beneath each of us, confirming just how alike we all are.

Hope you okay!!!?
Have you heard the news?
Call me when u get this!
Call me.
I love you.

Are you there?

We love you. X. Text me as soon as you get this.

I try to imagine a person whose phone doesn't ping, somebody truly free in the world, yet burdened with the responsibility of what that freedom means, its price, somebody truly alone.

On 9/11 I had been on a flight to LA which turned back to Heathrow halfway across the Atlantic, the ashen faces of the crew shading the *American airspace has been closed* line that came over the tannoy. Drinking at the bar (why not, the plane was probably fucked) we knew there was something they were not telling us. *We,* by which I mean myself and a complete stranger, an American lawyer, as this emergency (for how could it be anything but) had gifted us something in common (the event itself), which just being on the same flight had not.

Just like the storm.

*

That evening we attempted to eat our way through the menu at the new restaurant in the village, La Capra Pazza. I was with my publisher, his first time in the valley. The *Crazy Goat* was run by two young women cooking out of a compact domestic kitchen; they and their restaurant had appeared fully formed, as if by magic down on the main road. Full of passion for people, tradition, mischief and pleasure, with such an inquisitive energy, both emotional and kinetic, sparking off in so many directions that you think it can't last, that this enthusiasm must in the end be blunted by life, worn out by the very thing it celebrates.

But so far so good, why shouldn't it last? Perhaps the *Crazy Goat* was born of the storm itself, I had never noticed it before, there must be a God in there somewhere, a fabulous explanation, something mercurial wrought in the two women, mineral even, in their constitution, literally touchstones for pleasure and celebration, salt licks for our gastronomic vices.

By the time our antipasti arrived the rain was already constant, it can last for hours like this with no let up, so we settled in for a long night of food and wine, starting with a soft wild boar salami and a slate of cheeses (pecorino, Mucca and a dollop of Bruzzo) with honey and homemade chilli jam condiments. Salty food to get our juices flowing with which we slaked our thirst on a carafe of fizzy house white.

The downpour intensified, from inside you could hear an increase in volume as it hit the ground, bouncing off the tarmac of the road and off the stone steps up to the terrace, splashing back up into the air before running off, rain from below. The wind picked up, rattling the windows, whistling through drainpipes and working itself under loose roof tiles. The acoustics both amplified and shifted tonally. Trying to have a cigarette outside was proving impossible, and those that tried and failed ended up sharing a joke about it, how ridiculous and wouldn't they let us smoke inside just this once. So we came back inside and the cooks handed us towels, shaking their heads as they went back and forth from the kitchen, and later they did let us smoke inside. The thunder started, distant at first but coming closer and closer. I timed the intervals using the timer on my phone, which somehow wasn't the same as looking at a watch. Rivulets of water snaked under the door towards our feet. Lightning cracks soon followed, and the electricity cut out before we had even got to the second pasta dish – a simple burro e salvia ravioli – but our hosts brought candles and reassured us they had enough gas to cook with, so the evening would continue. A small cheer went up from the tables. The storm didn't perturb them, focused as they were on cooking and serving their guests. The scene reset itself. We could smell the twenty-four-hour slow and low braised beef bubbling away on the stove. Sensory overload: thyme, onion, capers, bay leaf and rosemary wafted from the kitchen, feelings of comfort contradicted by awareness of jeopardy, the intimacy suggested by soft candlelight punctuated by blinding flashes of white lightning arcs; cosmic portraits of us at our tables, while these pungent aromas and the skein of cigarette smoke hung in the air all around, reminiscent of times past. A nostalgic moment, characterised by wet feet, gusts of wind, staccato laughter edged with a subtle and skittish fear and the proximity of strangers, a moment out of time which loosened our tongues.

Next up was a dish of delicately sliced, almost shaved mushroom steeped in olive oil and lemon juice, sprinkled with Parmigiano, salt and pepper, which exploded onto our palates electrolysed by a sharp minerally white, not Vermentino, but something flat and full flavoured, possibly a Gavi from Alessandria just over the border in Piedmont. Crisp acidity with notes of peach, almond with a floral nose yet still bone dry like the best of German Rieslings. Wow, the alchemy of that combination, earthy mushroom, bass flavour to the high notes of both wine and the raging storm outside.

We soon grew accustomed to the uniqueness of the situation and re-focused on the task at hand, allowing it to be framed by unforeseen events come what may. In fact, the whole room took courage from the storm raging outside, drew on its power somehow, and fortifying our appetites as we worked our way slowly but surely towards the summit, the final dish, Capra e Fagioli! Roasted goat and beans that had defeated us on three previous attempts but tonight by some strange alchemy it was still firmly in our sights.

Huge slabs of focaccia Rosmario e Cipolle and blood-red sardinara both fresh from the oven kept on coming. *No more fucking bread!* we cried. They sent it out to sabotage us, to stop us getting to the end, to keep the summit tantalisingly out of reach, yet to edge us – sex and food as ever entwined – primed for another attempt, to go again; this was the essence of the cook's mischief, to tease our greed, to bloat us out, blocking up our guts, impossible as it was to take a shit in their small shared toilet and despite all the wine we drank to lubricate our bowels, aid our digestion, all of this did nothing other than kick the can down the road, to the biggest shit of all later on, perhaps after coffee, or so stuffed we were and would be, to the next day, after a night of wild dreams, burps and burbles. Yet we couldn't resist, whatever they brought we ate.

No more fucking bread! and the two women laughed and scolded us for being pussies, weak, not man enough, cuckolds almost, *a better man would eat it all and want more!* Instead, bringing us carafes of a heavier red – possibly a Sangiovese – to bolster us for the final ascent. First the beef, tender as the night (but not this night!), falling off the bone into the deepest of flavours, onion and thyme, wine, sage, garlic, marjoram with just a hint of cinnamon, foundational flavours of the earth to be topped only by the lightness of touch delivered by the roasted goat garlanded by the sweetness of nutmeg and clove that awaited us at the end.

Delirious, I imagined being fattened up for sacrifice, so eager were they to offer us up to the storm...

The cooks ladled second helpings onto our plates, holding back the goat until the whole room had polished off the beef. To a soundtrack of groans and by now tamped down laughter and little conversation – what more was there to say? – we ate on into the night while outside the storm worsened, building itself up to something, God knows what. The rain was now a wall of water and we diners sat as if under a diving bell. Whatever sounds we made took on a strange quality, a reverberation, rebounding off the rain itself. The eight of us sitting in the almost dark, immobile and immersed in the smell of food still piled on our plates and from the cooling pans in the kitchen, were paragons of gluttony, despite the tuts and sly long faces pulled by our hosts in mock horror at all the food we had left uneaten. Wood burned in the stove and over pudding (homemade ice cream, panna cotta, smears of raspberry jam) we enjoyed the crack, the fitful spits of sparks and hissing of the flames.

We were undone, and they ushered us out. We said our goodbyes which took the form of hugs, kissed cheeks, exclamations and handshakes. We left the safety of the restaurant and ran into a cataract of water. We groped our way to the car, which was only feet away. To drive back up the hill involved opening the windows and sticking heads out to make sure we didn't drive off the edge. The car immediately flooded, the windscreen liquified. Whatever light there was became the light you see underwater from sinking ships or cars in movies: milky, unreliable, occluding distances. Looking out through the windscreen was like being inside a bathysphere caught up in the turbulence of a riptide. I registered movement from the trees, smears of darkest green and browns against black filtered through three refractive surfaces, the rain, the windscreen and finally my glasses. Lightning flashes intermittently exploded inside the car, teasing us with glimpses of what was actually going on outside the car.

I get the car up to the house. Kit opens the passenger door and drops out of view, literally disappears through a curtain of water. I lean across and spy him lying in brambles on the edge of a fifty-foot drop to the terrace below. Unable to extricate himself, he flails about. I shout through rising laughter.

Don't move!

He was in danger of falling further into the brambles' clutches, probably forever. It was like being in vertical quicksand. Kit started laughing, then spluttering as the rain splashed across his mouth. It was a ridiculous situation. The iPhone torch did nothing in this type of situation, gave zero light. Unless I did something he would eventually fall through, thorns ripping him apart as he fell onto the terrace below.

I can't stop laughing as I lie in the road reaching with my arm, and water literally laps over me as it runs off the hillside. Somehow, I grab his hand, and start pulling him up; he clambers, getting purchase on the terrace wall. We roll over prone on the road, just out of range of the cars' headlights, in total darkness, we can't even see the silhouette of the house above us. Laughing until we almost drown. All that food and drink vapourised by adrenalin. Those fucking brambles will be the death of somebody…

Then I black out, and it's the morning. I get up and look out of the window.

Fuck me.

A terrace has collapsed into the road. The hire car sits under a dome of mud. The terrace below us obliterated. The cypresses, signatures of the house itself, have survived but the wood behind them looks devastated.

Downstairs the house is under a foot of water. I wade to the door and open it, letting the water pour out between my legs as I come outside. There is no sound, to be precise you could hear the absence of sound, you could hear the silence. The wind had blown itself out leaving an eerie vacuum.

Kit stumbles down in his boxers, punching his phone. It isn't working. I check mine, it's also out and I have only a little charge left. I check the lights, then the fuse box upstairs. There is no electricity. We venture down to the road like newborns.

What the fuck.

We dig out the car, in the expectation of finding it totally trashed. I didn't pay for excess insurance, who does? Goldcar will take me to the cleaners. God knows what it will cost to rebuild the terrace. Bit by bit we uncover the car and it emerges totally unscathed. Huge boulders and rocks pepper the road around it, but none seem to have hit it. A lucky break, although inside is a sea of mud from the open window, which will have to be cleaned out somehow. Rocks and tree branches block the main road, gouging huge holes out of the tarmac. We park up and walk down to the village. People stand about staring and prodding at phones that don't work. Others hold them up to try and snag reception like ravers in a club. People are talking about bridges knocked down, houses collapsed, the river breaking its banks and flooding both sides, washing away roads. Anybody dead? somebody asks. People shrug.

Who knows?

We walk up towards the next village, helping to shift debris as we go. Pickups, cars, tractors, Vespas stop and we help them get through, horns toot with thanks, hands shaken, jokes shared. A sense of a wonder at the power of nature creeps up on us. We share cigarettes and many exclamations of disbelief.

Madonna!

After a couple of hours we arrive, arms and legs aching, hungry and in need of a drink. It feels unseasonably warm and there is a strong wind gusting across the street and knocking over bins. Strange weather. A generator hums from the bar, we go inside and order some beers. Everyone is talking, repeating the same stories over and over, where they were last night, what they saw when they woke up, when was the last time something like this happened, what about the elderly in remote hamlets, people on ventilators, rumours of the dead, of livestock destroyed, hillsides collapsed. Faced with natural disaster we are left to deal with it collectively. We are our own first responders. Outsiders come later. Who knows how long the electricity will be out for? The oldest among us grew up before electrification, a fact they don't fail to remind us of. For now, it's gone. I half wished that this could be the new normal rather than an old one, as if electricity was a virus bringing with it all the problems of modern life.

A lot of food has to be cooked before it goes off, so barrels of charcoal are lit and people prepare for a huge communal lunch. A sense of festival energises us. Like a bank holiday but somehow pagan, granted to us, the survivors by nature. They bring trestle tables out from storage (a true sign of communality) and people come and go. A few emergency vehicles make it down from the top of the mountain and the villages beyond the pass. Their flashing lights and sirens add sound and fury to the drama, and we cheer them on their way down the valley to the hospital on the coast. Wine bottles appear from everywhere. The day feels like a scene from a movie, a movie without stars, just us, the extras.

Via walkie-talkie somebody hears that the valley road is cut off above Badalucco so these ambulances will have to go up and over the mountain and down into the adjacent valley, a two-hour trip instead of twenty-five minutes, and who knows if that route will stay open. Above and behind us (it feels like behind, but in reality the head of the valley lies north-east towards the border with France) from the villages of Creppo, Realdo and Verdeggia we have heard nothing. Half empty in the winter, those that live there are mostly old. Holdouts, the last of their generation they live under a huge sky, which they read like a newspaper. They sit by their porches and rate the storm against ones they have seen before.

The smell of barbecue, of roasting meat, wafts along the main street of the village. There is also the smell of diesel, woodsmoke and a strange scent of water and shingle, effluent from the river churned up by the storm. It has wiped out the Lago in the village leaving a sea of rock and silt but hardly a trickle of water. We stumbled around on it as if it were the surface of a stinking moon, amazed.

On the way back to the village we notice ochre patches on the surrounding hillsides where uprooted trees had dragged their roots down the steep hills and onto the riverbed. The hillsides are all now afflicted with these scabs, like scrofulous dogs.

After lunch there is music, an accordion, a guitar, for the first time in years something other than generic pop (I exaggerate). We lapse into a predictable appreciation of authenticity, in this authentic moment. We over-enjoy the moment. A perspective that always marks outsiders, bloodsuckers, culture vultures, parasites, cockroaches. I imagine Aldo here, centre of attention, hot and bothered behind a grill, handing out porchetta rolls, filling glasses with grappa and Ginepi, in his element, which was both people and nature, how we come together through food. He has always been a walker, foraging high on Mezzaluna and Monte Ceppo for mushrooms and herbs, sleeping in the most remote refugia. I hadn't seen him for a few years. Malik had left years ago also, to Sweden, where he would have had to learn another language. The few migrants that remained had blended in, faces in the village. They worked up and down the valley, cycled, took the bus, they spoke better Italian than most of us, vested as they were in surviving here. They were no longer that different, until perhaps the people on the posters that grew ragged on noticeboards between elections wanted to make something of it, some capital out of them again. Love and hate operate at either end of indifference, in the emotional cycles of humanity; they also beget each other through remorse. We can turn on a coin. It is hard to know our own true feelings, let alone those of others.

The woman who ran the witch shop also missed the storm, she had died in a fire or had caught and died of Covid after being burnt in a fire; I didn't have the powers of translation to divine which was the case. Either way, she was no longer around and her tourist trinket shop later became a popular takeaway pizza spot.

Eventually we got a lift home on the back of an Ape, the buzzing of its two-stroke engine ringing in my ears for hours afterwards. No more rain fell, but the temperature had plunged. Back at the house we built a fire and fell asleep in front of it fully dressed in our sleeping bags. It is never this cold in September, it's usually not this cold until February. Next morning there is still no reception (I wonder how many messages awaited me) but there is more traffic on the roads. We walk down to the river.

Our favourite spot had been obliterated, the riverbed scooped out, like a thumb had smeared away the details. Boulders, silt, earth had washed down from the hills surrounding the river, dragged down by the felled trees. The same trees that had smashed into bridges old and new. Sand and stones from upriver washed down in cascades of water surge, flushing out the whole of the valley into the sea. Like an enema. The mill tower had gone, its bricks thrown down into the river. Muddy mean-looking water trickled down a cleft in the middle, less than a foot deep. Nature's furniture had rearranged itself. People gathered themselves slowly. The storm had blown itself out; we were already living in the aftermath. Life took a breath, girding itself for what came next. In this space we experienced a magical two days out of our lives, yet firmly within the gyre of history.

The road had collapsed just below the restaurant, by the junction with the low road. Gloria had died of Covid only six weeks before. The place had been closed up, her son and granddaughter hadn't the heart to open for weeks. Now the road in front of the restaurant was in effect an extension of its covered terrace. Locals and others passing congregated in the street discussing what had happened, staring and pointing at the collapsed road and the puny-looking digger the council had got to clear the narrow stretch of tarmac that remained. Municipal police stood around smoking and offering opinions. Among the regulars the name on everybody's lips was Augustin, where had he been the night before, had anybody seen him. Augusto! Who was always around, sitting right here, it was like they had written him off, expected him to be part of the story of the storm and wanted nothing less than proof of this undeniable fact, the undeniable fact of his empty chair.

But he wasn't anywhere to be seen.

Giovanni came out of the kitchen with a couple of bottles of red, poured them all drinks and was soon deep in the telling of it with his friends and customers.

– There was this big crashing sound, my god I jumped out of bed to see what had happened, but it was hard to see anything because of the rain, I came outside the tarpaulin had ripped away, gone who knows where, my fucking torch was useless, I wasn't going out in that for it, but just then there was a huge flash and for a second everything lit up and right there...

He points with his finger at a spot right by the wall, a pile of rubble and a drop to the river.

– ...I saw a monster, a ghoul, a witch, a devil from children's stories, a face full of blood, strands of white hair stuck all over the face like seaweed, like a sea monster stumbling up from the river, clambering over the rocks, of course I didn't see all of that in a flash but my mind filled it in, in the darkness that came after I saw a face, as if burnt onto my retinas, a face I knew resolved there like in the darkroom of hell.

At this, he earns some cheers.

– One I could never forget, a face I knew too well. Augustin!

The small crowd explode with jeers and hoots of laughter, more wine is poured, and they toast the survival of their neighbour Augustin.

He had been on a bender since Gloria passed, as if you could tell the difference, nobody had seen him since the funeral. It was like the storm delivered him back from the dead!

Now, Giovanni was known for liking a drink but also for his florid language, which they say he learnt at college in Imperia. From books. Behind the bar were piles of them, thrillers mainly but some classics and also much-thumbed 1970s sex and horror pulp fiction. People borrowed them and they too enjoyed the florid prose, and tried them out on each other. People enjoyed how he talked and he enjoyed talking, which was why the restaurant had been such a success for so many years, the older locals remembered his father being a mean man of few words, and his mother, well...

– Imagine it, Augusto stumbling as if shipwrecked from the sea, dripping wet, a gash across his head, blood and water mingling, like Christ on his cross. I almost had a heart attack!

At this, chuckles and bravos.

– We embraced, and stumble inside together. I patch him up, we share a bottle and ride out the storm. My wife, she slept through the whole thing. Look, his Ape is right here below us, smashed to pieces, and he's only got but one scratch. What can we do with him, he's the bane of my family, my daughter wants to leave and set up her own restaurant anywhere so long as it's a place where he isn't, if you can believe that! Papa, she says, it's me or him! And he's not even family!

More laughter and the group retires to the terrace tables, now bereft of tarpaulin, an altogether more bucolic setting.

Giovanni's daughter Alicia brings out more wine, cheese and some salami, leaning into the table. The regulars peer at her, to see if the fire in her eyes is still burning.

– What are you looking at, idiots!

Yes! Smiles and a few more cheers, she reminds them of Gloria, they go quiet, emotions stirred by this storm.

She knows what they have been talking about, the rubbish her father can talk.

Augustin.

– Not even God can take him from us, she mutters.

– That man has nine, possibly even ten lives!

The conversation eventually moves on to other local characters and rascals, past and present, who seemed to survive no matter what. A natural response, joining the dots, making sense of life in the aftermath of a disaster. Who better to talk about than those who stuck two fingers up at the world, the rules and the people that followed them: *doing the right thing and for what?* Survivors, somehow charmed. Characters who live according to their own instincts and all the better for it. Folk Memory is nothing more than their tall tales, of the things they did, or wish they had done, the places they had been and others they only dreamed of, what the people had been like there, or how they imagined they were. But we were not them and they maligned us, but for all that they made us feel part of a bigger story.

Of Augustin himself there was no sign, it was enough to know that he had survived and by talking of him they shared his good luck in being alive, of surviving not just the storm, for that was just bad weather, but of everything else that plagued them. After the storm he became a sign, if only for a short while.

*

Mobile reception and electricity returned on the morning of the third day and after a flurry of texts and calls we head out, up and over the hill to reach the coast and a night in San Remo before catching the plane home the following morning. Three big climbs but only a few tree trunks blocking our path, which we cleared. Above the tree line we could see clear to the coast and the open sea. In the distance on a clear day – visibility is best in the winter or early spring – you can spy the shadowy outline of Corsica.

I once met an old woman in her mid-nineties who lived right up in the crux of our valley, in a high mountain village, who had never been to the coast, had never seen the sea. When she was young, many had left to find work, but mostly they just found trouble, by which she meant money, something she didn't like. She said people smelt of where they had been, she could smell the sea on them, a nasty stink. Perhaps she took metaphor literally, or was a little senile, or she meant the smell of fish, the stink of the sea on the clothes of those that got work on fishing boats.

Other people went to sea and never came back. Her son sent her packages from America. One package comprised a salami wrapped up in dollar bills. This became a village joke, the American salami and all the stamps it needed to reach them. We ate it, she said, shrugging, but it was tough and had little flavour. The money went into the drawer in her bedroom.

The sea appears fabulous to those who have never seen it or been on it, a place where the greedy seek their fortune, their eyes literally hungry to see beyond the horizon. Nothing good ever comes of that. The myopic prejudice of those that remain and only ever perceive the greater dangers of elsewhere.

I had half expected this old lady's grandson, Rafael, who I had met at a book event down on the coast, so a new friend, to tell me she was joking, winding me up, in order to see how gullible I was, but he never did, instead carefully translating the bits I didn't understand, and laughing along with her at the salami story which he had heard all his life. He had suggested we visit his grandmother because she was a curio, something to behold. Somebody who had never seen the sea in this day and age was almost a freak, a fairground attraction. He had never met his uncle, who he said had disappeared into America, as if it had eaten him.

The other reason to drive up to the village was lunch, to eat the local lemon chicken speciality, an odd dish I had seen nowhere else in the valley. Who had brought this dish here? Somebody new or somebody returned? Perhaps this chicken dish had come from across the sea, wowing us with its Bonnie-and-Clyde two punch of lemon and olive, a bitter-sweet alchemy. Cooks, those that like to cook, usually travel with stashes of spice, nubs of ginger, threads of saffron, easy to carry, their use learnt at the shoulders of mothers and older sisters. This is the flavour of home.

After lunch in the restaurant not two hundred yards from his grandmother's house – another place she had never visited – she made us coffee while he took me up to her bedroom to show me a musty roll of old dollar bills in the drawer, pinched by an elastic band. Twenty of them.

*

Fuel poured from under the wings as the plane arced sharply through the sky. Pressing my face to the window, I watched it evaporate. The sun swapped sides, crossing the fuselage and sweeping through the cabin accompanied by gasps and muted screams from some passengers. We had all seen the movies. I poured us both another gin and tonic from the bottle which had been left on the bar top. We drank silently. The lawyer told me he had just got married; this information à propos, I imagine, of our impending doom. He was the usual type you found in Upper class, rich, faceless, pleasant, one of life's ordinary winners. The crew hardly spoke and served the passengers in Economy class with rictus-like smiles and muted reassurances. With us the mask slipped and they presented as more vulnerable, even a little sullen. After an initial flurry of (rebuffed) questions we didn't probe them further, instead sharing a silent awkwardness. I almost suggested the hostess pour herself a drink.

We were all in this together.

By dusk we were back over London, circling for what felt like ages stacked among other jets in the sky above Heathrow, and as we finally descended (to a few cheers, claps) noses pressed up against windows, we saw the mayhem on the tarmac below, aircraft, baggage trucks and fire engines everywhere. What had happened? I had been on my way for a meeting about directing an American version of the French hit Taxi *starring Queen Latifah. A few weeks later I made it to LA. By then the project had been retitled* Taxi NYC. *I noticed that lots of cars on the boulevards were also flying* I Love NY *flags and bumper stickers. The hutzpah of Hollywood, of entertainment uber alles, Americans, who can turn on a dime while the rest of us remain trapped by so many headlights. I didn't get the gig but heard that Luc Besson was a monster to work with. Another bullet dodged. I did not disappear into America. It did not consume me.*

*

We hit gridlock on the coast road and crawled towards San Remo for another hour. As we cross back over our river where it reaches the sea it seems little changed, still a slow trickle over a wide basin of stones and pebbles, a mean estuary made worse by the smell of silage. A small fan of muddy water where the river bleeds into the sea was all there was to show for all the damage of the last few days. We took the car to a carwash and spent an hour cleaning it as best we could. That night we eat a shit pizza in a busy bar, drank but couldn't get drunk, and didn't really have much to say before going to bed early, deflated by feeling ordinary again. I couldn't sleep so went back out. Without motive I had another glass of wine surrounded by people enjoying themselves. It was a busy Thursday night; the weekend beckoned. Kit woke me up early, cursing me for snoring – we were sharing a room – and we drove in silence to the airport. At Goldcar check-in a young North African woman signed the car off with a big smile and no excess to pay. I wondered if she liked lemon chicken.

By the time we arrived back at Luton we had folded ourselves back into the routines of the ongoing pandemic and nobody seemed that interested in our storm. It was just that, *our storm.*

You had to have been there, I guess.

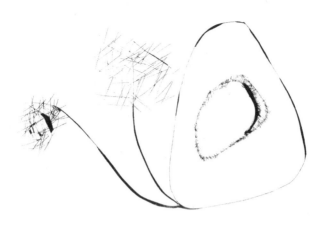

EPILOGUE

Istvan tossed and turned, he couldn't settle. When he finally fell asleep he was thrown into a recurring nightmare of sorts, or perhaps a vivid dream, illuminated by the flickering light from a burning cypress. He knew it was coming, drank dark spirits to summon it. He was on a stage which was also the terrace of the house he used to share with his wife in Italy. They sold it after the divorce. It had been the house they bought for him to paint in but all he had really done was drink in it – she said – so he sold it to an English arsehole, young, full of piss and vinegar. It had left a bad taste in his mouth. Nearly twenty years of his life. His mark, if not art, decorated the fabric of the house, paint on stone and wood. Afterwards, for years, he painted the house. Those twenty years became his practice; he exhibited endless sketches of it and paintings, drawings and plan elevations of all the improvements he had planned that now existed only in his head. He sold paintings of this house and its terrace under the stars which had taken up residence in his imagination.

A monster of some kind, but definitely not a dragon, lifted itself from the mountain across the valley and floated over to him, hovered over the terrace, blocking out the sky, smothering him, yet he could still see the orange flames from the burning tree and he had to get out from under it, to put the fire out, to stop the fire spreading and…

Writing up a dream you use a lot of *ands*, because dreams are just one thing after another, yearning for connectivity.

An eagle swoops, yet the prey feels the vertigo of diving from great height, in the moment before the talons…

Istvan woke with a start, sat bolt upright, sweat pouring off him, and called out. What did he cry out? A name, of a thing? A person? Word, words, snatched into the waking world. Contraband, obscene/absurd somehow for being carried over from the dream of a lifetime.

But there was nobody there to hear or answer him. He'd been alone for years, alone with the house that lived in his head, that took possession of him at night, however much he painted it, summoned it onto paper, *put it out there*, it came back.

And every time he woke up with words on the tip of his tongue.

ACKNOWLEDGEMENTS

TBC

ABOUT THE AUTHOR

Wayne Holloway is a writer and director living in London. After studying Philosophy at the University of Essex in the 1980's he started his career making music videos for the likes of Sinead O Conner, Awsad and Shane McGowan, before moving into commercials and film work, writing in the margins. He is the author of *Land of Hunger* (Zero, 2015), *Bindlestiff* (Influx, 2019) and *Our Struggle* (Influx, 2022).

Influx Press is an award-winning independent publisher based in London, committed to publishing innovative and challenging literature from across the UK and beyond.

www.influxpress.com
@Influxpress